SHADOWS OF GHOSTS

STEFAN HAUCKE

TABLE OF CONTENTS

"Battles are horrible things. The blood and moans and screams of the dying will haunt my dreams for the rest of my life. The dead stay with me. When I close my eyes, I can see the shadows of ghosts on every battlefield."

—General Grintar

ONE

MIDNIGHT ESCAPE

"It's started."

Cal Lanshire heard the words, but he didn't know who had spoken them. The darkness in his bedroom was thick; it robbed him of his sight. Was there someone in his room with him? Cal lay still, afraid to move, and listened. No more words were spoken. His bedroom was silent. The only sound he heard was the soft clomping of a horse's or a centaur's hooves on the cobblestone courtyard outside.

Maybe he'd dreamed the words. What had he been dreaming? Cal tried to remember. Faintly he recalled dreaming of a group of elves who were building a bridge over a river and of a large serpent that had been rapidly slithering toward his face. This didn't make any sense, but then dreams frequently didn't make sense.

A flickering yellow light abruptly reached under the bedroom door and dully illuminated a small patch of the floor. A voice began whispering. Cal wanted to jerk his head under the blanket. He wanted to curl up under the covers, making himself as small as possible, but he couldn't move. He tried to call out for his father, but he was too afraid to make a sound.

The whispering became slightly louder. There were two voices. Yes, he could definitely hear two voices, although the words weren't loud enough to be clear. The voices suddenly stopped. Then there came a muffled, shuffling sound of footsteps. The footsteps gradually grew softer, farther away, until they faded into silence. But there was still someone standing out there on the other side of the door. The flickering yellow light continued seeping into his room.

His bedroom door suddenly let out the soft, familiar creek it always made when opened. Cal wanted to close his eyes—yes, he desperately more than anything wanted to close his eyes—but he couldn't close them. He saw the door open and a figure step, almost glide, into his room. The figure was holding a small candle; however, the flickering light from the candle wasn't bright enough to illuminate the figure's face. All Cal could see clearly was a black, gloved hand that was holding the candle and two buttons on the figure's dark jacket. The figure drifted toward his bed, and when it reached the side of the bed it stopped. The candle was brought close to Cal.

"I see you're awake," a voice whispered.

The figure leaned down, and the light from the candle was finally close enough to reveal who had entered Cal's room. It was his tutor, Mr. Alden.

"Mr. Alden!" Cal called out. "What's happening?"

"Shhhh..." Mr. Alden put a finger over his lips for a moment. "We have to be quiet."

"What's happening?"

"It's started."

"What's started?"

"The war."

"Where's my father?"

"Your father sent me here to get you," Mr. Alden whispered. "We have to leave. Immediately."

"Why?"

"It's not safe here. Now get up and get dressed. Hurry."

"I want my father."

"He can't be here. He'll come to see you when he can."

"I don't want to go."

"You don't have a choice. We have to go."

Mr. Alden spoke with such authority Cal knew there was no point arguing with him. He climbed out of bed and quickly got dressed.

"Let's go," Mr. Alden said.

The long corridor outside his bedroom was flooded with darkness. The torches that normally kept the corridor lit had been extinguished. Mr. Alden put a hand on Cal's shoulder and led him through the corridor, their only light coming from the candle's dim, flickering flame.

At the end of the corridor, they reached a dark stairwell. Rapidly they moved down the stairs. When they reached the bottom of the stairs, they followed another dark corridor until they arrived at a large, thick wooden door. Mr. Alden removed a key from his pocket and unlocked the door. Outside was the courtyard. Only two torches were burning, and they were widely separated, giving off just enough light to be able to barely see. This confused Cal. The courtyard was always brightly lit. He squinted and saw two long rows of horses. Each horse had an armored solider on its back, and each soldier was holding a shield and a crossbow and was staring forward, expressionless. Nearby, two nervous-looking centaurs were busy loading supplies into a large wagon.

"This way," Mr. Alden whispered. He led Cal to a covered carriage. Two strong horses were hitched to the carriage. "Quick," Mr. Alden said. "Get in."

The carriage began moving as soon as Cal and Mr. Alden were inside. The faint firelight from the courtyard torches rapidly faded from view. The darkness was intense. Cal looked around, searching for some light, but found none. A thick cloud cover must have been keeping the stars and moon hidden. Cal closed his eyes. The darkness didn't seem so terrible when he had his eyes shut; he felt safer with his eyes closed.

He must have fallen asleep. When he opened his eyes, he felt groggy, and his back felt stiff from being in the same position for too long. He turned his head and saw that the stars were out. Cal smiled. "The stars," he whispered.

Mr. Alden leaned close to him. "Those aren't stars."

Cal stared at the stars, and as the sleepy grogginess disappeared from his mind, he realized something was wrong. The stars were all near where the horizon should be, and they were the wrong color. Instead of being the pale, bluish-white color that stars were supposed to be, these stars were almost golden.

"What are they?" Cal asked.

"The enemy," Mr. Alden whispered. "They're close. You're looking at their campfires."

Cal felt suddenly cold. He squeezed his eyes shut. He wanted the darkness back; the darkness would be so much better than seeing those campfires.

He listened to the soft creaking of the moving carriage and the rhythmic thumping of the horses' hooves and wondered where he was being taken.

TWO

AN UNEXPECTED ARRIVAL

Cal turned his face toward the sun and smiled. The sunshine and fresh air felt wonderful. After a minute, Cal moved his face away from the sun and rushed into the nearby forest.

During his afternoon lessons, which seemed to go on forever, Mr. Alden had tested Cal's knowledge of history. Cal was a good student and usually did well when tested, especially with history, but not this afternoon. It was such a beautiful day, all he could think about was how much he wanted to be outside. Because he kept thinking about being outside, he wasn't able to focus on Mr. Alden's questions. After a while, every time Cal gave an incorrect answer, Mr. Alden would scrunch up his eyes and push his lips together as if he'd just tasted the most bitter food in the kingdom. And each time Mr. Alden made this face, Cal had to seriously fight back the urge to laugh. Of course, eventually,

Cal did laugh. He caught himself and immediately wished he could take it back. He put on a serious expression and looked down at his lap. He was certain Mr. Alden was going to be mad. Cal started to apologize, but Mr. Alden cut him off.

"Let's make a deal," Mr. Alden said. "Since you obviously have other things on your mind this afternoon, I'm willing to let you go do whatever it is you'd rather be doing. But I want you to agree to start your studies an hour early tomorrow and promise to concentrate. Deal?"

Cal nodded.

"One more thing." Cal was just leaving the room when Mr. Alden said this. He stopped and looked back at Mr. Alden. He thought Mr. Alden had changed his mind; he thought he was going to be told to sit back down and work for another hour or more. Instead, Mr. Alden said something that Cal wasn't expecting to hear, and it took him completely by surprise. Mr. Alden told him that the war was almost over and that soon he would be allowed to go home.

Hearing this should have made Cal happy, but at first he didn't feel anything. A part of him didn't believe that he actually would be home soon. He'd been away for four and a half years, and as each of those years passed, home felt less and less real until now home seemed almost like something he'd dreamed. Cal had been sent with Mr. Alden to the little village of Shua because it was determined that in Shua he would be safe. But Cal didn't want to be in Shua. He didn't want to be away from his father and his home, and he didn't want to be stuck here in this village having to pretend to be someone he wasn't.

During the past four and a half years, he had only seen his father three times, and each time was only for a few hours at night. It was risky for his father to travel. When his father came to the village to visit, he had to do it secretly.

Many times Cal imagined his mother was with him, and frequently he would have imaginary conversations with her, telling her what was happening in his life, and this helped him get through the periods when he was feeling especially lonely and homesick. He'd never had a real conversation with her. His mother had caught a fever several days after giving birth to him, and the doctors were unable to bring the fever down. Cal had been told that his father refused to speak to anyone for more than a week after she passed away. His father spent days sitting in a chair near the bed where she'd died. Whenever Cal's mother's name was mentioned, his father's eyes would change, almost imperceptibly, but enough so that Cal could see the deep pain his father still felt.

Cal spotted his friend Mont. He was sitting on a branch near the top of one of the tallest trees. When Mont saw Cal, he stood up on the branch and waved enthusiastically with both arms, somehow managing not to lose his balance. Then, with an amazing agility that Cal envied, Mont rapidly maneuvered his way down the tree to the ground. He ran toward Cal, ran around him once, and then quickly moved in and playfully punched him on the shoulder.

"Hey, buddy, what took you so long? This is a perfect day for swimming."

"You're lucky I'm here now," Cal said. "Mr. Alden let me go early."

"I wish I had a private instructor," Mont said. "I wouldn't even care how much he made me study. Having a private instructor would be so much better than having to go to that stupid school."

"When are they letting you back in?"

"Next week. But it won't last. They'll throw me out again, and then I'll have used up all my chances. If I get kicked out again, it will be for the rest of the year." Mont picked up a stone and tossed it in front of him. The stone hit the ground, causing a small cloud of dirt to rise up. "I don't want to be held back a year. I don't want to have to deal with it."

"Why can't they figure out by now that you don't agree with what your father did?"

"Nobody wants to admit they're wrong. Everybody decided when my pap left that if I was older, I would have gone off to fight with the Congressers too. It doesn't matter what I say. Their minds are made up, and they're not about to change."

Cal and Mont moved rapidly through the woods. They were heading toward a pond that was hidden behind a thick mess of brush. They had discovered the pond several years ago when they were hanging out in the woods and had heard voices and had quickly pushed their way into the brush to hide. They had to hide because Cal was not supposed to hang out with Mont. If the villagers knew Cal spent time with Mont, they would strongly disapprove, and Cal and Mont would become the hot topic of village gossip. The boy from the royal family had made friends with the boy whose father had gone off to fight for the Congressers. What a scandal that would make. And Cal had been given strict instructions to keep a low profile. He had been told he was to stay out of trouble and was to do absolutely nothing that would draw attention.

Shortly after they arrived in Shua, Mr. Alden had arranged to have Cal introduced to some of the local kids who were his age. Cal tried to hang out with these kids, but when he was around them he always felt like an outsider. Even though the kids were all polite, Cal didn't sense any genuine friendliness behind their politeness. He could tell that they were impressed by the fact that he was a part of the royal family, and this made him smile because he could just imagine how they'd act if they knew who he really was.

Instead of spending time with the local kids, Cal used to disappear into the woods as soon as his instructions were over. He liked to explore; frequently he would follow one of the many narrow trails the deer had created. When he wasn't in the mood for exploring, he would sit and read, resting his back against a giant oak tree he'd discovered deep in the woods.

Cal and Mont met for the first time at the giant oak tree. One day Cal arrived at the tree and found Mont sitting on one of the tree's upper branches. This took him completely by surprise; he'd never seen anyone in this part of the woods before. Mont was sitting with one leg stretched out across a thick branch while his other leg dangled down. He appeared just as surprised to see Cal as Cal was to see him.

"Hello," Cal said. Mont didn't answer him at first. He stared at Cal for a moment, and then he climbed down to the ground and extended a hand and introduced himself. Cal shook his hand, and this surprised Mont. He gave Cal an odd look and said, "My pap is the one who went off to fight for the Congressers."

11

"I know," Cal said. "I've heard of you."

Mont stared at Cal, expecting a hostile comment or action. Cal looked back with a neutral expression, and this seemed to confuse Mont. He glanced down and nervously kicked at the ground with his heel.

"It's not your fault that your father joined the Congressers," Cal said.

Mont looked up. "Everyone else seems to think that it is." Mont told Cal that he'd been dismissed from school for the rest of the week for punching a kid. The kid had called Mont a dirty Congresser. Mont said he ignored most of the things that were said to him, but after a while he couldn't take it anymore. He said he hated having to constantly defend himself because of something Pap did. Especially since he didn't agree with what Pap did.

Cal told Mont that he hated that his father had chosen to get so involved in the war. Then he stopped himself. He was afraid if he said any more, he would give himself away.

"You were sent here so you'd be safe in case the Congressers managed to take over the capital?" Mont asked.

Cal nodded.

"You're the king's cousin?"

"A distant cousin," Cal said.

"I don't believe you," Mont said.

Cal shrugged. "I am. Not that it's any big deal."

Mont laughed. "You're the king's son. You're the prince."

"No, but I've met the prince a couple of times."

"You can trust me," Mont said, putting his right hand on his chest. "I won't tell anyone."

"I'm not the prince."

"Admit it." Mont pulled a small knife out of the leather sheath that was attached to his belt. He held the knife up.

Cal took a step back.

"Admit it," Mont said.

"I'm not."

"Admit it."

"It's not true."

"You can trust me. I won't ever tell anybody." Mont took the knife and suddenly sliced the tip of his thumb. He held his hand up.

"I..." Cal was too surprised to speak.

Blood ran down Mont's arm. Cal stared at the blood.

"I'll keep your secret."

Cal didn't say a word. His gaze was fixed on the flowing blood.

"You can trust me," Mont said. "I'll never break a blood oath."

Cal still didn't speak.

"Do you know what a blood oath is?" Mont asked.

Cal shook his head.

"It's a promise that you never can break. Once you make a promise and then cut yourself, you have to keep that promise forever because if you don't you'll soon die a terrible, painful death."

"Oh," Cal said.

"It may sound crazy," Mont said. "But it's real. The blood oath has been around since ancient times. The ancient people used to make treaties by using the blood oath."

Cal had never heard of this before and he didn't think he believed it, but Mont said it with such sincerity, Cal was almost convinced it was true.

"You're the prince," Mont said.

Cal stared at him.

"You can trust me," Mont said. "I've made a blood oath."

Slowly, Cal nodded his head.

"I knew it." Mont folded his thumb into his palm and squeezed his fingers around it, stopping the flow of blood. "But why did they have you pretend to be one of the king's cousins? Why not just pretend to be nobody? Wouldn't that have been better?"

"When my father's advisers sent me here, they knew that it would be just about impossible to keep the fact that I was from the royal family a secret. They thought if they tried to do that, people would get suspicious, and if they got suspicious, they would automatically suspect that I was the prince. My father's advisers were afraid there might be Congresser sympathizers here, and if they knew I was the prince, they might try to kidnap me and use me as a way to make my father surrender."

Cal and Mont talked for a long time. Mont told Cal that he lived with his pap's sister, Awl. He'd moved in with her when Pap left, but this really wasn't much of a change because he had always spent more time with her than he spent with Pap. Aunt Awl filled the role of ma in Mont's life. When Mont was three years old, his ma left. Mont told Cal that he didn't blame her for leaving. He said if he was her, he would've left too. Pap's moods were unpredictable; in a flash, he could go from smiling and laughing to yelling and pounding his fists on the nearest wall or table. Whenever Pap's temper erupted, Mont said he quickly made himself scarce. During the last two weeks before the war, Pap was in an almost constant state of anger. He hated the recent law the northern members of Parliament had managed to push through, banning the use of centaurs in the Western territories. He was furious at the king for not overruling this law. According to Pap, this law was just the first step toward banning the ownership of centaurs. Pap hated the abolitionists who called centaurs slaves. How could they be slaves when they were animals, not humans? No one was calling horses or cattle slaves. Just because a centaur had a head and torso that looked human, that didn't make it human. Pap said the Northern provinces had no right to push around the Southern provinces. When Jalk Dengon, the speaker of Parliament, walked out of Parliament to help the Southern provinces create their own government, independent of the kingdom, Pap was ecstatic. He openly referred to Jalk Dengon as a hero, and this was a dangerous thing to do in the village of Shua. The villagers fervently supported the king and the king's policy of keeping the kingdom together. Jalk Dengon was considered a traitor in Shua, and if anyone besides Pap felt otherwise, they kept it to themselves.

The war exploded two weeks after Jalk Dengon walked out of Parliament. Pap immediately made the decision that he would fight for the Congressional provinces—or Congressers, as the new government of the Southern provinces came to be called. When Pap was packed and ready to leave, he went to Mont and opened his arms, but instead of hugging him, Mont turned away. This infuriated Pap. He smashed his fist against the back of Mont's head. Mont lost his balance and tumbled forward, smacking his chin so hard on the wooden floor that his teeth cut almost completely through his lower lip. At first there wasn't any pain; his face was numb, and he wasn't aware that he was injured.

But when he sat up, he felt warm blood flowing down his chin, and he felt a throbbing in his jaw, which was faint at first but quickly intensified. Mont looked up, and Pap made eye contact with him for a brief moment. Then Pap slowly shook his head, looked away, and quickly walked out the front door. That was the last time Mont saw him.

It didn't take long before everyone in Shua knew that Pap had left to fight for the Congressers. The story spread as quickly as flames across a dry field. And just as quickly the residents of Shua began treating Mont and Awl with suspicion. Awl was a quiet, shy woman. She only had two close friends, and even though her friends didn't abandon her, it was clear that being seen with her made them uncomfortable. When Awl went to do her shopping, almost no one would smile at her or say hello. Those who did acknowledge her were people who felt guilty being mean; however, they never said more than they had to or kept eye contact for very long because they didn't want to have to associate with her any more than the short time it took for them to convince themselves that they weren't being mean.

For Mont, life in Shua was even worse because he was expected to go to school, and there he was constantly taunted. Sometimes the taunting took the form of name-calling and pushing, but mostly the taunting was subtle—his classmates giving him quick, angry looks, or rude gestures, or completely ignoring him. Mont was a pretty easygoing fellow, but he wasn't the type to allow anyone to walk all over him. Consequently, he frequently got into schoolyard fights.

Cal and Mont had been friends for almost three years now, and so far, no one in the village was aware of it. Their friendship was their secret.

"Boy, am I ready for the water," Cal said.

"So am I." Mont moved in front of Cal and then pushed his way into the thick brush that surrounded the pond. Although it was difficult to see, there was one spot where it was much easier to get through the brush. Cal and Mont had discovered this spot after they watched several deer use it to get to the pond for a drink of water. Cal followed Mont into the brush.

When Cal got to the pond, he found that Mont had already managed to strip down and jump into the water. "Hey, slowpoke!" Mont shouted. "What took you so long?"

Cal quickly stripped off his clothes and threw himself into the water. Mont crashed both of his arms down on the water, causing a wave to splash against Cal's face. Cal slapped at the water, splashing Mont back.

"I wish I could swim all day," Cal said.

"Maybe you can talk Mr. Alden into having your instructions here."

"For some reason I don't think he would agree to that."

Mont started laughing. "I can just imagine you and Mr. Alden swimming around in the pond here."

Cal splashed Mont and then dove under the water before Mont could splash him back. He stayed under as long as he could hold his breath. When he came up for air, he was ready for a major splashing assault from Mont. But Mont didn't move. He was wearing a nervous, worried expression and was staring past Cal. Suddenly Cal felt cold, afraid. He wondered what Mont was staring at. He wondered what was behind him. Quickly, Cal turned around.

Standing at the edge of the pond, near the spot where they had dropped their clothes, was a large, overweight man. He was wearing a hat, and the shadow from the brim hid his face. The man's arms were crossed, and he was staring at the boys.

THREE

IMPORTANT NEWS

The large man uncrossed his arms.

If this man meant to cause them trouble, there was very little Cal or Mont could do. The brush that surrounded the pond had many thorny vines woven through it, and the man was standing by their clothes, so running away wasn't an option. Just the thought of rushing naked through the thorny brush made Cal wince.

"What do you want?" Mont called out.

The man didn't answer.

"What do you want?" Mont called out again.

Still the man didn't answer.

"What do you want?" Mont's voice had deepened. He was angry.

Slowly, the man reached up and removed his hat. Cal couldn't believe it. Could it really be? He rapidly swam to the edge of the pond, and as he got out of the water he stumbled, landing on his hands and knees, but he instantly got up. "Zinn!" Cal shouted. A huge smile spread across his face. He ran to the large man and hugged him.

"Cal," Zinn said. "I wasn't sure if that was you in the water. You've grown up in the four years since I last saw you." The man took a step back and looked at Cal and smiled.

Cal noticed that he had gotten Zinn's shirt wet. "Sorry," Cal said, pointing at the shirt.

"It doesn't matter." Zinn smiled.

Mont got out of the water. He stood beside Cal.

"This is Zinn," Cal said to Mont. "He and my father have been friends since they were kids. He's my father's best adviser."

"You're Zinn Dymar," Mont said. "Cal's told me about you."

"This is my friend, Mont Felder," Cal said to Zinn.

Mont and Zinn shook hands.

"Don't tell Mr. Alden that Mont and I are friends," Cal said. "I'll explain it to you later, but Mont and I shouldn't hang out together."

"It doesn't matter," Zinn said. "Alden knows that you and Mont are friends. He was the one who told me to come here to find you."

"How could he know?"

"His job was to take care of you. He's been watching you."

"Watching me? You mean he's been *spying* on me?" Cal had never suspected Mr. Alden had been following him, spying on him. A bitter mixture of anger and betrayal gripped Cal.

"No," Zinn said. "He wasn't spying on you. He watched you to make sure you stayed safe. Your safety is very important."

"He had no right to spy on me."

"Alden had to watch you. It was his job to keep you safe."

"He had no right to spy on me. He—"

"There's no time to debate this now," Zinn said, cutting Cal off. "Get dressed. I have important news to tell you."

"What's wrong?" From the tone of Zinn's voice, it was obvious something serious had happened. The anger that had gripped Cal was now pushed aside by worry.

"It's not something that can be discussed here. We need to go to the house where you and Alden are staying."

"What happened?" Cal asked as he quickly got dressed.

"I told you, it's not something that can be discussed here."

Fear joined the worry Cal felt. There was a sadness in Zinn's eyes, which he tried to hide by quickly looking away from Cal. What could be wrong? Had the kingdom lost the war? No, that couldn't be possible. Mr. Alden had just told him that the kingdom was on the verge of winning the war. The Congressers hadn't won a battle in months.

But what if Mr. Alden was wrong? What if Mr. Alden had lied to him? Maybe the Congressers were actually on the verge of winning the war. What would happen if the Congressers won?

The worry that had gripped Cal was so intense now it was causing him to feel nauseous. He swallowed and did his best to will the nausea away.

"Come on," Zinn said. "We need to hurry."

Cal turned to Mont and said, "I'll see you tomorrow." He wondered if he actually would be able to see Mont tomorrow. He suspected he was going to be taken from Shua.

"Yeah, I'll see you tomorrow." Mont's voice was flat. It was obvious he didn't believe that Cal would be able to meet him here in the woods tomorrow, or probably ever again.

Cal followed Zinn. He was surprised by how fast Zinn was walking. He needed to know what the important news was, and all he could think of was the war. He couldn't imagine any other reason why Zinn would be here. The news had to be about the war, and the news had to be bad. Maybe the Congressers had somehow managed to win. Maybe now he and his father were going to be forced into exile.

"Did the Congressers win the war?" Cal asked.

"No."

"Then what's wrong? What's the news you have to tell me?"

"Wait," Zinn said. "We're almost there."

Why couldn't Zinn tell him the news now? Why did he have to wait?

The small house where Cal and Mr. Alden had lived for the past four and a half years came into view. Attempting to at least momentarily push the worried thoughts from his mind, Cal focused his attention on the front door. He watched the door as they got closer and closer to it. When Zinn reached the door, he didn't stop to knock. He opened it and walked in as if he'd lived in the house all his life. Cal followed Zinn inside, closing the door behind them.

Without saying a word, Zinn turned and walked down the hallway that led to Cal's bedroom. He went into the bedroom, and Cal followed him. Standing beside Cal's bed was Mr. Alden. He appeared both nervous and sad. He gave Cal a sympathetic look, and then he turned his gaze to Zinn. "Everything is ready," Mr. Alden told Zinn.

Cal noticed that there was a fully packed backpack on his bed. He looked at Mr. Alden and then at Zinn, expecting an explanation, but neither of them spoke. Mr. Alden and Zinn glanced at each other, and from their expressions Cal could tell that they were trying to figure out who should be the one to give him the news.

"Sit down," Zinn told Cal.

Cal sat down on his bed, next to the backpack. He looked at Zinn and waited to be told the news. Zinn emitted a soft sigh, glanced at Mr. Alden, and then he leaned forward and put a hand on Cal's shoulder. "This is going to be difficult for you," Zinn said. "But you're going to have to remain strong."

"I will," Cal said. Anxiety had caused an intense tingling to erupt in the pit of his gut. He felt like he was going to be sick.

"The night before last your father was assassinated. His death has not been officially announced yet. Right now almost everyone believes the king was only wounded." Zinn's fingers squeezed Cal's shoulder. "Your father went to a play. During the second act, one of the actors, Jac Buratt, ran onto the stage with a crossbow he'd smuggled into the theater. He shouted something, and then before anyone knew what was happening, Buratt shot your father."

Cal felt numb. He understood the words he was hearing, but at the same time his mind didn't want to accept them. The room no longer seemed real, and he felt disconnected from his body as if he were having a dream.

"Your father was a strong man. He wasn't conscious, but he managed to live through the night. His death hasn't been announced because we needed time to prepare things."

Zinn looked at Cal, anticipating an emotional reaction to this news, but Cal was too numb to react. Cal thought he should say something, but his mind was confused, and he couldn't find any words.

"Buratt was killed. This morning." Zinn hoped that this would at least somewhat help the pain he was certain Cal was feeling. "Buratt managed to escape from the theater, but your father's guards were able to track him. He hid in a hay barn, and the guards set fire to the barn. When Buratt ran out of the barn, he put up a fight and the guards killed him." Zinn frowned. "Buratt was a Congresser sympathizer, but we had no idea. He never spoke out, never made any effort to help the Congressers. When Buratt's house was raided last night, they found his diary, and it was full of hatred for the kingdom. He knew the Congressers were about to lose the war, and he felt he had to do something to help them. He wanted to redeem himself. He felt he was a coward for not joining the Congressers and fighting for them."

Cal looked at Zinn and blinked, but he didn't speak. Zinn gave Cal's shoulder another squeeze and said, "I'm sorry."

Everything still felt unreal. Cal still felt as if he were dreaming.

"Now I need to explain to you why you must stay strong," Mr. Alden said. "Things are going to be very difficult for you."

Cal gazed down at his hands.

"Are you listening to me?" Mr. Alden asked. "It's very important that you listen to me."

"I'm listening." Cal looked at Mr. Alden. The numbness he'd been feeling was going away, and it was being replaced by a combination of sadness and anger. He was never going to see his father again. Never. The reality of what had happened grabbed him. His father had been murdered. His father was dead.

Zinn saw anger appearing in Cal's eyes. "Stay strong, Cal. Don't let your emotions take over. There are some very important things you must do soon. You have to stay strong."

"I will."

"You're going to be the king," Mr. Alden said. "But you can't become the king until you reach the age of thirteen."

"I'm almost thirteen." Cal's birthday was only fifteen days away. How would he be able to take on the responsibilities of the kingdom fifteen days from now? He didn't know enough to be able to make all the decisions the king would need to make. How could he become the king?

"Until you turn thirteen, General Macton—because he is the speaker of the Parliament—will be the provisional head of our government."

General Macton was Cal's father's first supreme commander. He had been in charge of the military during the first year and a half of the war. At first Macton was full of enthusiasm and energetically drew up several battle plans that he claimed would guarantee the kingdom a swift victory. However, Macton never put his plans into action; he preferred to defend the kingdom's undisputed territory rather than go on the offensive. When forced into battle, Macton always ended up retreating. Frustrated by Macton's unwillingness to go on the offensive, the king relieved him from his position as supreme commander. This infuriated Macton; he claimed the king was militarily incompetent and would destroy the kingdom. Macton resigned from the military and then ran for Parliament. He soon proved his real skills were as a politician. Macton was elected to the Parliament, and then he managed to convince his fellow members of Parliament to elect him speaker of the Parliament. As speaker, Macton's power and influence was second only to the king.

"Are you going to take me back to Enara?" Cal asked.

"No," Mr. Alden said. "You can't go back there. Not now."

"Why not?"

"Your life is in danger."

"My life has been in danger since the war started. That's why I was sent to live here."

"You were sent here because your father was afraid the Congressers might attack Enara, and if they did he didn't want you caught in the battle. He wanted to keep you in a safe place. Your identity was kept a secret here because we were afraid that if the Congressers knew you were here, they might try to kidnap you so that they could trade you back to your father for concessions. You were a potential bargaining tool. But your life was never in danger because no one would have gained anything by killing you."

"What would they gain now?"

"A lot."

"That doesn't make sense."

"You're the last member of the royal family who has a direct lineage to be able to inherit the throne." Mr. Alden crossed his arms. "If you were to die, the speaker of the Parliament is the next in line to become king. General Macton would be our new king."

"You think that Macton is going to order someone to kill me?"

"Probably not," Zinn said. "If it ever became known that he ordered your death, he would be convicted of treason and executed. Macton wouldn't want to risk that. But I believe he wouldn't do anything to discourage his followers from coming after you."

"His followers would like to kill me?" Cal couldn't believe this.

"No," Mr. Alden said. "Not all of them. But there are a handful of people who have very close ties to Macton, and they would love to have close ties to the king. Their careers would dramatically advance if Macton were to become the king."

"And then there's the Congressers," Zinn said. "Having Macton become the king would be a dream come true for them."

"Why?"

"Macton isn't opposed to the Southern provinces becoming an independent nation. All he would require of them is that they agree to have open trade with the kingdom. Even though we are on the verge of defeating the Congressers, the terms Macton is willing to offer are tantamount to the kingdom surrendering. The Congressers would get just about everything they want."

"Parliament would never allow him to do that," Cal said.

"Parliament wouldn't have the authority to stop him. The king, and only the king, has the authority to declare war and sign peace treaties. You know that," Mr. Alden said. "Besides, Macton is an amazing politician. He has the ability to convince most of the members of Parliament that he's doing the right thing. He's a very charming man. He knows how to stab a person in the back and make them think that he's doing them a favor."

"We can't allow Macton to take over," Zinn said.

"I want to go back to Enara," Cal said.

"No." Zinn shook his head. "You can't go back. Not yet. Until you're thirteen, Macton has authority over you. He could have you sent somewhere that would make it easy for someone to assassinate you. You would be committing suicide if you went back to Enara now."

"Then where am I going?" Cal looked at the backpack on his bed. "Where are you sending me? I don't want to run away."

"Cal," Zinn said. "You have to stay strong. Don't get angry or upset. Don't let your emotions take control. The things you're going to have to do now are going to require that you stay calm and in control of yourself."

"We have a plan," Mr. Alden said.

"Where are you sending me?"

"To the Western territories," Mr. Alden said.

"Why?" Cal was confused; this didn't make any sense. The Western territories were mostly wilderness; very few people had settled in the territories. The kingdom had claimed the territories, mostly so that another nation couldn't claim them; however, the territories were not an official part of the kingdom.

"Yesterday afternoon I met with General Grintar," Zinn said.

Cal's father had appointed General Grintar to replace Macton as the supreme commander of the military. Soon after his appointment, General Grintar proved himself to be a master of military strategy. He went on the offensive, attacking the Congressers hard, and managed to win every major battle. His intelligence, loyalty, and bravery impressed the king and made him a hero throughout the Northern provinces.

"General Grintar is currently traveling to the Western territories," Zinn said. "When I met with him, he agreed to go to the territories. He said he would bring as many troops as would voluntarily follow him. I imagine he has the majority of the military with him. I'd bet there's only a handful of his men who would rather stay behind than follow him."

"Why would General Grintar and his troops go to the Western territories? That doesn't make any sense." Cal was confused.

"He went there because he didn't want to be under Macton's control," Zinn said. "If General Grintar stayed in the kingdom, he would be obligated to follow Macton's orders, or he would have to openly rebel against Macton. In the Western territories, Macton has no authority. By going to the Western territories, Grintar can avoid having a confrontation with Macton and Macton's followers.

"We must make sure you get to the Western territories. After you reach the Western territories, you will stay there with General Grintar until you turn thirteen. Once you're thirteen, you'll be the king. Then General Grintar and his men can bring you back to Enara, and you can take your place at the head of the government. Grintar can then finish off what is left of the Congresser army, and you can bring the Southern provinces back into the kingdom."

"Now we have to hurry," Mr. Alden said. "It will be best if you are well on your way before news of the king's death reaches the village here."

Zinn opened the backpack and removed a set of clothes and told Cal to put them on. They were the type of clothes a poor farmer boy would wear. "You'll be traveling through the countryside where most of the inhabitants are poor," Mr. Alden told him. "These clothes will help you to blend in."

"I must change also," Zinn said. He left the room for several minutes, and when he came back he was dressed like a farmer. He had a backpack on that was similar to the one that Cal was to carry. "Let's get moving," Zinn said.

"After you've been gone for about an hour, I'm going to tell some of the people in the village that I'm taking you back to Enara for the king's funeral," Mr. Alden told Cal. "I want them to think you're with me. That way when they come looking for you, they'll be told you're with me and will, hopefully, come after me."

"We're going to leave the village by following a small trail in the woods," Zinn told Cal. "With luck, no one will see us."

Cal put on his backpack and followed Zinn to the front door.

Mr. Alden went to Cal and gave him a quick hug, and this took Cal completely by surprise because Mr. Alden had never hugged him before. "Good luck, and be careful," Mr. Alden said. "The kingdom needs you."

FOUR MEN ON HORSEBACK

Cal followed Zinn. He was amazed that Zinn was able to maintain such a fast pace. Zinn was overweight and had always moved slowly and carefully; Cal had never imagined that Zinn was capable of moving so fast.

"It's important that we get as far away from the village as we possibly can before the sun goes down, before we have to make camp," Zinn told Cal. "When they come looking for you, they're going to thoroughly search all around the village first. The farther away from the village you are, the safer you are."

Zinn sounded out of breath, but he showed no sign of slowing down. Cal wanted to tell Zinn that he should rest or at least slow down, and then he decided against saying this because he thought it might hurt Zinn's pride and would make him even less likely to rest, no matter how much he needed to. Zinn wiped sweat from his forehead. Cal worried that Zinn might end up having a heart attack. If that happened, Cal didn't know what he would do. The sun was getting low, but there was still at least an hour of daylight left. Cal was sure Zinn couldn't keep this pace up for that long. Cal thought that maybe he should pretend like he needed to rest—maybe that way he could get Zinn to rest without hurting his feelings.

"I'm getting tired," Cal said.

"We have to keep moving," Zinn said.

"Let's rest for a couple of minutes."

"No. I'm sorry, but we have to keep moving."

"Can't we rest for a minute?"

"No. Right now we can't afford to waste a second."

"But—"

Zinn abruptly spun around and clasped a hand over Cal's mouth. With his other hand, Zinn put a finger over his lips, signaling silence, and then he took his hand away from Cal's mouth. Cal watched Zinn, hoping for an explanation. Zinn pointed at his ears. *Listen.*

Cal didn't hear anything. He shrugged.

Again, Zinn put a finger over his lips, signaling silence. Cal nodded. He wondered what it was that Zinn had heard. Cal kept listening, but all he heard were several birds chirping and the faint rustling of leaves caused by the gentle breeze that was blowing. Zinn was so nervous he probably mistook the sounds of the birds for voices. Well, Cal had to smile to himself because at least this false alarm had caused Zinn to stop and get some rest.

Just as Cal was about to point to his mouth to inquire if it was OK to say something now, he heard the snort of a horse. Before Cal knew what was happening, Zinn grabbed him and shoved him toward some thick brush and whispered, "Hide, quick. Don't come out until I tell you."

Cal took his backpack off and clutched it to his chest, held his head down, and pushed his way into the brush. Some of the branches were sharp, and he felt scratches on his cheeks and hands. He pushed his way as far into the brush as he could go, and then he lay down on the ground, curled around his backpack. There was a long, thin scratch on the back of his right hand that was bleeding. He brought his hand up to his mouth and sucked away the blood; the scratch stung.

There came the sounds of trotting horse hooves. Cal could see out, although not very well, between the tangled branches and leaves of the brush. Four men on horseback had appeared. They surrounded Zinn. They were dressed like local farmers, but from the way they held themselves in their saddles it was obvious that they were military men. Congressers. Cal could feel his heart pounding. His throat felt suddenly dry and tingly, and he had to fight back the urge to cough.

"Identify yourself," the apparent leader of the group of men commanded.

Zinn didn't answer.

"Identify yourself," the man repeated.

"My name is Lar Nann," Zinn said. There was anger in his voice.

The leader jerked a sword out of a scabbard that was attached to the saddle of his horse. He touched the tip of the sword to Zinn's throat and said, "What is your real name?"

"Lar Nann."

The leader stared at Zinn, deciding whether or not he was being lied to. "Tell me," the leader said. "Where is the boy?"

"What boy?"

The sword was yanked away from Zinn's neck, and the leader raised the sword up and swung it down, smashing the flat part of the sword against Zinn's left cheek. Zinn stumbled backward from the blow and almost fell down. The leader raised his sword again. "Where is the boy?"

Zinn reached in his pocket and pulled out some coins. "Here," he said. "Here is my money. Take it. I don't have much. You're wasting your time robbing someone like me." He held the coins out, offering them to the leader.

The leader brought the sword down, smacking the flat side against Zinn's face, this time sending Zinn tumbling to the ground. Zinn threw the coins at the leader, and then he reached into his other pocket and removed more coins and threw these at the leader too. "That's all I have!" he shouted. "That's all. Take it and leave me alone. Go on."

"Tell me where the boy is."

"I have no more money!" Zinn shouted. "Leave me alone!"

The leader cursed and yanked on the reins, and his horse reared up. When the horse came down, one of its hooves landed on Zinn's right ankle. There was a loud snapping sound like a thick branch being broken in two. Zinn let out a high-pitched yell and curled up, holding his ankle.

"Search him," the leader ordered.

Two of the men got down from their horses and went to Zinn's backpack, opened it, and dumped its contents on the ground. All the backpack held was some clothes, food, and a small knife. The men looked at the food and clothes and grunted. One of the men picked up the knife and looked at it and then, deciding he didn't want to steal it, threw it on the ground. The men searched the backpack for secret pouches and, finding nothing, tossed it aside.

Next, they went to Zinn and searched his pockets. He cursed them and tried to push them away, but he was in too much pain to put up much of a fight. The men looked at their leader, and one of them said, "He's got nothing."

The leader's eyes narrowed with anger, and he stared at Zinn for a minute, and then he said, "Move." He turned his horse away from Zinn and galloped off. His men got back on their horses and followed their leader. However, one of them came back. He slowly looked around as if he'd seen or heard something. He directed his horse close to the brush where Cal was hiding, and Cal was sure he'd been seen. Cal's heart pounded against his ribcage as if it were trying to escape. His muscles tensed; he was ready at any second to get up and run even though he knew he had no chance of being able to outrun or outmaneuver four men on horse-back. The man stared at the brush, and Cal was certain the man could see him. Cal wondered why the man didn't come after him or call out to his companions.

It felt like the man was staring at him for hours. Why didn't he do something? Cal thought that maybe this was some sort of a trap, that maybe the other men were on their way back and would surround the brush. Cal thought that maybe he should get up and run now. But, before Cal moved, the man suddenly turned his horse away from the brush and galloped off in the direction his companions had gone.

What now?

Cal wanted to go to Zinn, but Zinn had told him to stay in the brush until he said that it was OK to come out. Cal had to stay where he was. He sat up and carefully positioned himself so that it was easier for him to see Zinn. He hoped Zinn would signal for him to come out, but Zinn didn't. Zinn didn't even glance over at where Cal was hiding. How long would he have to stay here? Zinn started slowly crawling toward a nearby tree. When he got to the tree, he grabbed the trunk and used it to help stand up. He wasn't successful. Zinn was almost standing, and then the pain in his ankle became too much for him. He let out a loud hissing sound and collapsed, grabbing his ankle and squeezing his eyes into tight, wrinkled pits.

Cal rushed to Zinn. He knelt down beside him and said, "I'll go find help."

Zinn's eyes opened. "What are you doing out here? Hide!"

"The men are gone."

"They might be tricking us. One of them could come back on foot, and we wouldn't hear him. He could be hiding anywhere, watching us."

Cal looked around.

"If one of the men is coming back on foot, he may not be here yet. There might still be time. Hide. Now!"

Hesitantly, Cal stood up and stepped back, away from Zinn.

"Hide," Zinn ordered.

Cal looked at Zinn, uncertain if he should obey, or if he should run off to find someone who could help.

"*Hide*," Zinn repeated.

Cal turned and ran to the brush, but before he could begin pushing his way back into the brush, someone lunged out of it. Cal lurched out of the way and tripped over a rock and landed on his hands and knees. He got up immediately and started to run. He was going to run faster than he'd ever run; they weren't going to catch him. He wasn't going to let them catch him.

"Wait! Cal, wait!" A voice Cal thought he recognized called out.

It couldn't be, could it? As he ran, Cal looked over his shoulder and saw the person he'd thought the voice belonged to. Mont. Cal stopped running. Was Mont the person who had come out of the brush?

"How'd you get here?" Cal asked.

"I've been following you," Mont said. "I knew you were in trouble, and I didn't trust him." Mont pointed at Zinn. "I wanted to make sure you were going to be all right."

Zinn swore. Cal and Mont looked at him, and he frantically motioned for them to hide. They went into the brush and sat down next to Cal's backpack. Cal was out of breath.

"What's happening?" Mont asked.

Cal told him everything. Mont listened to Cal without interrupting, and when Cal was finished speaking, Mont still didn't say a word; he needed time to mentally digest what he'd been told. After a minute, Mont reached out and touched Cal's arm and said, "I'm sorry about what happened to your father."

Cal nodded and looked away. He didn't want to talk about what had happened to his father. For now, he wanted to block it out of his mind. It was important that he stay strong. That's what Zinn had told him, and Zinn was right. He couldn't let his emotions take over. There was too much at stake.

"Let's go get help for Zinn," Mont said.

"We can't."

"Why not?"

"Zinn thinks that those men might come back. They might be hiding, watching him, waiting to see if I show up."

"I'll go make sure they're not around."

"You can't. What if they see you?"

"It doesn't matter. They're looking for you, not me."

"Yeah, but they might think that you're me."

Mont grinned. "Don't worry. I know my way around the woods. My pap taught me how to hunt and how to survive in the woods, you know that."

"If they catch you, they'll kill you."

"First, I'll make sure they don't see me, and second, even if they do see me, I'll disappear so fast they won't have any idea where I went."

"I don't think that's a good idea."

"They won't see me. I promise." Mont winked at Cal. "I've been following you guys, and neither one of you had any idea, did you?"

"No," Cal admitted.

"See? I know what I'm doing. You don't need to worry about me."

"All right," Cal said, giving up. He knew he wasn't going to be able to talk Mont out of looking for those men. "Just be careful."

"I'll be fine. Don't worry." Mont pushed his way out of the brush.

"What are you doing? Hide," Zinn said the second he saw Mont. There was anger in Zinn's voice.

"I'm going to see if those men are around."

"Don't. They're dangerous." Zinn started to pull himself across the ground, toward Mont. "This isn't a game."

"I'll find out where they went," Mont said. "I won't be gone long." Before Zinn could respond, Mont scurried away.

Zinn frowned, and his eyes narrowed. He glanced around as if expecting the men to appear at any second. He tried to get up by balancing all of his weight on his uninjured leg, but he wasn't able to do it. Zinn tumbled over, swearing loudly. He curled up, holding his ankle.

Cal had to use all of his willpower to keep himself from going to Zinn. He hated just sitting there and hiding, watching Zinn and doing nothing. Cal tried to think of something he could do to help, but he could think of nothing. He felt like he'd go crazy if he had to sit there much longer. He wondered how long Mont would be gone. What if the men caught Mont? No, Cal didn't want to think about that. He didn't want to think about anything. He wished he could make his mind go blank.

A bird landed on the top of the brush and quickly fluttered away, and the sound of its wings made Cal jump because, at first, he didn't know what it was. He crossed his arms. He wondered how long Zinn was going to make him stay hidden. He hoped there was someone nearby who could help.

All of a sudden, Mont appeared. He was strolling toward Zinn, and he had a big smile on his face. "They're gone," Mont said. "Don't need to worry about them right now. Cal can come out."

Zinn looked up at Mont. "How do you know they're gone?" Both Zinn's expression and tone of voice make it clear that he didn't trust Mont.

"I tracked them," Mont said. "None of them circled back. All four of them stayed together. They headed northwest."

"How do you know this?" Zinn asked.

"My pap taught me how to track," Mont said. "He used to take me with him when he went hunting."

"How do you know you followed the right tracks? Maybe you followed someone else's tracks."

"I followed their tracks right from here." Mont was offended that his tracking abilities were being questioned.

Cal pushed his way out of the brush. "We need to find someone who can take care of your leg."

"And we better hurry because it's going to be dark pretty soon," Mont said. "Once it gets dark, we'll have to walk so slow to keep from tripping over every branch and root that it will take us forever to go the distance we could walk in five minutes in the light."

"Mont and I can go look for a village," Cal said. "There must be a village nearby."

"There is," Zinn said. "But you can't go there. The village has a lot of known Congresser sympathizers."

"If we don't go there, how are we going to get help for you?" Cal asked.

"There's an abolitionist family that can be trusted. They've helped many centaurs who have run away from their owners," Zinn said. "The abolitionist family has a farm that's not far from here."

"Where is it?" Cal asked. "Mont and I will go there."

Zinn shook his head. "It's not far, but it's difficult to find from here. There are no paths from here that go near it."

"What direction is it?" Mont asked. "If you tell me, I bet I can find it."

"If you don't find it, you'll be stuck in the dark somewhere."

"I won't get lost."

"I'm not so sure about that."

"We can carry you," Cal said. "Mont and I will carry you to the farm. You said it's not far."

"I'm too heavy for you to carry."

"No you're not," Mont said. "If we get a couple of big, sturdy branches and tie our shirts to them, we can make a stretcher to carry you."

"I'm too heavy."

"We have to try," Cal said.

Cal and Mont started looking for a pair of branches that they could use. It took them a good fifteen minutes before they were able to find a pair of branches that looked thick enough and strong enough to be able to hold Zinn. Cal and Mont took off their shirts, and Mont tied the shirts to the branches. "This should work," Mont said. "It won't be comfortable, but it should hold him."

Zinn looked at the stretcher and shook his head. "I'm too heavy."

"I think it'll work," Cal said.

Cal and Mont helped Zinn get on the stretcher. Then they carefully made sure that Zinn's injured leg was supported and wouldn't slip over the side of the stretcher as they were carrying him. Next, they picked up the contents of Zinn's backpack that had been dumped on the ground and put it all back in the pack. Mont slipped his arms through the straps of Zinn's pack. Cal picked up his pack and put it on.

"Ready?" Mont asked.

Cal nodded, and Zinn muttered, "I'm too heavy for this."

"We have to try," Cal said. He went to one end of the stretcher, and Mont went to the other end. They lifted at the same time, slowly, making sure the stretcher could support Zinn. Cal was surprised to find that lifting Zinn wasn't as difficult as he'd thought it would be. The stretcher held. This was going to work. Cal smiled.

"Which way do we go?" Cal asked.

Zinn pointed.

"Ready?" Mont asked Cal.

"Yeah. Let's go."

They began walking in the direction Zinn had pointed.

FIVE

RALT AND ILY

The sun was gone. It had turned the western horizon a deep orange, but now the orange was starting to fade, taking away what little light was left. Mosquitoes were coming out for their evening feeding. They buzzed around Cal's ears, landing on and biting his neck, back, shoulders, and arms. Because he was carrying the stretcher, he was unable to slap them away. All he could do was shake his head to keep them away from his ears and twitch whatever part of his body they happened to land on, but this did little good.

Cal's hands and shoulder muscles hurt from carrying the stretcher. He wanted to rest, but he didn't say anything because he didn't want to seem like a wimp. The weight of the stretcher didn't appear to be bothering Mont at all. Mont looked as if he could carry his end of the stretcher for miles without having to stop.

"The mosquitoes are hungry tonight," Zinn said.

"They sure are," Mont answered.

"We're very close now," Zinn said.

"Do you mind if I rest for a minute?" Mont asked.

Finally, Cal thought. He didn't think Mont was going to ask to rest, and he knew he couldn't go on much farther. His hands were becoming numb, and his shoulder muscles were hurting so much he knew that if he didn't stop soon he would drop his end of the stretcher.

"I should have made you boys take a rest before this," Zinn said. "I'm surprised you were able to carry me this far."

"We're stronger than we look," Mont said with a proud smile.

A mosquito landed on Cal's arm, and he slapped it. Then he waved his arms around, temporarily pushing back the swarm of mosquitoes that were stalking him. It felt so good to be able to freely move his arms.

"You see that big tree over there?" Zinn asked. He pointed at a tree in the distance that towered over the other trees. "Just past that tree the ground slopes down, and at the bottom of the slope is a field that belongs to the farm we're going to."

"That's nothing," Mont said. "Let's get moving. You ready, Cal?"

"I'm ready." Cal swung his arms at the mosquitoes one last time, and then he and Mont simultaneously lifted the stretcher.

They quickly made their way to the large tree. Its trunk was enormous. Cal guessed that the tree must be at least a couple of hundred years old. Soon after they walked past the tree, the ground suddenly sloped down steeply. Cal and Mont stopped and stared at the steep slope. Carrying Zinn down the slope on the stretcher wasn't going to be easy. They decided that the best way to go down the slope would be to walk sideways. If they walked straight down, the person in front would be burdened with most of the weight. Taking each step slowly and carefully, they began walking sideways down the slope. At one point some of the dirt under Cal's left foot came loose, and his foot slid forward, almost causing him to fall.

"Are you all right?" Zinn asked.

"Yeah," Cal said. "I'm fine."

"Just a little bit more to go," Mont said. "We'll be at the bottom in a second."

When they got to the bottom of the slope, they put the stretcher down.

"That's the farmhouse," Zinn said.

They could see several illuminated windows on the other end of the field. Cal thought he could faintly smell the scent of something cooking. His stomach grumbled, and he realized that he was hungry; he hadn't eaten anything since lunch, and it was now later than the time he usually had dinner. A mosquito began buzzing around Cal's ear, and he swatted at it.

"I wish you could carry me straight to the farmhouse from here," Zinn said. "That would be the quickest way to go, but this field's been planted. You're going to have to follow along the edge of the field to the farmhouse."

"Let's get moving," Cal said. "These mosquitoes are making me crazy."

"I'm ready," Mont said.

They picked up the stretcher and started walking along the edge of the field. Cal got another whiff of whatever was being cooked. He guessed it was a stew. A hunger pang hit him. He hoped he would be able to eat soon. The muscles in his arms and shoulders were demanding rest. Cal focused his attention on one of the illuminated windows. Almost there. The window was getting bigger, closer.

When they finally reached the farmhouse, they set the stretcher down on the front porch. Zinn shifted his weight and looked as if he wanted to stand, but then he frowned, frustrated, and gave up.

"How does your leg feel?" Cal asked.

"It doesn't hurt as much as it did, but it still hurts."

Mont went to the front door and knocked. "Hello," he called.

The door opened about a foot, and a short woman with brown eyes and black hair stuck her head out. She appeared nervous, as if at any second she might jerk her head inside and slam the door shut and lock it. Her brown eyes gazed at Mont, at Cal, and then locked on Zinn. She saw that he was hurt, and she looked as if she wanted to go to him to help him, but she was too scared. Maybe she suspected they were robbers trying to trick her into letting them inside the house. "What do you want?" she asked.

"My name is Zinn Dymar. I met your husband a couple of years before the war started. I met him at the abolitionist gathering that was held in Enara. He was there to organize a network to help runaway centaurs."

"Help runaway centaurs?" The woman's forehead wrinkled, her eyes narrowed, and her lips pushed tightly together. She looked like she'd just bitten into a sour apple. "We've never had anything to do with centaurs. They're filthy, crude animals." The woman withdrew her head into the house and closed the door.

"What are we going to do now?" Cal asked. He was worried that Zinn would ask them to carry him somewhere else; Cal didn't think he had enough strength left to carry Zinn anywhere.

"Knock on the door again," Zinn said.

Mont knocked. The woman didn't come back.

"Keep knocking," Zinn said.

Mont pounded on the door. He kept pounding, without stopping, for almost a full minute. "Go away!" the woman suddenly shouted. She didn't open the door.

"I need to speak to your husband," Zinn said.

"He's resting. It's almost dinnertime. Leave us alone."

"I need to speak to your husband," Zinn repeated. "It's very important."

The woman didn't respond.

"Should I start knocking again?" Mont asked.

"No," Zinn said. "I think she left to get her husband."

They waited for a while. "I think I should start knocking again," Mont said.

"Not yet," Zinn said.

They waited for another minute. Then, abruptly, the door swung open. A broad-shouldered man stepped into the doorway and looked at them. His hair was uncombed, and his eyes appeared sleepy; he wasn't fully awake. "What do you want from me?" the man asked Zinn. The man's voice was deep, and he sounded annoyed.

"My name is Zinn Dymar."

The man stepped out onto the porch and leaned forward to get a better look at Zinn. At first he didn't appear to recognize Zinn, and then a smile slowly spread across the man's face. "Zinn," he said. The man's smile dissolved into an embarrassed expression. "You're hurt, you need help," the man said. "I'm sorry, I just woke up from a nap. My mind isn't clear." The man went to Zinn. "Let me help you inside."

"We can carry him," Mont said.

"Bring him into the living room," the man said. "Follow me."

Cal and Mont carried Zinn into the house. As Cal entered the house, he was hit by the wonderful scent of cooking food, and this made his stomach gurgle. He hoped he would be able to eat soon. They carried Zinn through a short hallway that led to the living room.

"Here," the man said, motioning toward the sofa. "Bring him here."

They brought the stretcher to the sofa, and the man helped Zinn get from the stretcher to the sofa. Zinn winced as he moved his injured leg. The man gently took Zinn's boot off and looked at his ankle. The outside of the ankle had turned a deep purple, and there was a lump pushing against the skin.

"I'm no expert, but it looks to me like your bone is broken in more than one place," the man said. "I'll go get the doctor."

"No," Zinn said. "Not now."

"Why not?"

Zinn explained the situation. The man listened to Zinn without interrupting, but his face appeared more and more worried as he listened. When Zinn finished, the man opened his mouth as if he wanted to speak, but no words came out. He closed his mouth, looked down at the floor for a moment, and then he looked at Cal with a sad expression. "I'm sorry," he said in a voice not much louder than a whisper. "Your father was a great man. He did great things."

Cal nodded. The sadness that he had so far managed to keep away wrapped around him, and he had to mentally push it away. He didn't want to cry. Not now.

The man looked at Cal as if there was something more he wanted to say, but he didn't speak.

"I don't want the doctor to come here tonight because if someone sees the doctor coming here, they'll want to know why, and word will quickly get around the village, and I want to keep our presence here tonight a secret," Zinn said. "The Congressers are looking for us, and I know there are Congresser sympathizers in the village."

"You're right," the man said. "But unless we get the doctor, there's nothing I can do to help your leg."

"The pain is tolerable," Zinn said. "I can make it through the night without a doctor's help."

"What's going on?" the man's wife asked as she entered the room. She was wiping her hands on the apron she was wearing. "I couldn't leave the bread I was baking, or it might have burned," she said, explaining her absence.

The man quickly told her what was happening. Her face went pale, and she nervously clasped her hands together. "What are we going to do?" she asked.

"I don't know yet," Zinn admitted.

"First," the man said, "we should introduce ourselves. My name is Ralt Graton, and this is my wife, Ily."

Cal and Mont said hello.

"I'm sorry I didn't let you in," Ily said. "At first I thought you might be criminals, but when you mentioned my husband helping centaurs, I was sure you were Congressers. If the Congressers find out that we've been helping runaway centaurs, they'll burn our house down. We have to be very careful."

"I understand," Cal said.

"There's no way you'll be able to lead Cal to General Grintar," Ily said. "That leg will take weeks to heal."

"I'll lend you three of my horses," Ralt said. "It won't be easy, but you should still be able to ride."

"No." Zinn shook his head. "We can't use horses. We have to be able to hide quickly, and it would be impossible to hide if we had horses."

"Then you won't be able to take him to the general," Ily said. "Cal will have to find the general by himself."

"Not by himself," Mont said. "I'm going with him."

"No you're not," Zinn said. "Tomorrow morning you're going back home."

"I'm not going home tomorrow," Mont said.

"Listen to me," Zinn said. "This isn't a game. Getting Cal safely to General Grintar is both extremely important and dangerous. Your presence will only make a complicated situation even more complicated. You have to leave."

"I won't leave."

"You don't have a choice," Zinn said.

"I want him to stay with me," Cal said.

"He can't." Zinn sounded exasperated.

"Mont is staying with me."

"No. He can't."

"I want him to stay."

Zinn stared at Cal, and Cal stared back. "I want him to stay with me," Cal said.

"He can't."

"I want him with me."

"Fine," Zinn said. "If that's what you want. But you better understand that you're putting your friend's life in danger. If he stays with you, there's a good chance he could be killed."

Cal looked at Mont and said, "You don't have to come with me. If you want to go back home, I won't hold it against you."

"I'm not going home," Mont said. "We're friends. I'm staying with you. I'm not afraid. Together we'll find General Grintar. You know I'm good at finding my way in the woods."

"Cal, you and Mont cannot do this by yourselves," Zinn said. He looked over at Mont and said, "You may know how to get around in the woods, but you don't have the experience needed to navigate such a huge distance. If you don't move exactly in the right direction, you could easily end up a hundred miles away from where you want to be."

Mont didn't say anything; he couldn't argue with what Zinn had said.

"I know someone who can take the boys to the general," Ralt said.

"Who?" Zinn asked.

"His name is Ellsben."

"And you're confident he can lead them to Grintar, and that he can be fully trusted?"

"Yes." Ralt nodded. "Ellsben is one of the first centaurs I helped. He—"

"No," Zinn said. "Having a centaur with them would leave them with the same problem they'd have if they had a horse. Hiding would not be easy, and—"

"Centaurs are not horses," Ralt said. He was angry. "They have brains the same as you and I. In fact, I've met centaurs who are smarter than the two of us together."

"I wasn't questioning the centaur's intelligence," Zinn said, frowning. "What I meant was the size of the centaur would make it difficult for him to hide. Besides, they're going to have to travel through parts of the Southern provinces, and this would be dangerous for a centaur."

"Do you have a better idea?" Ralt asked.

Zinn's frown deepened.

"Do you have a better idea?" Ralt asked again.

"I don't think it would be wise for the boys to travel through the Southern provinces with a centaur."

"Then forget it," Ralt said. "Come up with a better way to get them to the general. I don't have any other idea how to do it."

Zinn looked away for a moment. Then he looked at Ralt and asked, "Are you sure this centaur knows how to navigate? If I show him on a map where Grintar is, he'll be able to get there?"

"Yes." Ralt nodded. "Ellsben's family was sold to different owners. That's what made him run away from his master. He wanted to get his wife and son back, but he couldn't find them. So he made his way north. He's studied navigation for years because he wants to go back to the Southern provinces after the war to find his family, and he knew that if he didn't learn to navigate, he'd never be able to find all the places where he thinks his family might be."

"And you're sure this centaur can be trusted?"

"Absolutely. Ellsben's been a loyal friend for years."

Zinn grunted. "I still don't like the idea of them traveling with a centaur."

"Then forget it."

"Wait." Zinn abruptly squeezed his eyes shut. The corners of his mouth tightened. He appeared to have felt a sudden, deep pain in his leg. He leaned his head back against the sofa's armrest for a moment, and then he slowly opened his eyes. He looked at Ralt.

"I think I should get the doctor," Ralt said.

"No." Zinn shook his head. "I don't want the doctor tonight. I'll be all right."

"Are you sure?"

"Yes," Zinn said. "Now go get that centaur."

"If you don't have confidence in Ellsben, I'm not going to waste his time or my time by bringing him here."

"Ralt, I trust you. If you trust Ellsben, I'll trust him."

"All right," Ralt said. "I'll get him." Ralt put his boots on and grabbed his hat.

"What about dinner?" Ily asked. "You need to eat before you go. Dinner will be ready soon."

"I can't wait," Ralt told her. "You know how far I have to travel. I want to get moving right away."

"At least let me make you a sandwich," Ily said. "I'm not going to let you leave here without eating." Ily quickly went back to the kitchen.

"Don't wait up for me," Ralt told Cal and Mont. "You need to rest for your journey tomorrow. I won't be back until early tomorrow morning."

Ily brought a sandwich to Ralt. He hugged her and gave her a quick, affectionate kiss, and then he took a bite of the sandwich and turned and walked toward the front door.

"Ralt," Zinn called out.

Ralt stopped, turned around, and looked at Zinn. Zinn held out his hand. Ralt went to him and clasped his hand. "Thank you," Zinn said. "Thank you."

"You're welcome."

Soon after Ralt left, Ily announced that dinner was ready. Since it would be impossible for Zinn to eat at the kitchen table with them, Ily suggested that she could serve dinner on the little table that was near the sofa. Cal and Mont helped her bring the plates, napkins, silverware, and food to the table. The main course was lamb stew. Cal was so hungry he gulped down his bowl of stew, and then he felt embarrassed by his rude behavior. Ily asked him if he would like some more stew, and he gave her an embarrassed smile and said, "Yes, please. It's very good."

The fresh bread Ily served was delicious. "This is the best bread I've ever eaten," Mont said. "I mean it too." Ily smiled at this compliment.

Zinn only took a couple of spoonfuls of the stew. Ily asked him if there was anything else he would like to eat; she said she would be happy to prepare him something else.

"No," Zinn said. "The stew is wonderful. I don't have much of an appetite right now."

"Well," Ily said, concerned, "if there is anything you would like, please let me know."

When they were finished eating, Zinn told Cal that he needed to speak with him. "I'll help Ily clean up," Mont said. "That way you guys can talk in private." Mont and Ily quickly cleared the table.

"Cal," Zinn said, "I want you to bring my backpack over here."

Cal brought Zinn's backpack to him. Zinn opened it up and reached inside, moving around the contents of the backpack, searching for something. Eventually, he found what he was looking for. His knife.

"Please hand me my right boot," Zinn said.

Cal gave Zinn his boot. Holding his knife, Zinn stuck his hand into his boot and began cutting away the stitching that held the material at the bottom of his boot in place. Next, he peeled back the material from the area where his heel rested, and then he turned the boot upside down, and what appeared to be a coin fell out. Zinn gave it to Cal.

"What is it?" Cal asked. The coin was gold, and it easily fit in the center of his palm. No, it wasn't a coin. The gold disk had a detailed image of a heraldic crest on it; the heraldic crest consisted of a powerful eagle flying, holding arrows in its talons, symbolizing the kingdom's readiness for war, and in its beak it was carrying an olive branch, symbolizing the kingdom's desire for peace. Cal turned the disk over. On the back, written in the Old Language, were the words, a vow to uphold the laws of the kingdom, which every king had to swear to when ascending the throne.

"This came from the royal crown," Zinn said.

"Why are you giving me this now?"

"It's your identification. You haven't been seen in Enara for over four years, and you've grown and changed a lot in those years. Grintar was afraid, and I agreed with him, that when you're brought back to the castle, Macton could challenge your right to the throne by claiming that you're not really Calton Lanshire. He could claim that you're an imposter being presented by the enemies of the kingdom, to work as their puppet."

"Would this work?"

"It would work long enough to cause a lot of unnecessary trouble." Zinn pointed at the heraldic crest. "This should prevent that trouble from happening."

Cal stared at the heraldic crest resting on his palm, and he remembered his father's coronation. He remembered seeing the crown being placed on his father's head. No. Cal closed his fingers over the crest. He didn't want to think about that; he didn't want the sadness to come back.

"Give me your right shoe," Zinn said.

Cal took his shoe off and handed it to Zinn. Zinn took his knife and cut away the stitching inside the shoe that held the padded material over the heel in place. Next, he pulled the material back and carved out an area in the heel of the shoe just big enough for the crest to fit in. "Give me the crest," Zinn said. He took the crest from Cal and pushed it into the space in the shoe that he'd carved out. The crest fit perfectly. Zinn then pushed the padded material back in place, over the crest. "I only took out a little bit of the stitching, so the padded lining should still stay in place," Zinn said. "Put the shoe on and walk around. Make sure it's comfortable."

The shoe felt the same as it had before Zinn put the crest in it. Cal walked around the room to see if after a bit of walking he'd begin to feel the crest pushing against his heel.

"How is it?" Zinn asked.

"Perfect," Cal said. "I can't feel it at all."

"Good," Zinn said. "Now you can go help Mont and Ily in the kitchen, if you want. I'm going to rest." Zinn closed his eyes.

Cal went into the kitchen. "Is there anything I can do?"

"You've got excellent timing," Mont said and grinned. "We just finished."

"Is there anything Zinn needs?" Ily asked.

"No." Cal shook his head. "He's resting."

Mont raised his arms and stretched and yawned. "Rest sounds pretty good to me. I know it's not late, but I'm beat."

The sight of Mont yawning made Cal yawn too.

"We don't have an extra bed," Ily said. "I wish we did. What I can do is give each of you a bunch of blankets to put on the floor. I hope you'll be comfortable."

"Sure," Mont said. "We'll be fine." Cal agreed.

Ily went to get the blankets, and Cal and Mont followed her. They helped her carry the blankets to the living room. Zinn was asleep. Ily went to him and gently, trying not to wake him up, spread a blanket over his legs and body. Zinn twitched and muttered something, but he didn't wake up. Cal and Mont each picked a spot on the floor to put their blankets, and then they lay down. Ily gave them each a pillow and whispered goodnight. She left a small candle burning on the coffee table so that they would have some light in case they needed to get up.

Mont fell asleep immediately. Cal listened to Mont softly snoring, and wished he could fall asleep. He was exhausted, he wanted to sleep, he wanted to shut down his mind, but he couldn't. His shoulders ached, and the many mosquito bites he had on his arms, back, and neck itched. He lay still, forcing himself not to move, hoping this would cause him to fall asleep. But it didn't. He scratched a mosquito bite on his neck that presently itched more than the other bites. Then he rolled over on his left side.

Although he tried not to, he couldn't keep himself from thinking about his father. With his eyes closed, he could clearly see his father's face. He remembered last year when his father had come to visit him. That was the last time he'd seen his father, and at the time the idea that he might never see his father again had never entered his mind. The idea that his father was dead still didn't seem real to Cal. But it was real. He wouldn't be here now if it wasn't real. Cal was suddenly overcome with anger. He wanted to kick his blanket off, he wanted to get up, he wanted to knock furniture over, he wanted to swear and yell. Cal remembered what it was like before the war when he lived with his father in their house on the royal grounds. His life was normal then, he lived with his father, he had a home; that's the way his life was supposed to be.

His father shouldn't have sent him away. Cal hadn't wanted to leave; he wasn't afraid of the Congressers, and if the Congressers had managed to overtake Enara, he and his father could have escaped together. Or died together. He didn't care. He wasn't afraid; all he'd wanted was to stay with his father. He'd been so angry at his father for sending him away that there were many times he wished the Congressers would win the war. Cal used to imagine going into exile with his father, after the Congressers had won, and having his father admit to him that he shouldn't have sent Cal away and begging Cal to forgive him.

The flame burning on the candle Ily had left on the table was diminishing. Cal stared at the tiny flame. Remembering the anger he'd felt toward his father made him wish he could take it all back; he wished he'd never felt that way. Now that his father was gone, he'd never have the chance to take it back, to let his father know that he was sorry for being angry with him.

The candle's flame, twisted, flickered, and went out. Darkness. Tears that Cal had been holding in flowed from the corners of his eyes.

SIX

ELLSBEN'S STORY

C al heard voices. Before he opened his eyes, he knew the sun had risen because he could feel the sun's warmth on the side of his face. When he opened his eyes, he immediately squinted from the bright sunlight that was streaming in through a window. He sat up, bringing his face out of the direct sunlight, and saw a centaur standing beside him. The centaur was talking to Zinn and Ralt. It had been years since Cal had seen a centaur, and he'd forgotten how big they were. There were no centaurs in Shua, and the only place Cal could remember seeing centaurs was in the royal gardens where the centaurs worked as gardeners. Cal had had almost no contact with these centaurs. He'd only exchanged a brief hello with them on the several occasions when he'd been close enough to them to be able to speak to them; exchanging these brief hellos was the closest Cal had ever come to having a conversation with a centaur.

"Good morning," the centaur said to Cal.

"Good morning." Cal was amazed at how big this centaur was. But no, maybe this centaur wasn't much bigger than the average centaur; he just looked bigger here in this house that had been built for people. The centaur had to slightly bow his head to keep it from touching the ceiling.

Cal wished he'd had a chance to spend time with centaurs because, after all, they were the main reason for the war. Everything he knew about them was from what he'd been taught and what he'd read. Centaurs came from the continent of Zana. Although centaurs were physically strong, they were not as technologically advanced as those on the other continents, and because their weaponry was primitive, they were easily defeated in battle. Centaurs were first brought to the Southern provinces two hundred years ago when smalta became the primary moneymaking crop in the area. Smalta was a fibrous crop that was used to make clothing and other materials. Harvesting smalta was very labor intensive, and the growers couldn't find enough labor to harvest the amount of smalta that was in demand, mainly because there weren't enough people living in the Southern provinces. Centaurs were captured and brought from Zana to the Southern provinces as slaves. Their slavery was justified, and had continued to be justified, by the fact that although a centaur's head and torso was identical to the head and torso of a human, centaurs had the body and legs of a horse, and this, according to some, made them nonhuman.

"Cal," Ralt said. "This is my friend Ellsben."

Cal stood up and shook hands with Ellsben.

"Did you sleep well?" Ralt asked.

"Yes. The blankets were comfortable."

"I wish we had an extra bed or sofa for you and your friend."

"I was fine. Honestly, the blankets were comfortable." Cal looked at Zinn. He was about to ask Zinn how he felt, but this question was answered without being asked. Zinn's face was pale, and the flesh under his eyes was dark and swollen. Zinn smiled at Cal, but this smile obviously took effort. "How much sleep did you get?" Cal asked.

"I was only able to sleep for about an hour. The throbbing in my leg kept me up."

"I'm going to get the doctor," Ralt said.

"No." Zinn sounded angry. "Not yet. I've waited this long; I can put up with the pain for a few more hours."

Cal could smell eggs and bacon cooking. From the kitchen, Ily called, "It's almost ready." Cal went over to Mont and woke him up. "Hey," he said. "Get up. It's time for breakfast."

Mont sat up, stretched, sniffed the air, and smiled. "Smells good," he said. Then he saw Ellsben. He stared at Ellsben for a moment, and the smile on his face broadened. He got up, went over to Ellsben, stuck out his hand, and said, "Hi. My name's Mont."

Ellsben shook Mont's hand and introduced himself.

"Everybody come and get a plate," Ily said, walking into the room. "I'll bring the food out here so we can eat with Zinn."

"Eat in the dining room," Zinn said. "I'm not hungry."

"Are you sure?" Ily asked.

"Yes," Zinn said.

"Is there anything I can bring you? Some toast maybe?"

"I'm thirsty. I'd like a glass of water," Zinn said.

"Sure." Ily brought him a glass of water.

"All right, boys," Ralt said. "Let's eat." He led them to the dining room.

Ily and Ralt brought out the food, and they all sat down. Ellsben knelt on the floor, but he was still too tall for the table; he had to hunch down to be able to reach anything. Ellsben held his plate up with one hand while he ate so that he wouldn't have to keep hunching down.

"Eat as much as you can," Ily said. "You have a long journey ahead of you."

"We should leave soon," Ellsben said. "We don't want to waste the daylight."

"Thank you for helping us," Cal said.

"I'm glad to help," Ellsben said. "I'd either still be a slave, or I'd be dead if it wasn't for the help I received. Now it's my turn to give back."

"How did you escape from your owner?" Mont asked.

This was the same question that was in Cal's mind, but Cal didn't ask it because he felt it wasn't a polite thing to ask. The experience of escaping had to be traumatic and might be something Ellsben didn't want to discuss, especially with people he'd just met.

Ellsben set his plate on the table and looked at Mont. "I escaped twice," he said. "The first time I escaped, I was captured and brought back."

"How did you finally manage to get away?" Mont asked.

Ellsben didn't say anything, and Cal was sure that Mont had offended him. Cal started to apologize, but Ellsben cut him off. "Let me finish my breakfast," he said. "Then I'll tell you about how I escaped."

After they were done eating, Ily and Ralt cleared the table, and Ellsben told Cal and Mont about himself.

———

Ellsben had a happy childhood. He was lucky enough to grow up with both of his parents; their owner, Mr. Kand, believed that families should be kept together. Mr. Kand was a religious man, and he believed that God intended for families to stay together, and that he would be going against God if he broke apart a centaur family he owned by selling the members of the family to different owners. Mr. Kand worked them hard, and he had no tolerance for even a hint of laziness, but he was never mean.

When Ellsben was twenty, Mr. Kand bought a centaur to help tend Mrs. Kand's gardens because Mrs. Kand, now in her late seventies, had become too frail to do much of the work that the gardens required. The new centaur's name was Ona, and she was so beautiful Ellsben could barely talk when he met her. He blushed and tried not to stare at her, and he believed that he'd acted so stupid she must have thought he was a complete idiot. But he was wrong. At the end of the day, when their work was done, Ona found him and asked him if he would go for a walk with her and show her around. They began spending many hours together after their work was done, and soon they were in love. They decided to get married, and with Mrs. Kand's permission, they had the marriage ceremony in the area near the main flower garden. A year after they were married, Ona gave birth to a son. They named him Dar. Ellsben was as happy as he'd ever been; however, this happiness was tempered when, two days after Dar's birth, Ellsben's father collapsed while he was in the field harvesting smalta. He was brought back to the main barn and died while his wife cradled his head. No one knew for sure why Ellsben's father collapsed, but it was believed that his heart had failed.

For the next four years, Ellsben and Ona watched their son grow. Dar was a happy boy, full of energy and intelligent curiosity. Ellsben's mother loved to spend time with Dar, and she frequently let him spend time with her while she worked, caring for the smalta. She told him stories and sang songs to him as she worked. Ellsben and Ona talked about having another child.

Then Mr. Kand died, and everything changed. Mr. Kand's health had been gradually deteriorating; his hands had become so arthritic he could barely use them, his vision was failing, and he had trouble breathing. One day Mr. Kand had a coughing fit and fell to the floor, barely able to breathe, and he had to be carried to his bed. That night he was attacked by a terrible fever, and he became delirious. He muttered prayers and flapped his head from side to side. Shortly after the sun peeked over the horizon, Mr. Kand's body gave up. After witnessing her husband's death, Mrs. Kand decided she had no reason to continue living. She refused to eat, and several weeks after her husband passed on, she too was gone.

Mr. Kand's nephew took over the plantation. The new Mr. Kand treated the centaurs as if they were unfeeling machines. He showed them no kindness or consideration. The new Mr. Kand considered himself a businessman, and he was determined to run the plantation efficiently, cutting what he considered waste to maximize production. The first area of waste that he decided to eliminate was all the excess centaurs. All centaurs who were too old or too young or too weak to work efficiently in the fields were to be eliminated. He considered his uncle's idea of keeping inefficient centaurs so that they could stay with their families a foolish idea.

When the new Mr. Kand announced that Ellsben's mother, wife, and son were to be taken to the market and sold, Ellsben pleaded with him not to do it, but the new Mr. Kand refused to listen. To keep Ellsben from causing trouble, the new Mr. Kand had him brought to the main barn and locked in a stall. Ellsben kicked the door to the stall and shouted and paced until he was so exhausted he collapsed. He curled up on the floor of the stall and covered his face with his hands and wept.

Ellsben was kept locked in the stall for a week. When he was released, he tried to find out where his family had been sent and who had bought them, but none of the centaurs he worked with knew anything about what had happened to his family. Ellsben wanted to die; he thought about taking his life, but then he told himself he couldn't give up. He had to find his family. If he ran away and secretly talked to centaurs on other plantations, maybe he'd find out where his family was. There had to be centaurs who knew who had bought his family and, most importantly, where his family was. Ellsben vowed that he would find his family and bring them to the Northern provinces where they could start a new life, a free life. He had no idea how he was going to accomplish this—he'd never been more than a mile away from the Kands' plantation—but he swore he'd find a way to do it. He was going to find his family, and he was going to bring them to the Northern provinces where they'd be free, and nothing was going to stop him.

Ellsben ran away at night. He followed a road, having no idea which direction he was going, or whether he was traveling closer to his family or farther away from them. He stayed on the road until the sun started to rise. At night the road was empty, but Ellsben knew that the road would be used in the daylight, and if he was caught without a pass he would be taken into custody. Centaurs were not allowed to leave their master's property without a pass. A pass was a document written by the centaur's master explaining why the centaur was not on his property and what the centaur had been sent to do. At the bottom of the pass the centaur's master placed his seal. If a centaur was caught without a pass, the centaur was considered a runaway and was taken into custody and was kept locked up until the centaur's master came to collect his property. Ellsben went into the woods to look for a place where he could hide and rest until the sun went down. He didn't want to get too far away from the road, but he soon got mixed up and couldn't figure out which direction the road was. He felt panicky and wanted to keep moving until he could find the road, but he knew it would be incredibly risky and foolish to keep moving around. He had to hide. He found an area where there was a lot of brush, and he went into the brush and lay down. He tried to sleep because he needed to rest, but he was too worried that he wouldn't be able to find the road. If he couldn't find the road, he might not be able to get out of the woods. He could end up walking deeper and deeper into the woods, or he could end up walking in circles forever. Ellsben had no idea how to find food in the woods; he had no idea which plants were edible and which plants were poisonous, and he knew nothing about how to hunt. He imagined himself starving to death, alone in the woods.

As soon as the sun began to set, Ellsben got up and started trotting toward where he'd convinced himself the road was. But he never found the road. In the darkness, Ellsben felt completely disoriented; he didn't think he could even find his way back to the spot where he'd lain down for the day. He heard noises that he didn't recognize, and these noises frightened him. He'd never once in his life been completely alone; he'd never been lost. All he could think of to do was charge forward. He galloped blindly, straight ahead, through the woods. Branches struck his arms and face, scratching him and cutting him, but he barely noticed. He continued galloping straight ahead, and suddenly, just when he was about to collapse from exhaustion, he found himself in a field of planted smalta. He stopped. His lungs burned, and the muscles in his legs quivered. In the distance there were lights coming from a house. Abruptly, dogs began barking. Ellsben saw them, four large hunting dogs, racing toward him from the direction of the house. He was too tired to run, and besides, where could he run to? He didn't want to go back into the woods.

The dogs surrounded him. They barked and snarled and took turns lunging forward, trying to bite his legs. He kicked at them. One of the dogs managed to bury its teeth into Ellsben's left rear hock. He kicked his leg furiously until the dog released its bite. The dog, now that it had the taste of blood in its mouth, lunged at Ellsben with an insane determination. Ellsben kicked the dog with all his strength. His hoof hit the side of the lunging dog's skull, causing a loud cracking sound. The dog collapsed, blood dripping out of its nostrils, and didn't move. The intensity of the barking of the other dogs increased.

A deep male voice shouted, "What in the hell is going on out there?"

Ellsben looked at the house and saw a man looking out of one of the upstairs windows. The man saw Ellsben and began cursing wildly. He disappeared from the window. Suddenly there came the sound of a loud whistle. The whistle was an alarm signal. Men began shouting back and forth. Ellsben knew he should gallop away, but he was more afraid of being lost in the woods than he was of the men.

Three men were coming toward him. One of the men was armed with a bow and arrow, and the other men were each holding a bullwhip. The men with the whips moved behind Ellsben, and the man with the bow and arrow stood about twenty feet in front of Ellsben and kept the arrow aimed at Ellsben's chest. The man with the bow and arrow let out a quick whistle, and the dogs backed away from Ellsben. "You filthy naggie," the man with the bow and arrow said. "You killed Mal. He was my best dog."

"Let's kill the naggie," one of the men behind Ellsben shouted. His companion whooped in agreement.

"No," the man with the bow and arrow said. "I want the reward money. This runaway naggie isn't worth anything if we kill him."

One of the men behind Ellsben snapped his whip across Ellsben's flanks. "Come on, naggie, get moving." Ellsben felt the whip again. He started moving forward. The men herded him to the barn, which was located at the end of a short road that stretched out from behind the house. Once Ellsben was in the barn, they hobbled him.

"Don't even think about trying to run away again," the man with the bow and arrow said. "My dogs are outside the barn, and if you so much as stick your nose outside of this barn, they'll start up with their barking." The man's eyes narrowed, and he took a step toward Ellsben. "If I catch you outside of this barn, I'll kill you. To hell with the reward money. I can't be spending all my time chasing after a run-away naggie."

As soon as the men left, Ellsben tried to walk, but he fell down before he could complete more than a couple of steps. He'd never been hobbled before, and he had no idea how to walk while hobbled. There was no point even trying to get up; Ellsben decided he'd lie on the floor until somebody came and forced him to move. He wiped away tears from his cheeks. He was a failure; he'd failed his family, and he'd never see them again.

Ellsben had been lying on the floor, thinking about his family and sobbing, for about an hour when a centaur came in the barn. The centaur had red hair on his head and a sorrel coat. The centaur looked at Ellsben and frowned and shook his head. "You're an idiot," the red-haired centaur said.

Ellsben didn't respond.

"You're lucky they didn't kill you, or at least beat you," the red-haired centaur said. "But I bet your master's going to give you a beating. I'm sure he will."

"Go away," Ellsben said.

"I've brought you a cup of water and a sandwich."

Ellsben hadn't noticed what the red-haired centaur was holding. In one hand the red-haired centaur held an old, dented tin cup, and in his other hand he was holding a small sandwich made from the crusty end pieces of a loaf of bread. "Thank you," Ellsben said. "But I'm not hungry."

"Here." The red-haired centaur set the cup and sandwich on the floor, beside Ellsben. "You better eat. They're sure not going to feed you, and if they knew I was feeding you, they'd give me a beating, so I don't know how much food I'll be able to bring to you. Eat now while you've got the chance."

Ellsben drank the water and made himself eat the sandwich. The bread was stale and difficult to chew. "Thank you," Ellsben said. He wished the red-haired centaur would go away because right now he wanted to be alone. He didn't want to talk to anybody, and he didn't want to have to listen to anybody.

"Why did you run away?"

"I just decided to."

"You didn't just decide to. You had a reason. What was your reason?"

"My family was sold. I wanted to find them."

The red-haired centaur started laughing. "You ran away because they sold your family, and you thought you were going to find them?" The red-haired centaur kept laughing. "You're one stupid naggie, you know that?"

"If you had a family and your family was sold, you'd run away to find them."

"Like hell I would."

"You would."

"Boy," the red-haired centaur said, laughing even louder. "You've got to be the stupidest naggie I've ever met."

"Go away."

"I've been married. Twice."

"Go away."

"I'm not lying. With my first wife I had a son and a daughter."

"What happened to them?"

"They were sold. My boy was three years old, and my girl was one." The red-haired centaur looked down at the floor in thought for a moment. "It's hard to believe, but my boy's twelve years old now, and my girl's ten. I probably wouldn't even recognize them anymore."

"You never saw them after they were sold?"

The red-haired centaur shook his head. "Not once. I don't even know where they went."

"And you never tried to find them?"

"I didn't run away. I'm not a stupid naggie like you." The red-haired centaur crossed his arms. "I got remarried. My second wife and I had a boy."

"Were they sold too?"

"No. I was sold. Two years ago, and I haven't seen them since the day I was taken to the auction house."

"And you never tried to go back to them?"

"I told you, I'm not a stupid naggie like you." The red-haired centaur smiled. "All running away would get me is a beating. You've got to accept the way things are. If you try to change things that can't be changed, all you'll accomplish is creating a lot of trouble for yourself. If they don't need us or want us anymore, they sell us. That's the way it is. You've got to accept it."

"I don't have to accept it."

"You better. If you keep trying to run away, they'll decide that you're a troublemaker and they'll kill you. That's what will happen. So, you better learn to accept things the way they are."

Ellsben was kept hobbled in the barn for three days. Each day the red-haired centaur managed to bring some food and water to him, and even though Ellsben had no appetite, he forced himself to eat. Several ill-tempered men came and had Ellsben, still hobbled, put in a wagon. They brought Ellsben back to the new Mr. Kand. They dragged him out of the wagon and dropped him on the ground in front of Mr. Kand's house. The new Mr. Kand came out, looked down at Ellsben, spit on him, and said, "You cost me a lot of money. I had to pay the son of a bitch that caught you, and I had to pay the sons of bitches that brought you back here." Mr. Kand kicked Ellsben. "Now get up and get to work."

Ellsben refused to move. He didn't want to move; he didn't want to do anything.

"I said, get up and get to work."

When Ellsben still didn't move, Mr. Kand started swearing loudly. He kicked Ellsben several times, and then he went into the main barn. He came out with a bullwhip. "Get up and get to work!" Mr. Kand shouted.

Ellsben didn't move.

"Get up!"

Ellsben looked at him—that was all.

The whip hissed across Ellsben's shoulders. He squeezed his eyes shut and covered his head with his arms. "Get up!" The whip slashed him again. And again, and again, and again. And he didn't care because he wanted to die; he wanted the darkness of death to engulf him and carry him away.

Then, in his mind, he heard the sound of his son laughing and shouting, "Daddy, run with me! Come on, run with me, Daddy!" He remembered the many times he'd cantered around the outside of the smalta field with his son struggling to keep up. After a while he always slowed down so that Dar could race past him. "Look how fast I can run, Daddy! Look how fast I can run." Ellsben remembered the first time he'd kissed Ona; he remembered her hands gripping his shoulders, the way her lips felt touching his.

"Get up!"

With a sudden flailing movement, Ellsben threw his arms away from his head and lurched into a standing position. Because he was hobbled he almost fell over, but he managed to keep his balance. Blood oozed out of the stinging wounds the whip had left on Ellsben's shoulders and upper back and trickled down his torso in tiny streams.

"I don't know what's gotten into you," Mr. Kand said. "But you better understand now that I'm not going to put up with any stubbornness. And if you try running away again, you're dead."

Ellsben stared at Mr. Kand.

"I'm not going to waste my time trying to smarten you up. You run, you're dead. Do you understand me?"

Ellsben nodded.

"Good. Now get to work."

He worked. He went to the field every day and worked hard and did his best to appear as if nothing was bothering him, as if he was content. The new Mr. Kand, however, refused to remove Ellsben's hobbles. He kept Ellsben hobbled because he didn't trust Ellsben, and he wanted to punish him for running away. At night, when he was alone, Ellsben studied the metal locks on the hobbles, trying to figure out how he could break them open. He couldn't smash the locks with a rock or a hammer because they were fastened firmly against his fetlocks. There was no way to smash the locks without injuring himself. It seemed he didn't have any choice but to wait for Mr. Kand to decide to remove the hobbles. How long would Mr. Kand keep him hobbled? Another week, a month, or longer? The thought of wearing these hobbles for months, maybe even a year or more, made Ellsben feel sick. He had to find a way to break the locks. But how?

One night Ellsben awoke to the sound of his name being whispered in his ear. He opened his eyes and saw Eta, an old female centaur who cooked for the Kands and did their laundry. Because Eta never worked in the fields, Ellsben had had very little contact with her. She appeared frightened. Why was she here?

"Ellsben," Eta whispered.

"Eta, what's wrong?" Ellsben started to stand up, but she put a hand on him, indicating that she wanted him to lie still. "What's wrong?" he asked again.

"Don't move," she said. "And talk quiet."

"What's wrong?" Ellsben whispered.

"I know why you ran away. When you ran away, I was happy. I was sure you'd find your family and you would take them to the Northern provinces. I was sure of it." Eta suddenly stopped speaking and glanced around as if she'd heard a noise. After a moment, when she was satisfied that the noise was nothing to worry about, she continued speaking. "I know you want to try again, and I want you to try again.

A person's family is important. They shouldn't be split up. I remember when they sold me when I was a little girl. My mama and I were both crying like crazy, and she wouldn't let go of me, so they started beating her until she couldn't hold on to me any longer." A tear slipped down Eta's cheek. "That's why I decided never to have children, because I didn't want to have to go through that again."

"Eta, I'm going to run. As soon as they take these hobbles off me."

"They're not going to take those things off. I overheard Mr. Kand say that you're going to wear them until the day you die."

"I'll find a way to get them off Eta. I'll figure out some way."

"I've got the way."

"What?"

"Here." Eta pushed a thick metal key into Ellsben's hand. "I stole this from the drawer where Mr. Kand keeps his keys."

"Eta, if he finds out—"

"Shush. He won't find out because I'm going to put the key back. Now unlock yourself."

Ellsben used the key to open the locks on his hobbles, and then he gave the key back to Eta.

"Now, Ellsben, I want you to promise me something."

"What?"

"Promise me that you won't let them catch you. If they catch you again, they'll kill you, and I don't want that on my conscience."

"I won't let them catch me."

Eta smiled. She leaned down and kissed him on the top of his head and said, "Good luck." Then she quickly, quietly, hurried away.

Ellsben waited until he was sure Eta had enough time to return the key and get back to her sleeping quarters before he stood up. If he was caught escaping, he wanted to make sure Eta wouldn't be implicated. Ellsben stretched his stiff legs; it felt wonderful to be able to fully move his legs again.

Moving as quietly as possible, Ellsben went outside and looked around. There was no moon, and the darkness was thick. He listened. Nothing. Ellsben took in a deep breath and then began walking as softly as possible past Mr. Kand's house, toward the woods. As soon as Mr. Kand's house had disappeared into the darkness, Ellsben began trotting. He wanted to gallop, but he didn't dare gallop because he could only see a short distance ahead, and if he was moving fast he wouldn't have enough time to avoid running into trees or tripping over fallen branches or rocks.

North. Ellsben concentrated on the word *north*, hoping that by doing this he would cause himself to move in that direction. He wanted to go to the Northern provinces. He'd heard rumors that in the Northern provinces there were people, *abolitionists* he believed they were called, who would help runaway centaurs. Ellsben knew he was going to need help if he was going to find his family. He had no idea where his family was, and he now knew there was probably no way he'd ever be able to find them on his own. If he went searching for them again, he'd most likely end up getting captured again. He needed to get to the Northern provinces where there were people who would help him.

When the sun began to rise, Ellsben found a place where he could hide and rest for the day. He was only going to travel at night when there was much less chance of someone seeing him. And this time he was going to stay away from roads and farms. He was going to try his best not to do anything that might cause him to be captured. He had to get to the Northern provinces.

How would he know when he'd reached the Northern provinces? Ellsben believed that when he crossed into the Northern provinces, he would sense it—he would feel as if a heavy weight had slipped off his back. When he reached the Northern provinces, he would know—he was certain he would know.

Ellsben traveled for two nights. During this time he was able to suppress his hunger by drinking lots of water when he came across a stream or large puddle. But by the third night, his hunger became too intense to be satisfied with water. There were plants everywhere, and probably many of them were edible, but Ellsben had no idea which ones were safe to eat and which ones were dangerous. All he could do was pick something and hope that it wouldn't poison him. He had to eat. Ellsben grabbed a branch of a nearby tree and studied its leaves. He'd never heard of anyone getting sick from eating the leaves of a tree. Ellsben put a leaf in his mouth and slowly chewed it. The leaf tasted waxy and slightly bitter. He swallowed the leaf and waited for something bad to happen. Other than a soft gurgling noise from his stomach, nothing happened. Ellsben plucked a handful of leaves from the tree and stuffed them into his mouth. He chewed them and then swallowed. His hunger pangs began to subside. He plucked more leaves and ate them.

Suddenly he felt full; he felt as if he'd eaten twice as much as what he'd actually eaten. Ellsben rubbed his stomach. He belched, and this relieved some of the pressure that was building in his gut, but this relief didn't last long. Soon the pressure in his gut was so severe he had to hunch his torso. Now he felt incredibly thirsty.

Ellsben started walking, and this made his gut hurt even more, but he couldn't stop walking because his need for water had become overwhelming. He had to find water. He tried to trot, but it was too painful. The ground began to feel as if it were moving like waves on a lake. Ellsben stumbled. His vision blurred. He curled up on the ground, clutching his stomach and squeezing his eyes shut. He was certain he was going to die.

His abdominal muscles rapidly tightened and relaxed, tightened and relaxed, making him feel as if he was being kicked in the gut. Watery saliva pooled under his tongue. Suddenly, everything that was in his stomach came gushing out of his mouth. When it was finally all out, he spit several times, trying to get rid of the bitter taste of the puke.

He opened his eyes and looked at the withered leaves on the ground, not far from his face. He wanted to get up. He still desperately needed to find water, but he had no strength; it took all his energy just to be able to blink. An insect buzzed near his ear, and he couldn't even bring his hand up to swat it away. He was in a state somewhere between consciousness and unconsciousness. All he could do was look at the leaves on the ground. He watched as the leaves' color turned from the blue tint of the moonlight to the orange hue of the morning sun. His tongue felt swollen and dry.

"You poor soul," a female voice whispered. He would've been startled by the suddenness of this voice, but the voice was so gentle it soothed rather than startled him. "You poor, poor soul." A cool hand stroked his forehead. He looked up, but didn't see anybody. "You need water," the voice said. "Let me get it for you." The speaker went away. Ellsben could tell he was alone, but the speaker quickly returned.

"Here, drink." A white hand, fingers curled, palm holding water, appeared in front of Ellsben's face. Somehow he thought he could see through the hand. "Drink," the voice said. The hand moved closer to Ellsben's face, and he felt cool water trickle into his mouth. He swallowed the water. The hand came back with more water several more times. "That's enough," the voice said. The muscles in Ellsben's legs and arms twitched; his paralysis was seeping away.

"When you get up, walk east, toward the sun, and you will find a path. When you are on the path, turn so that the sun is on your right side," the voice said. "Do you understand?"

"Yes." Ellsben nodded.

"The path will lead you to a house. In front of the house there is a wagon with a broken wheel. Go to the house; you'll find friends there."

The speaker of the voice was gone. It was as if she'd become part of the air and had drifted away like smoke in a breeze. Ellsben stretched out his arms; his muscles were stiff, and it hurt to move. Trying his best to ignore the pain, Ellsben twisted his body to get his legs and hooves underneath him so that he could push himself up, so that he could stand. The muscles and tendons in his legs shot waves of pain through him as he moved, but he did manage to stand up. At first he felt dizzy and was afraid he was going to fall over. He closed his eyes and concentrated on his balance, and after a minute, the dizziness went away.

Feeling almost as if invisible hands were pushing him, Ellsben turned toward the morning sun and started walking. He walked for about half an hour before he came to the path the voice had told him about. It was a narrow footpath that appeared to be rarely used; in places small, young branches were growing into the path. Again feeling as if invisible hands were pushing him, Ellsben turned left on the path so that the sun was on his right side. He followed the path, pushing aside the branches that were growing into it. He walked for almost a mile. The path ended at the edge of the woods. Not far from the end of the path was a small house. In front of the house was a wagon with a broken wheel. Feeling as if he were in a trance, Ellsben walked toward the house. When he was near the wagon with the broken wheel, the strength he'd gotten from the water left him. His legs gave up, and he collapsed.

Just as Ellsben collapsed, Ily came out of the house. She was bringing a basket of wet laundry out to hang on the clotheslines. When she saw him, she dropped the basket and ran to him and asked, "Are you hurt?"

He couldn't answer her at first because he was surprised. The moment he saw her drop the laundry basket, he was certain she was going to scream and men were going to come and hobble him, and then he would probably be killed. The new Mr. Kand wouldn't pay for his return, and nobody would want to take a naggie who keeps running away. However, once he heard her ask if he was hurt, he knew none of what he'd just imagined was going to happen. He knew the voice in the woods had directed him to friends.

"Are you hurt?" Ily asked again.

"I'm thirsty and hungry," Ellsben said. His voice sounded scratchy and deeper than usual. Ellsben told her about the leaves he'd eaten, how they'd made him sick, and then he told her that someone had brought him water this morning and told him to come here for help.

"We will help you," Ily confirmed. "Let me get my husband."

When Ralt arrived the first thing he did was ask Ellsben if he could stand. "You can't stay here in plain sight," Ralt said. "We've got to hide you."

"I think I can get up," Ellsben said.

Ily brought him a cup of water, and he quickly drank it. He took a deep breath and then, carefully, stood up.

"Here," Ralt said. "Put your hand on my shoulder. You'll be able to steady yourself that way."

Ellsben put his hand on Ralt's shoulder. He'd never had a twoer treat him like an equal before; the twoers who were friendly always made it subtly clear, through their body language and tone of voice, that they believed they were superior. Optimism swelled inside Ellsben, and this optimism gave him strength. These twoers were his friends, and he knew that they would help him find and rescue his family.

Ralt brought Ellsben into his barn. At the back of the barn there was a large pile of hay. Ralt picked up a pitchfork and began moving the hay. Behind the hay was a door. Ralt opened the door and motioned for Ellsben to follow him. Ellsben walked though the doorway and found himself in a small room. "This is where you can stay until you get your strength back. If anyone comes around looking for you, they won't find you here," Ralt said. "We've hidden half a dozen runaway centaurs in here over the past five years."

"Thank you," Ellsben said.

"Ily's gone to brush away your tracks, so no one will be able to follow them. I'll bring you some food."

After several days of rest, Ellsben regained his health. Ralt made arrangements with a friend to find an apprenticeship for Ellsben. "Now that you're free, you'll need to be able to support yourself," Ralt said. "You're going to have to learn a trade."

Ellsben told Ralt that he couldn't consider himself free until he was with his family. He was going to go back and find his family. Ralt said there were people who could help Ellsben find where his family was, but it would take a while to arrange this because finding his family would be difficult. "While the arrangements are being made," Ralt said, "you need to begin learning a trade so that you can support your family once they're free."

Ralt's friend found a carpenter who was willing to teach Ellsben carpentry. This carpenter lived and worked deep in the Northern provinces, so Ellsben wouldn't have to worry about the bounty hunters who frequently slipped over the border to search for runaways. Bounty hunters were hated by most of the North, and they rarely dared to go more than several miles into the Northern provinces. Ralt told Ellsben that bounty hunters showed up on his property several times every month. That was why Ellsben had to be kept hidden in the barn.

Ellsben enjoyed learning carpentry; he was fascinated by how things were built. During the period he was learning carpentry, Ellsben spent his free time studying navigation and wilderness survival. He learned navigation and survival skills from an old man who had spent many years exploring the Western territories. Unfortunately, before Ellsben had mastered his survival skills, the war began. Once the war started, Ellsben didn't dare go back to the Southern provinces because the new Congresser government had issued orders to have all runaway centaurs killed. He wasn't afraid of being caught, because he was confident he could keep out of sight, but he was afraid if he tried to bring his family to the North, they might get caught, and there was no way he was going to risk that. To make matters even more complicated, when the war started, Ralt's friends lost their ability to communicate with their sources in the South. Because of the war, it had become impossible for Ralt's friends to figure out where Ellsben's family was.

———

"We need to leave now," Ellsben said. He glanced out the window and frowned. "I've been talking too long. We should have already left."

"Mont," Ily said. "I've got a pack for you. It's in the living room, next to Cal's pack."

"Thanks," Mont said.

"I've packed a blanket for you and some of Ralt's work clothes. The clothes are a bit too big for you, but if you roll up the shirtsleeves and pant legs, you should be able to wear them."

They went into the living room. Zinn was pale, and he was gently massaging the muscles around the knee of his injured leg. Ralt asked him how he felt, and Zinn said the pain was getting worse.

"We're leaving," Mont said to Zinn. "Ralt can get the doctor for you now."

"Listen," Zinn said. "You're going to need a story to tell people when you meet them."

"Don't worry," Mont said. "I can come up with plenty of stories."

"No." Zinn flashed an angry look at Mont. "If you try to make up a story on the spot, a perceptive person will catch the inconsistencies, even subtle ones, in your story." Zinn turned his attention to Cal. "When you meet people, tell them that you and Mont are brothers. Say you're the Graton boys. Cal, your first name will be Lang, and Mont's name will be Cron. You can tell people that Ellsben belonged to your father, and your father died in the war, so you're bringing the centaur to your uncle. Tell them that you're moving in with your uncle because your farm is in debt, and now that your father is gone, there's no way you'll be able to get out of debt. You have to get rid of your farm. Your mother is going to come to your uncle's farm in several weeks, as soon as she takes care of some business. Act like you're in a hurry, so that you won't have to talk to anyone for very long. Say as little as possible."

"And Cal," Ralt said. "You need to be careful when you speak. You have an upper-class accent. With that accent there's no way anyone's going to believe that you grew up in the Southern provinces. You're going to have to do your best to mimic the accents of the people you meet."

"Don't worry, I can do the talking," Mont said with a realistic-sounding Southern accent. "I can talk just like those Southern boys."

"That's pretty good," Ralt said. "I'm impressed."

Zinn looked at Mont and shook his head. "You're over-confident. Don't assume that your accent is going to fool everyone. Say as little as possible."

"I won't say any more than I have to," Mont said to Zinn.

"You know, I still don't like the idea of you going along with Cal," Zinn said. "Your presence is going to complicate the journey and could cause it to fail."

"I think Mont's presence will help," Cal said. "He's dependable. I trust him."

Zinn looked like he wanted to contradict Cal, but he didn't. He said nothing.

"We need to leave," Ellsben said.

"Yes." Zinn nodded. "You should go."

Cal and Mont picked up their packs. Mont asked Ralt to contact his aunt and tell her that he was OK, that he was helping a friend and would be back as soon as he could. "Try to convince her not to worry," Mont said. "She worries about me a lot." Ralt said he would do this. Mont gave him directions to his aunt's house.

Zinn motioned for Cal to come close to him. He grabbed Cal's hand and clasped his shoulder. "Be careful," Zinn said.

"I will," Cal said. "I promise."

Ily hugged the boys and told them she'd put enough food in their packs to last them a week as long as they were careful and didn't eat too much of it right away. Ralt shook hands with Cal and Mont and wished them luck.

They went outside, and Ellsben led them directly to the woods.

SEVEN

SAMA'S GHOST

With the exception of several quick stops to rest, Ellsben kept them moving until the sun started to set. "We've got to cover a lot of territory as quickly as possible," Ellsben said. He looked at the boys, hoping they weren't mad at him. They both smiled at Ellsben, letting him know that of course they weren't mad.

"This hiking has been pretty tough," Mont said. "But is sure as heck beats sitting in a classroom all day."

Cal agreed, and Ellsben laughed.

As soon as they had their camp set up for the night, Cal sat down and took off his shoes. His feet hurt. The paths they'd followed today were narrow, and most of them were overgrown. They had to push branches and vines out of the way as they hiked, and they also had to frequently step over brush that was beginning to grow in patches on the paths.

Ellsben made a small campfire, and then they began eating their dinner. When they were finished eating, Mont looked at Ellsben and asked, "Did you ever get to meet the person whose voice you heard when you were sick from eating those leaves, the person who brought you water and directed you to Ralt and Ily?"

"No." Ellsben shook his head once.

"The person obviously knew Ralt and Ily."

"She did."

"And Ralt and Ily don't know who it was?"

"They have their suspicions."

"Did they tell you who they think it was?"

"They didn't need to tell me. I know."

Mont raised his eyebrows. "Who was it? How come you never saw her again?"

Ellsben glanced around as if he was about to do something wrong and was afraid he might get caught. "I don't know if I should tell you."

"Why not?" Mont asked.

Ellsben was silent for a moment, and then he said, "I'll tell you only if both you and Cal promise never to mention what I'm about to tell you in front of Ralt or Ily."

Cal and Mont both promised.

"It was their daughter," Ellsben whispered.

"Why can't we mention that their daughter helped you?" Cal wanted to know.

"Because she's dead."

"How come you never met her?" Mont asked. "Did she die right after she helped you?"

"No. She died before she helped me."

"That doesn't make any sense."

"It was her ghost that helped me."

"How do you know that?" Mont leaned his head back, and his expression made it clear that he strongly doubted what Ellsben had just told him.

"When she gave me water, I could see right through her hand. That's how I knew it was a ghost helping me. I didn't know that she was their daughter until one night when Ily told me about her daughter. Her name was Sama, and she was the one who convinced her parents that they should help runaway centaurs. When she was twelve years old, she saw a runaway centaur who had been caught by bounty hunters. The centaur had been captured only a short distance from her home. Sama was outside in her yard hanging laundry on the line when she heard a bunch of noise down the road from her home. She went to see what the noise was and found four bounty hunters beating and hobbling a runaway centaur. She'd never seen anything like this in her life, and she couldn't stand to see it . She ran home screaming and crying. She told her mother and father about what she'd seen, and she told them that they had to start helping runaway centaurs. At first Ralt and Ily refused to even consider this because of the danger it would put them in if they were caught, but Sama wouldn't give up. She kept on them until they finally agreed to help. She even went with her father when he went to his first abolitionist meeting. He joined a secret local abolitionist group, and she joined too."

"Did she die helping a runaway centaur?" Mont asked.

"No. Ily told me that Sama hit her head when she dove into the river near their house, and she drowned. Sama was only eighteen years old. Ily told me that she and Ralt still haven't gotten over Sama's death. Ily said that her absence is a pain that they feel every day."

"You think Sama's ghost haunts the woods near her house?" Cal asked.

"She doesn't haunt the woods," Ellsben said. "She's just sort of there, invisible. She only makes her presence known when there's somebody who needs help."

Ellsben scooped up some dirt and threw it on the campfire, putting it out. "Time to get some sleep," Ellsben said.

Cal and Mont got their blankets out, and they each searched for the softest spot on the ground to lie down. Cal spread his blanket out on the best piece of ground that he could find. When he lay down he felt a small rock that he hadn't seen pressing against his lower back. Cal rolled over on his side, reached under his blanket, found the rock, and tossed it into some nearby brush.

Ellsben had settled near where the campfire had been. "Goodnight," Ellsben whispered.

"Goodnight," both Cal and Mont returned.

Cal fell asleep almost instantly. He was exhausted. If he had any dreams, he didn't remember them; he sank into a deep sleep that both his mind and body needed. He'd been asleep for a little over an hour when a hand grabbed his shoulder. Cal's eyes flashed open, and adrenaline surged into his system. He started to yell, but the hand quickly covered his mouth, stopping him.

"Shhh. Cal, it's me. It's Mont." Mont leaned close so that Cal could see his face. There was no moon; the only light came from what the stars were dimly emitting.

Cal pulled Mont's hand away from his mouth. "What's the matter?" Cal whispered.

"I couldn't sleep," Mont said. He sounded out of breath. "So I decided I might as well get up and explore the area around here a little bit."

"What happened?"

"I went in that direction," Mont said, pointing to his left. "I went about half a mile when I saw a couple of men. They didn't see me. I stayed hidden."

Cal sat up. "Where are the men now?"

"They're coming this way. I think they're looking for you. They're walking around like they're searching for something. We've got to hide. Hurry."

"We need to wake up Ellsben." Cal hurriedly put on his shoes and then scrambled over to where Ellsben was. "Ellsben," Cal whispered. He touched Ellsben's arm, and Ellsben opened his eyes.

"What's wrong?"

"There are men coming this way," Cal said. "Mont saw them."

"Quick, get into that brush over there," Ellsben said. "Stay out of sight until I signal that it's OK to come out. You might have to spend the rest of the night hidden. Now go. Disappear."

Cal and Mont grabbed their packs and blankets and ran to the brush and tried to push their way into it, but the brush was too thick. The tangled branches made it impossible to penetrate. They went around the brush and into an area of the woods where the branches of several trees growing close together almost completely blocked out the light coming down from the stars. They dropped their packs, stuffed their blankets in their packs, and lay on the ground. From where they were they could still faintly see the dark shape of Ellsben. He hadn't gotten up; he was pretending to be asleep.

"Maybe those men you saw won't show up here," Cal said.

"Maybe," Mont said. "But when I saw them they were headed straight toward our campsite."

"How'd you see them in the dark? You must have been right next to them."

"No. One of them was carrying a lantern and—" Mont abruptly stopped talking. He nudged Cal with his elbow and pointed. A light had appeared in the woods directly in front of them. The light rapidly grew brighter, closer.

Soon Cal and Mont could see the faces of two men. The man carrying the lantern had curly black hair and narrow, mean eyes. The other man, who appeared to be the leader, had a thin red beard and straight red hair that hung down to his shoulders. Both men were dressed like farmers, but their choice of clothes didn't disguise them because, unlike farmers, both men had swords in scabbards attached to their belts. The man with the red hair was also holding a crossbow.

"Those are bounty hunters," Mont said. "I'll bet you anything that's what they are."

"Do you think they'll hurt Ellsben?"

"They better not."

The men suddenly saw Ellsben. They stopped walking, and the man with the lantern held it out so that its light illuminated Ellsben's face. Ellsben was still pretending to be asleep. The men glanced around to see if there was anyone else nearby. They didn't see anyone, but from the way they kept looking around it was obvious that they believed Ellsben had companions nearby.

"Naggie," the red-haired man said. His voice was deep and rough sounding. "You wake up, naggie."

Ellsben opened his eyes. He pretended to be half asleep and confused.

"What are you doing here, naggie?" the red-haired man asked.

"Huh?" Ellsben blinked several times, still pretending to be confused. He rubbed his eyes with the palm of his right hand.

"You better answer me, naggie. What are you doing here?"

"My master was hurt in the war. He's not able to walk. I was sent to get him and bring him home. His wife's sick with worry."

"Liar." The red-haired man's arm twitched as if he was considering lifting the crossbow and aiming it at Ellsben. "Tell me the real reason why you're here."

"I didn't lie to you, sir."

"You're an escapee, aren't you?"

"No sir."

"I think you are."

"No sir, I'm not. I've got a pass. If you want, I can show it to you."

"A pass doesn't mean a damn thing. Someone could've forged a pass for you."

"No sir, the pass is real. I'm telling you the truth."

Cal and Mont were amazed by Ellsben. He was now speaking with a heavy slave accent and was acting completely subservient to the man who was questioning him. This was a new Ellsben—or maybe this was the old Ellsben, the way Ellsben had to act when he was a slave.

"Are you traveling with anyone?"

"No sir." Ellsben shook his head.

The red-haired man looked Ellsben up and down as if the sight of Ellsben disgusted him. "We're looking for a couple of boys."

"Boys?" Ellsben looked confused.

"They're twelve years old. Have you seen any boys around here?"

Ellsben shook his head; he still appeared confused. "I haven't seen no boys."

"Don't lie." The red-haired man took a step toward Ellsben. "The boys we're looking for, their lives are in danger. There are people who want to kill these boys. We were sent to find them and protect them."

Ellsben stared at the red-haired man.

"They're lying," Cal whispered to Mont. "Ellsben better not believe them."

"Get ready to run," Mont whispered back. "If he does believe them, we've got to get out of here."

"Where are the boys?" the red-haired man asked.

"I haven't seen no boys."

"Are you sure?"

"Yep." Ellsben nodded. "The truth is, you gentlemen are the first folks I've seen since the day before yesterday."

The red-haired man stared at Ellsben for a long time. Then he said, "You better not be lying."

"It's the truth. I haven't seen no boys."

"We're not going far," the red-haired man told Ellsben. "If we catch you with those boys, if we find out that you've lied to us, you're dead." The red-haired man pointed his crossbow at Ellsben.

"I told you the truth, I swear. I haven't seen no boys." Ellsben held his hands out as if begging. His eyes were wide.

"You better be telling the truth." The red-haired man turned and made a signal with his right hand to the man holding the lantern. The man nodded, acknowledging the signal, and then he raised the lantern up so that its light reached farther in front of them. They walked off into the area of the woods that was located to the right of Ellsben.

Cal and Mont watched the light from the lantern until it disappeared. "I think we should stay here," Cal whispered.

"I agree," Mont said. "I've got a feeling those men are going to circle back so that they can check on Ellsben. We should stay here until the sun comes up. Then we can see what Ellsben thinks, but I think we should try to get away from this area as quick as possible."

"Are you going to sleep?" Cal asked.

"I don't think I can now," Mont said.

"I don't think I can either."

Cal and Mont watched for the light from the lantern, and they listened for sounds from the men. They didn't see the lantern again, and the only sounds they heard were crickets and the occasional hooting of an owl. After a while both Cal and Mont began to feel tired, and although they fought it, sleep, like a strong current, eventually overwhelmed them.

EIGHT

SOMETHING BAD

Cal heard birds chirping. He opened his eyes. The sky was covered with thick gray clouds, and since he couldn't see the sun's position in the sky, Cal couldn't estimate what time it was. He hoped it was early.

Mont was asleep and so was Ellsben. Cal sat up. The muscles in his shoulders and back were stiff from lying on the hard ground. He reached his arms over his head and winced from the pain he felt as he stretched. He stood up. "Ow," he muttered. Even the muscles in his legs were stiff. "Hey, Mont," Cal said.

Mont mumbled in his sleep.

"Hey, get up," Cal said.

Mont's eyes fluttered open. He yawned. "I didn't mean to fall asleep," Mont said. "I wanted to stay up and keep a lookout for those men. You shouldn't have let me sleep."

"I fell asleep."

"That's no good." Mont frowned. "We shouldn't have both gone to sleep. What if those men had come back?"

"Ellsben fell asleep too."

Mont stood up and looked at Ellsben. "I shouldn't have let myself fall asleep," Mont said. He swore and angrily kicked the ground with his heel. "We've got to be more careful in the future."

Cal nodded. "I tried to stay awake. I just couldn't keep my eyes open."

"I should have gotten up and walked around. That would've kept me awake," Mont said. "That's what I'll do from now on. If I'm keeping watch, I'll move around. I should've followed those men last night. It would have been good if we knew where they went."

"We can worry about what we'll do next time when next time comes," Cal said. "Right now we need to get moving." Cal picked up his pack and walked over to Ellsben. Mont picked up his pack and followed Cal.

"Ellsben," Cal said.

Ellsben's eyes opened, and he immediately stood up. Cal was startled by how quickly Ellsben got up. "Have you seen those men again?" Ellsben asked. He looked around.

"No," Cal said.

"We just woke up," Mont said.

"Those men are probably nearby," Ellsben said. "We need to get away from this area, but let's quickly eat something before we go. Once we get moving, I don't want to stop until it gets dark."

They ate some of the food that Ily had put in each of their packs. Ellsben and Mont appeared calm, but Cal felt nervous. Maybe it was just his imagination—he hoped it was just his imagination—but he had a feeling that something bad was about to happen.

"How many miles do you think we'll be able to cover today?" Mont asked.

"Depends on the terrain," Ellsben said. "The area we're going to travel through today is pretty flat, so that should help. But if we run into a lot of underbrush, that could slow us down quite a bit."

When they finished eating, Ellsben led them into the woods. They didn't return to the tiny path that they had been following the day before. "I want to stay away from that path because those men or others might be watching the path," Ellsben said. "Staying in the woods right now is the safest way to travel. But if the clouds don't go away, it's going to be difficult to know for sure that we're traveling in the proper direction because during the day the sun is the best thing to navigate by."

"It looks like it's going to rain," Mont said.

"I hope not," Ellsben said.

Mont looked at Cal and said, "Why are you being so quiet? You're not sick, are you?"

Cal shook his head. "I'm all right."

"Good." Mont smiled and slapped Cal on the shoulder.

Even though Cal had said he was all right, he honestly didn't feel all right. He still had the feeling that something bad was about to happen. There was a nervous tingling in the pit of his gut that wouldn't go away.

"If it rains, I'm going to take my shoes off," Mont said. "I hate walking in wet shoes. They start making this squeaking sound when they're wet, and then they always end up making my feet smell."

"Won't it hurt your feet to walk without shoes?" Ellsben asked.

STEFAN HAUCKE

"Nah," Mont said. "My feet are tough. I walk around barefoot all summer."

"I'm glad I have hooves," Ellsben said. "Feet are too fragile. If I had feet, I'd hate to have to stuff them into shoes or boots."

"I wish I had hooves," Mont said. "What do you think, Cal? Wouldn't you rather have hooves?"

"Yeah, I guess so," Cal said.

Mont looked at Cal. "What's the matter?"

"Nothing's the matter," Cal said.

"You're acting like you don't feel well," Mont said. "Are you sure you feel all right?"

"Yeah. I'm fine."

"Do you want to stop and rest for a minute?" Mont asked.

"No. I'm—" Something whooshed past Cal's head, and then there was a sharp cracking sound. For a moment Cal's mind caused him to feel as if time had stopped; he saw no movements and heard no sounds. Then time abruptly seemed to be flowing at more than twice its normal rate. Cal turned his head and saw that the cracking sound he'd heard had come from a bolt that had been shot from a crossbow and had hit a tree. The bolt had knocked away bark and had deeply penetrated the tree's trunk, causing a large split to appear above and below the spot where the bolt had entered the trunk. Cal's strength suddenly left him, and he almost tumbled over as he realized that the whooshing sound he'd heard had been the bolt passing by his head. He'd almost been killed. That bolt had been shot at him.

"What was that?" Mont asked. He appeared both scared and confused.

With amazing speed, Ellsben reached down and wrapped his left arm around Cal's waist and his right arm around Mont's waist. He lifted them up, hugged them close to his chest, and then charged forward. Another whooshing sound. Ellsben let out a grunt. Cal looked back and saw that Ellsben's left flank was bleeding; he'd been hit by a bolt from a crossbow. "Are you OK?" Cal asked.

"Yes, it just grazed me. It didn't go in," Ellsben said. "Now climb on my back. Both of you. I can run faster if you're on my back."

Cal held on to Ellsben's arm as he twisted his body until he was able to swing his right leg over Ellsben's withers. Cal straddled the equine part of Ellsben's back and wrapped his arms around Ellsben's waist to keep himself from falling. Mont managed to get behind Cal; he held on by hooking his right arm around Cal's chest.

Ellsben galloped with all his might. The world around Cal and Mont turned into a blur, and Cal had to close his eyes because seeing the speed they were moving was making him nauseous. Cal could feel a jolt every time one of Ellsben's hooves contacted the ground. Never once had Cal imagined himself riding a centaur. Being ridden was considered degrading by centaurs; they felt it brought them down, made them appear to be horses. Free centaurs never consented to be ridden.

When Ellsben became tired and had to slow down to a canter, Cal had no idea how far they had gotten from the place where they had been attacked because everything had happened so fast his sense of time was distorted, and without a clear sense of time he couldn't begin to guess the distance they'd traveled. Ellsben stopped cantering and started walking.

"You boys are going to have to get down now," Ellsben said. He was gasping for breath. "I've just about used up all my energy."

Cal and Mont climbed down from Ellsben's back and walked beside him. Sweat was trickling down Ellsben's face from his forehead. He stopped and clutched his sides. "I don't think I've ever galloped so fast in my life," he said.

The wound on Ellsben's left flank was still bleeding, but the flow of blood was beginning to slow. A scab was starting to form.

"Does it hurt?" Cal asked.

Ellsben looked back at his wound. "Nah," he said, shaking his head. "It stings a little, but that's all. It's not very deep; it's barely more than a scratch."

"Everything happened so fast I didn't even see anybody," Mont said.

"I did," Ellsben said. His breathing was returning to normal. "It was those two bounty hunters from last night. I saw the man with the red hair."

"When?" Cal asked.

"After he shot the first bolt. The bolt that hit the tree."

"Do you think we lost them?" Mont asked.

"No," Ellsben said. "Those men will easily be able to follow the tracks I left when I galloped away. They're following us now. We've got to keep moving, and we've got to stay in the woods and away from any clearings. It's going to be almost impossible to make it so that those men can't track us."

NINE

THREE CENTAURS

They traveled for almost an hour without speaking. They were nervous, every sound—the snapping of a stick that was stepped on to the rapid fluttering of a bird's wings as it flew up into the air—caused them to cringe. Cal's back tingled; he kept imagining a bolt from a crossbow slamming into him, knocking him to the ground, tearing his flesh, causing his warm blood to gush out and soak into the dry dirt beneath him. It would be a miracle if they ever made it to General Grintar.

Ellsben abruptly stopped walking.

"What's wrong?" Mont whispered.

Ellsben pointed at his nose. Cal sniffed the air and caught a faint whiff of woodsmoke. "There's a campfire nearby," Ellsben whispered.

"What should we do now?" Cal asked.

"Keep moving. Be as quiet as you can. The smoke is coming from that direction." Ellsben pointed to his right. "We'll go in the opposite direction. Come on."

As they walked, Cal was acutely aware of every dried leaf and fallen twig that softly crunched under their feet. He knew the sounds they were making as they walked were barely audible, but to his ears they sounded as loud as overhead thunder. Even his breathing seemed loud to him.

Relax, Cal told himself. *Relax.*

Mont cupped a hand over his mouth and sneezed. "Sorry," Mont whispered.

Ellsben stopped walking. He tilted his head as if he was listening for something, and then he shrugged and resumed walking. Mont scrunched up his nose, trying to hold back another sneeze.

Someone, somewhere let out a high-pitched yell that echoed through the woods. Cal was ready to run, but he wasn't sure which direction he should run because he couldn't tell which direction the yell had originated. Ellsben grunted and pulled Cal and Mont close to him. "Get ready to climb on my back," Ellsben said. "We might have to get out of here fast."

Another yell. Then the sounds of hooves pounding the ground. Suddenly three centaurs came into view. Each centaur had a sword raised above his head. They galloped up and surrounded Cal, Mont, and Ellsben. All three of the centaurs had scruffy beards and long, unkempt hair. Their shirts were filthy, and they smelled of body odor and woodsmoke. The biggest centaur was the apparent leader. He put his sword in a scabbard and approached Ellsben. This centaur had a deep scar on his chin and, Cal noticed, he was missing his left thumb.

"Who are you?" the leader asked Ellsben.

"My name is Ellsben."

"What are you doing with these twoers?"

"We're going to the Western territories. To meet some friends," Cal answered.

The leader's eyes narrowed, and he frowned. "Is this here your naggie?" The leader pointed at Ellsben.

"No," Cal said. "He's—"

"Liar!" The leader took a step toward Cal and loudly stomped his right front hoof. "That's your naggie. He's your naggie."

"He's not my naggie," Cal said. "He's my friend."

"Your *friend*?" The leader let out a loud, angry laugh. Then he looked down at Cal and said, "Do you think I have manure for brains?"

Cal sensed that anything he said would make the leader angrier, so he decided it would be best to keep his mouth shut.

"This naggie is your slave," the leader said. "You're from the upper class—I can tell from your accent." The leader snorted and then did a poor imitation of Cal's accent, "He's not my naggie, he's my *friend*."

The leader's followers both laughed.

"How many naggies does your family own?" the leader asked.

"None," Cal said. "My family is from the Northern provinces. We've never owned slaves."

The leader ripped his sword from its scabbard and thrust the tip of the sword against Cal's chest. As soon as this happened, the followers stepped back and held their swords out, ready, if given the order, to attack.

"Don't lie to me, boy," the leader said. He brought his sword up so that its tip was touching Cal's neck, right under his chin.

"I'm not lying." Cal's voice sounded far calmer than he felt.

"He's telling the truth," Ellsben said.

The leader turned his attention to Ellsben. "Do you consider this twoer your friend?"

"Yes," Ellsben said.

"You're an idiot." The leader loudly cleared his throat and spit on the ground. His spit almost hit Cal's feet. "You've been raised in the north. Up there the twoers pretend to like us naggies. You don't know what it's like to be one of their slaves."

Ellsben scowled. "I was born a slave. My wife and son are still slaves. They were sold, and I don't know where they are, and not knowing where they are or how they are eats at me every day. I know what it's like to be a slave—I know what it's like."

"Twoers sold your family, and then you become friends with towers? You're crazy." The leader shook his head as if he was trying to rid his mind of a disgusting thought.

"Not all twoers are bad," Ellsben said. "There are good twoers and there are bad twoers, just like there are good naggies and bad naggies."

"Bah! All twoers are bad." The leader stomped his right front hoof. "Even the abolitionists. They act oh so nice, but they don't really believe that we're equal to them. They feel sorry for us the way somebody would feel sorry for an animal."

"Have you ever met an abolitionist?" Ellsben asked.

"I don't want to meet one. When the war started, my friends and I escaped because most of the twoers who oversaw us went off to fight. It was easy to escape. But we never tried to find any abolitionists. We don't need their help, and we sure as hell don't want their pity. We've taken care of ourselves for four years. It hasn't been easy—we've had to steal, and we're not proud of it—but at least we've never had to accept charity from any twoers."

"You don't need to accept charity," Cal said. "There are people in the Northern provinces who can teach you and your friends a trade. You could work. That's what Ellsben did."

"Isn't the little boy nice? What a nice little twoer—it's so nice that he's willing to give us dumb naggies such wonderful advice." The leader leaned forward and shoved Cal, knocking him down. "Do you have any more advice for us dumb naggies?"

"Leave him alone!" Mont shouted.

With unbelievable speed, the leader twisted his torso toward Mont and swung his arm down, smashing the back of his hand across Mont's face. Mont was knocked off his feet. He landed on his back, letting out a loud, "Omp!" Mont sat up, and blood streamed out of his nostrils. He wiped his face and looked at his hand, and when he saw the blood his face tightened with anger. He got to his feet and clenched his hands into fists and lunged at the leader.

"No!" Ellsben shouted. He grabbed Mont by the back of his shirt and pulled h
.0im away.

"Let me go!" Mont yelled. He squirmed, trying to slip out of his shirt, trying to get away from Ellsben. "I'm not afraid of him," Mont said. "Let me fight him."

"No." Ellsben hooked his arm around Mont's chest and tightly held him, preventing him from breaking free. Mont flailed his arms and kicked his legs and swore loudly.

The leader's lips retracted, creating an angry grin. He waved his sword over his head and kicked his hind hooves and shouted, "Kill the twoers! Kill them!"

The followers whooped and held their swords out and started circling Cal, Mont, and Ellsben. "Give us the two-ers," one of the followers said to Ellsben.

"Stop." Ellsben looked the leader in the eyes. "If you hurt these boys, I'll gallop out of here and find the local law, and I'll send them after you. I'll make sure they find you. And you know what will happen when they find you."

The leader kept his gaze locked on Ellsben's eyes. He wanted to see if Ellsben was bluffing, and when he realized that Ellsben wasn't bluffing, he let out a loud, angry screech. Then he slammed one of his front hooves down on the ground, spraying dirt into the air. The leader motioned for his followers to back away from Cal, Mont, and Ellsben. His followers obeyed.

"Take your twoers and get away from us, you damn twoer lover," the leader said to Ellsben. "Get away."

"Let's go," Ellsben said to Cal and Mont.

Ellsben made sure Cal and Mont were in front of him as they left because he wanted to keep himself in between them and the centaurs just in case the centaurs decided to charge at them. If the centaurs charged, Ellsben would kick them and fight them and hopefully buy enough time for Cal and Mont to get away.

But the centaurs didn't charge. All they did was scream, "Twoer lover! Filthy twoer lover!" until Cal, Mont, and Ellsben reached a point where the centaurs could no longer see them.

TEN

THE FARMER

When darkness arrived, they were not in a place where they could camp for the night. They were in an open area, and this made Ellsben nervous. Even though a thick cloud cover was blocking the stars and moon, making it almost impossible to see anything, Ellsben insisted that they keep moving. It was difficult walking in the darkness; they had to take small steps to prevent themselves from stumbling over any unseen objects on the ground. Cal couldn't even see his feet.

"We could stop and camp right here," Ellsben said. "The darkness will protect us. But if the clouds go away after we fall asleep, this area will light up from the moon, and anyone looking for us will easily be able to see us. We need to camp in a forest with the trees and brush to hide us."

"I don't mind walking in the dark," Mont said. "Besides, I'm not sleepy, so I'd rather be walking than lying down, tossing and turning."

"I'm not sleepy either," Cal said. "I feel like I should be walking."

They continued walking for what seemed like an hour, but because they were moving so slowly, Cal felt like they hadn't even walked a mile. He wondered how much longer, how much farther they would have to walk before they would get to a place where it would be safe to camp.

Ellsben suddenly stopped.

"What's wrong?" Cal asked.

"I'm not sure what direction we're going anymore," Ellsben said. "Without the stars, there's no way to know for sure which direction we're facing. I've got a bad feeling that we've just walked in a big circle."

"Maybe we should stop and camp here," Cal said.

"I'm still not tired," Mont said. "Why don't you guys rest here, and I'll stay awake. If the clouds go away, I'll wake you up, and we can get moving again."

"If we do stop here, you can't fall asleep," Ellsben said.

"Don't worry, I've learned my lesson," Mont said. "I won't even sit down. As long as I'm standing, there's no way I'll fall asleep."

"I guess stopping here is the best thing to do," Ellsben said. "But I wish we didn't have to stop. Sleeping out in the open like this makes me nervous."

"I'll stay awake, I promise," Mont said. "If the moon comes out, or if anything happens, I'll—"

Suddenly half a dozen tiny, blinking green lights surrounded Cal, Mont, and Ellsben. The green lights swarmed around their heads and then fluttered down to the ground in front of them.

"Fireflies," Cal said.

The green lights lifted up into the air and began moving away.

"Follow them," Ellsben said.

"Why?" Mont asked.

"I've been told fireflies always travel from east to west," Ellsben said.

"They do?" Cal had never heard this before.

"Yes. I've been told they travel from east to west because they're trying to follow the sun. When they wake up in the evening, they are attracted to the last rays of the sun's light. If we follow the fireflies, we will be going west, the direction we're supposed to be going."

They followed the fireflies, but the fireflies were difficult to keep up with. They had to move twice as fast as they'd been moving, and this caused them to stumble over objects on the ground. Cal tripped over a rock and fell forward. He thrust his arms out, and his hands smacked the ground. Sharp pebbles scraped his palms.

"You all right?" Mont asked.

"I'm fine," Cal said. He stood up and rubbed his hands together, brushing the dirt from them. His palms stung.

Up ahead the fireflies descended to the ground as if waiting for Cal, Mont, and Ellsben to catch up.

"Don't move toward them," Ellsben said. "If we scare them, they might scatter. We've got to let them fly the way they want to go, toward the direction the sun set."

The fireflies rested on the ground for maybe a minute, their green lights slowly blinking, and then they abruptly lifted up and flew into the darkness.

"Quick," Ellsben said. "Follow them."

Cal, Mont, and Ellsben did their best to keep up with the fireflies, but the fireflies were gradually getting farther and farther ahead. Their blinking lights were getting smaller and smaller. Cal's heel sank in a small hole, and he stumbled, but didn't fall. The fireflies descended as if they were about to land, giving Cal, Mont, and Ellsben a chance to catch up. However, the fireflies only hovered near the ground for a moment before they lifted back up and continued moving forward. Their blinking green lights shrank to barely visible pin dots in the distance and then quickly disappeared.

"What should we do now?" Mont asked.

"Let's walk a little farther, and then we can camp for the night," Ellsben said. "Do you still want to take the first watch, Mont?"

"Yes," Mont said. "Right now I'm wide awake. I'll keep watch while you and Cal sleep."

A dog started barking. Cal tried to figure out what direction the barking was coming from, but he couldn't figure it out because the barking was echoing and seemed to be coming from every direction. A light from a lantern appeared in the distance. "Who's there?" a voice called. The dog's barking was getting louder.

"Run," Mont said.

"No," Ellsben said. "It's not the bounty hunters. It's a farmer. There's no point running away from him. Just act calm and stick to our story. Remember, you're taking me to your uncle's farm."

"Why should we talk to him?" Cal asked. "We should leave, we should hide."

"We can't hide," Ellsben said. "That dog will follow us. If we try to hide, that farmer will think something suspicious is going on, and then he'll most likely get his neighbors and maybe the local sheriff to come out here to see what's going on. We've got enough people looking for us right now—we don't need any more people looking. I'm almost positive that farmer won't cause us any trouble as long as we stick to our story."

The dog suddenly appeared; it was less than half the size Cal had imagined it to be. The dog seemed to be elderly; it had many gray hairs around its otherwise dark muzzle. It stood several feet in front of Ellsben and lowered its head and barked wildly.

"Who's there?" the farmer called out. He was almost close enough so that the light from his lantern could reach Cal, Mont, and Ellsben.

"Hello, sir!" Mont shouted.

"I can't hear anything," the farmer said in a loud voice. "Mak, be quiet!"

The dog was silent for a moment, and then he defiantly resumed barking.

"I said, be quiet! Get over here."

The dog stopped barking and ran to the farmer and pressed up against his leg. He let out a low growl and then barked. "Quiet!" the farmer shouted. The dog whimpered and looked up at the farmer.

"Hello, sir," Mont said. To Cal's ears Mont sounded exactly like a Southerner; if Cal didn't know Mont, he would have been willing to bet everything he owned that Mont had grown up in the South. Cal knew there was no way he could fake an accent as well as Mont, and he worried that if his accent sounded phony the farmer would know immediately that he and Mont weren't brothers. Cal hoped he wouldn't have to do much talking; he could probably get by if all he had to say was hello and his name.

As the farmer got closer, they saw that he had a significant limp. The farmer wasn't tall, but he had broad, strong shoulders and a large belly that hung over his belt. He had round cheeks, which gave his face a boyish quality. The farmer stopped walking and held up his lantern so that its light first touched Cal's face, and then he moved the lantern so that its light touched Mont's face, then Ellsben's face. "What are you doing on my property?"

"We got lost, sir," Mont said. "We should have stopped when it got dark, but we weren't tired and we've got a long way to go, so we kept walking. It's my fault, actually. We left the road we were on because I thought I knew a shortcut, but without the stars I got confused, and now we're lost."

"Where are you going?" the farmer asked.

"We're taking our naggie to our uncle's farm," Mont said. "We're going to live with our uncle. Our daddy got killed in the war, and even though our farm wasn't very big, it was too much for Mama to take care of. She's selling our farm." Mont looked at his feet.

A small tear traveled down the farmer's cheek; he didn't bother wiping it away. "I'm sorry about your daddy. This war's been a terrible thing. I fought in it for two years. Last year they sent me home."

"Why?" Mont asked.

"Because of this. Look here." The farmer gave Mont his lantern and told Mont to hold it so that the light from the lantern illuminated the farmer's legs. Slowly, the farmer pulled up his right pant leg. Dark wood, shaped like the lower part of a leg, extended from where the farmer's knee should have been down into his boot. "I got hit with an arrow in my calf. The wound got infected, and the field doctors had to saw the lower half of my leg off. It was the most pain I'd ever felt. I don't even know how to begin to tell you what the pain was like. It still hurts. If I walk around too much, this leg gets throbbing so much I can't think about anything else."

The sight of the farmer's missing leg made Cal feel sick, but he couldn't pull his gaze away. Cal had frequently heard about horrible injuries that people suffered from the war, but this was the first time he'd actually seen a war wound. The base of the farmer's real leg, where it attached to the wooden leg, was crisscrossed with thick pink scars and dried, flaking skin. The farmer rubbed the scars and winced, and then he gently pushed his pant leg back down into place.

"If you want, you boys can stay with your naggie in my barn tonight," the farmer said.

"Thanks, but we wouldn't want to inconvenience you," Mont said. "We can find a place around here to camp out."

"It wouldn't be any inconvenience to me at all," the farmer said. "Besides, you boys don't want to camp outside tonight. If those clouds up there let loose, and I'm betting they will, you'll get soaked. The truth is, if you don't stay in my barn, I'll feel terrible when I hear the rain coming down tonight. I won't be able to sleep because I'll keep thinking about you boys being stuck out in the rain."

"We don't mind the rain," Mont said.

"Don't be foolish. You'll be a lot more comfortable in my barn."

"We hate to bother you."

"You won't be bothering me." The farmer smiled and held out his hand. "My name's Stro."

Mont shook Stro's hand. "My name is Cron, and my brother's name is Lang. He can't speak. This winter he got a fever, and it took his voice."

Cal was impressed by Mont's quick thinking. Now he didn't have to worry about faking a Southern accent. Stro stuck out his hand, and Cal shook it and smiled.

"We expect his voice will come back soon," Mont said. "Mama told us that when she was a girl she had a fever and it took her voice. It took almost half a year before her voice came back."

"Is what took his voice contagious?" Stro asked.

"No sir," Mont said. "I mean it probably was when he had the fever, but his problem with his voice isn't contagious anymore. I've been around him all the time, and I haven't caught it."

"Damn," Stro said. "I was hoping he was contagious. I've got a neighbor who keeps coming over and complaining because I haven't fixed my side of the fence that runs between our property. I'm tired of listening to him. If your brother was contagious, I'd invite my neighbor over and your brother could cough or sneeze on him."

Mont grinned.

Stro led them to the barn. As they were walking, Stro said, "I never should have fought in the war. I was a fool. What did I have to gain from the war? Nothing. I risked my life so those rich plantation owners could keep their naggies. I've never had a naggie in my life, never could afford one." Stro stopped walking. He turned and looked at Ellsben, and then he gave Cal and Mont an embarrassed smile. "Boys, I'm sorry if I offended you."

"You didn't offend us," Mont said. "This is the only naggie we own. We're not rich. Our folks could barely afford this naggie."

Stro started walking. "I have to farm my land by myself. Now with half my leg gone, it's going to be almost impossible to do all the work that needs to be done. I could lose my farm. I could end up losing this land that my family has owned for three generations. I lost my leg, I'll probably lose my farm, and you boys lost your father. Why? All because those rich bastards want to keep their naggies. And what are those rich bastards going to do to help us? Nothing. Even if we win the war, those rich bastards won't be willing to let go of one cent to help people like us."

They reached the barn. Stro opened the barn's side door and went inside, and Cal, Mont, and Ellsben followed him in. Stro grabbed a lantern that was hanging on the wall, lit it, and handed it to Cal. The barn wasn't very big. One side of the barn had three stalls; the first stall was occupied by a huge, sleeping sow, the second stall was occupied by a cow, and the third stall was empty. On the other side of the barn there was a pile of hay, and beside the hay was a smaller pile of straw. Next to the straw was a ladder that led to the loft.

"You can hang the lantern here," Stro said. He pointed to a hook that was attached to a support post.

Cal hung the lantern on the hook that Stro had indicated.

The cow let out a long, low moo.

"I'm going to get some blankets for you boys," Stro said. "I'll be right back."

As soon as Stro was gone, Mont smiled and whispered, "I did pretty good, didn't I? He believed every word I said."

Ellsben didn't smile back. "You said too much. Don't you remember that you were told not to say any more than you have to?"

Mont's smile dissolved. "I'm sorry."

"We shouldn't be here," Ellsben said. He was angry. "The more we interact with people, the greater our chances of being caught. When he comes back, tell him that we are going to leave early tomorrow."

"I will." Mont looked like he wanted to curl up in a corner and hide.

"And make sure you—" The barn door opened, and Ellsben shut up.

Stro came in, and a little boy, about ten years old, was with him. The boy's arms were wrapped around several large blankets, which were almost too much for him to carry, but he had a determined look on his face. The boy brought the blankets over to the pile of hay and set them down. Stro went to the hay and made two small piles, which he shaped like beds, and then he laid a blanket on each pile. "Not as good as a real bed," Stro told them. "But this sure will be a lot more comfortable than sleeping outside on the ground."

"Thanks," Mont said. "We appreciate this."

Stro made a dismissive gesture with his hand. "It's nothing."

The little boy started to climb the ladder that led to the loft. "Han, come here," Stro said. The boy frowned and looked as if he was considering ignoring what Stro had just told him, and then he let out a dramatic sigh and slowly climbed down the ladder and went to Stro. Stro smiled at the boy and put an arm around him. "This is my son, Han."

"Hello," Mont said. He introduced himself and Cal.

"Glad to meet you," Han said, but he didn't sound like he meant it; he was only saying it because it was what he'd been taught to say. Han looked back at the ladder.

"Well," Stro said, "I should get moving. I still have a few chores to do before I can go to bed."

"We might not see you in the morning," Mont said. "We've got a long way to go, so we're going to leave just as soon as it gets light."

"I'll see you in the morning," Stro said. "Work starts early around here. I'm always up before the sun."

"OK," Mont said. "Goodnight."

"Goodnight, boys." Stro smiled at them and then turned and left the barn.

Han did not follow his father. He went over to Mont and looked up at him and asked, "Have you seen my cat?"

"No, I haven't." Mont shook his head.

"My cat's about this big." Han moved his hands around to show the size of his cat. "He's big and fluffy. His face is white and black."

"We can let you know if he shows up," Mont said.

"He's probably in the loft. He likes to hide up there." Han started walking toward the ladder. A deep frown appeared on Han's face as he walked past Ellsben. When he reached the ladder, he turned around and looked at Cal and Mont and said, "I hate naggies."

"Why?" Mont asked.

"Because all they do is cause trouble. If it wasn't for the naggies, we never would have had this war. My daddy lost his leg in the war, and he almost died. I wish there was no such thing as naggies."

A cat started meowing. Han quickly climbed the ladder and went into the loft. "There you are, you bad kitty. Trying to hide again. Bad kitty."

The cat answered Han with a soft *mrrow-mrrrrrr*.

"Come here bad kitty. It's time for bed."

Mrrrow.

Han appeared at the edge of the loft. He was holding a large black-and-white cat under his left arm. The cat's front and hind legs were limply dangling; Han was holding the cat the way a child would absentmindedly hold a doll. Cal was surprised the cat allowed itself to be held this way. Slowly, still holding the cat under his left arm, Han climbed down the ladder.

"I've got to go to bed now," Han said to Cal and Mont. "I'm actually supposed to be in bed right now, but Daddy let me stay up so that I could find my cat." Han hugged his cat to his chest and went to the door. As Han was going out the door, Mont said, "Goodnight." Han gave a halfhearted wave in response and pushed the door shut with his shoulder.

Ellsben made a bed for himself with some of the straw. "Now let's get to sleep," Ellsben said. He still sounded angry. "We need to get up and get out of here first thing tomorrow morning."

Cal and Mont went to their hay beds. Mont took his blanket off his hay bed and offered it to Ellsben. "You didn't get a blanket," Mont said. "Take mine. I don't need it."

"Keep it," Ellsben said, sounding annoyed. "I don't think Stro would be pleased if he came in here and saw me with the blanket he gave you."

"You're right," Mont said. "I'm sorry."

"I've got a blanket in my pack," Ellsben said.

"That's right," Mont said. "I forgot."

"But I'm not going to use it."

"Why not?"

"Because Stro expects me to lie on the straw just like the animals, and I think it's best to do what he expects. I don't want to start any trouble. Now I don't want to discuss this anymore. Let's get some sleep." Ellsben lay down on the straw and closed his eyes.

"Goodnight," Cal said.

"Night," Mont answered.

Cal lay down and closed his eyes, but he wasn't tired. In his mind he saw Stro's leg—he saw the thick pink scars that crisscrossed the end of Stro's leg where his knee should have been. Cal felt sick to his stomach. He couldn't make the image of Stro's mangled leg leave his mind. Stro was a nice man, a kind man, and he was also the enemy. He'd been one of the men Cal's father's army had fought. How many other men like Stro had fought in the war on both sides? How many men had fought and maimed and killed each other when, if they'd met under other circumstances, they could have easily become friends? How could a man like Stro be one of the enemy?

Suddenly there was the soft sound of scattered raindrops striking the roof of the barn. The sound of the rain calmed Cal. Sleepiness seeped into him, and soon he was asleep.

———

"Cal, get up."

"What's wrong?" Cal muttered. He felt like he'd just fallen asleep.

"It's morning."

Cal opened his eyes. Ellsben was standing next to him. "Get up," Ellsben said. "We need to get moving."

Cal sat up. There was very little light coming in through the barn's windows. There was still the sound of rain striking the barn's roof.

"Get up, Mont," Ellsben said.

Mont muttered something and covered his head with his arms.

"Get up." Ellsben tapped Mont on the shoulder.

Mont opened his eyes. He appeared momentarily confused, as if he didn't know at first where he was. "Is it morning already?" he asked.

"Yes," Ellsben said. "We need to get moving."

The barn door creaked open, and Stro appeared. He held the door open for a dark-haired, heavyset woman who was carrying three plates. After the woman stepped through the doorway, Stro came into the barn and closed the door. The woman smiled broadly and said, "Good morning, boys."

"This is my wife," Stro said. "Eda."

"Good morning," Mont said. "It's a pleasure to meet you."

"I made you boys and your naggie eggs and toast," Eda said.

"Thank you," Mont said when she handed him one of the plates.

Cal smiled and nodded his head when he accepted his plate.

"Thank you, ma'am," Ellsben said. He took the plate without making eye contact with her; he kept his gaze down.

The eggs were fresh and tasted wonderful. Cal soaked up the egg yolks with his toast. Mont took a huge bite of toast and said, "This is great. Thanks a lot for making us breakfast."

"I was glad to do it," Eda said. "You boys should have a warm breakfast if you're going to be walking in this raw weather all day."

"You know," Stro said, "you're welcome to stay here until it clears up. I'm sure the rain will stop by this afternoon."

"We can't stay," Mont said. "We've got to get to our uncle's farm. He's expecting us. If we don't show up when we're supposed to, he'll start worrying."

The barn door opened, and Han came in. He was wearing his work clothes; he had to come into the barn to do his morning chores. Han's eyes were only half open. He'd apparently woken up recently and wasn't yet fully alert. He yawned and grabbed a pitchfork and walked toward the cow's stall. Abruptly he stopped walking and stared at Ellsben. Han's face got red, and he frowned and turned and faced his father. "That naggie's eating our eggs!"

"Yes," Stro said. "He is."

"Why are you wasting our eggs on a naggie?" Han shouted.

"That naggie belongs to our guests," Stro said. "It would be rude to our guests if we didn't feed their naggie."

"You don't have to feed him eggs!"

"I want you to apologize to our guests right now," Stro said.

"*No.*"

"Apologize to our guests."

"I won't apologize. I hate naggies, and I don't want a naggie eating our eggs. I won't apologize because I'm not sorry." Han threw the pitchfork to the ground and rushed out of the barn.

Stro let out a long sigh. "I apologize for him."

"It's OK," Mont said. "You don't have to apologize."

"Yes, I do," Stro said. "That's not the way I raised him to behave."

Cal, Mont, and Ellsben quickly finished their breakfast. Mont thanked Stro and Eda for their hospitality and then said they needed to leave now. Stro shook hands with Mont and Cal and wished them luck.

Cal, Mont, and Ellsben stepped out into the rain.

ELEVEN

RIVER SNAKES

"Didn't Stro say he thought this rain would stop by the afternoon?" Mont asked.

"That's what he told us," Ellsben said.

"I hope he's right," Mont said.

They had left Stro's property several hours ago, and during this time the rain, which had initially been a drizzle, had turned into a heavy downpour. Cal walked with his head down so that the rain wouldn't hit his face. The combination of the sounds of the falling rain and the steady tapping of the raindrops on his head and neck put Cal into a trance. He walked without thinking about anything, and this felt really good.

Lightning flashed overhead and was instantly followed by an enormous boom, which snapped Cal out of the trance he'd been in.

Another flash. A louder boom.

Cal cringed and quickly looked around for some sort of shelter.

"We've got to get away from these trees," Ellsben said. "Lightning likes trees."

"Over there," Mont said, pointing to his right. "In that clearing I think I see a couple of boulders. We could hide beside them. I've never heard of lightning hitting boulders."

A bolt of lightning stabbed a tree not far from where they were standing, and the booming of thunder and the cracking of the tree made their ears ring. Cal shook his head.

"Get away from these trees," Ellsben shouted. "Now."

They ran to the boulders Mont had pointed out. The boulders jutted up from the ground, and Cal guessed that the boulders had more of their mass underground than aboveground. Cal crouched down close to the largest boulder, and Mont crouched down beside him. Ellsben knelt down and protectively leaned his torso over Cal and Mont.

A huge gust of wind drove the rain against them with such force that the raindrops actually stung their skin. Lightning flared across the sky, and the exploding thunder made Cal feel as if an invisible hand had struck his head. He looked over at Mont and was surprised to see that Mont was grinning. "Isn't this great?" Mont said, looking up at the sky. "This is one of the best storms I've ever seen."

Cal tried to smile, but couldn't. He turned his face toward the closest boulder; he didn't want to look at the lightning, and he especially didn't want Mont to see that he was afraid of the storm.

Out of the corner of his eye, Cal saw a flash of bluish light and then heard and felt an enormous pounding of thunder. He closed his eyes. There came more thunder, a rumbling thunder that made Cal think of a giant growling dog.

The wind, the lightning, and the thunder continued for what felt like hours but was probably no more than fifteen minutes before it abruptly stopped. The driving rain turned into a drizzle. "It's over," Mont said, sounding disappointed.

Ellsben looked up at the sky as if he suspected the lightning hadn't really gone away, but was hiding, waiting to strike the moment they believed they were safe.

"Might as well get moving," Mont said. "The storm's over."

"I hope so," Ellsben said.

They went back into the woods and continued following the tiny path they'd been on before the lightning storm forced them to get away from the trees. The dampness intensified the odors of the dirt and the decaying leaves that covered the forest's ground. A bird somewhere overhead let out a rhythmic squawking sound. Another bird answered it.

When the drizzle finally dissipated, the mosquitoes decided it was time to feed. Cal and Mont waved the mosquitoes away with their arms. Ellsben kept the mosquitoes back by waving his arms and swishing his tail.

A thin fog drifted into the woods. Seeing the fog made Cal think about what it would be like if the forest was on fire; he imagined the fog was smoke. If smoke suddenly swirled around them, would they be able to figure out how to get away? Or would they run directly into the flames? What if the flames came at them from all sides? Cal imagined the heat becoming more and more intense. He imagined choking on the thick smoke and feeling his skin blister.

Ellsben abruptly stopped, and Cal almost walked into him. They had come to the edge of a bluff; below was a huge river. The river water was muddy and slow moving.

Mont started taking off his clothes. "I'm ready for a swim."

"No." Ellsben grabbed Mont's arm. "We can't swim across."

"Sure we can." Mont grinned and nodded his head toward the water. "That current isn't fast. We can easily swim across. Don't worry."

"Look," Ellsben said. He pointed at several spots on the banks of the river.

Cal stared at the spots where Ellsben had pointed, but he couldn't see anything unusual.

Mont squinted, put his hands on his hips, leaned forward, and said, "What were you pointing at? I don't see..." Mont's eyes suddenly widened, and his hands dropped from his hips. "I see them now. I see them. Those sons of bitches are all over the place."

"What?" Cal asked. He still didn't see anything unusual.

"River snakes," Mont said.

"Where?" Cal asked.

"They're all over the place," Mont said.

Ellsben and Mont pointed to at least a dozen spots on both sides of the river. Cal looked at all the places where they had pointed, but he still didn't see them.

"I guess I'm blind," Cal said. "I can't see any—" Cal abruptly stopped speaking when what he'd thought was a stick suddenly slithered into the river.

"We can't swim across," Ellsben said. "We'd never make it. Those snakes are poisonous, fast, and aggressive. In fact, this time of year they're especially aggressive because they're protecting their eggs."

"If we can't swim across, we're going to have to follow the river until we come to a bridge that connects to the nearest main road," Mont said. "If we wait until late at night, it should be safe to cross the bridge. It's unlikely anyone will see us."

"No," Ellsben said. "Any bridge that connects to a main road is dangerous. The bridges are being watched all the time."

"How are we going to get across?" Cal asked.

"I honestly don't know," Ellsben said. "If we follow the river for a while, maybe we'll come across an abandoned raft."

"Do you really think we'll find a raft?" Mont sounded doubtful.

Ellsben shrugged. "It's unlikely, but right now that's the only logical solution I can think of."

They followed the river south, staying a good distance away from the river's banks so that they wouldn't cross paths with a river snake. Although occasionally a river snake would move inland, they almost always spent their time in the water or no more than several feet from the water. River snakes were nervous when they were on land because they were slower and far less agile than in the water.

A mosquito bit Cal on the side of the neck, and he slapped it. He looked at his hand and saw a large splotch of blood in the center of his palm from the mosquito. The sight of the blood made Cal feel sick, and he quickly wiped it away by rubbing his palm against his pant leg.

"I've got an idea," Mont said.

"What's your idea?" Ellsben asked.

"I'll distract the snakes," Mont said. "I'll take a long branch and start smacking it on the water so that the snakes will attack the branch, and while they're going after the branch, you and Cal can swim across." Mont looked at Cal and gave him a smug smile. "What do you think?"

Cal didn't like the idea of getting into the water with all the river snakes, but he knew he could do it if he had to. The river would probably take him a little more than a minute to swim across, and he was sure Mont could keep the snakes distracted for that amount of time. Cal looked at the river. He couldn't jump in; he would have to slowly wade in because he had to make sure he didn't make even the slightest splash because any sounds or sudden movements could cause the snakes to come after him.

"That's a pretty good plan I came up with, isn't it?" Mont looked proud.

"No," Ellsben said. "Your plan is no good."

Mont appeared confused. This wasn't what he was expecting to hear, and he studied Ellsben's face to see if Ellsben was just joking. When Mont saw that Ellsben wasn't joking, he crossed his arms and said, "What's wrong with my plan?"

Ellsben raised his eyebrows and said, "Those snakes are deadly. If one of us were to get bitten, we'd die. Your plan might work, but we can't risk what would happen if it doesn't work."

Mont frowned, and for a moment Cal was sure Mont was about to get angry. However, Mont's expression softened, and he shrugged his shoulders and shook his head. "I still think it's a good plan."

"Keep thinking," Ellsben said. He put a hand on Mont's shoulder. "Eventually we'll figure out a way we can safely get across that river."

A thick cloud of mosquitoes buzzed around them. Cal wildly flailed his arms, but the mosquitoes persisted. Cal walked faster, hoping this would keep the mosquitoes from being able to easily follow him, but this didn't work. Running would be the only way to get away from them, and that would only last for as long as he could run. Once he stopped running, the mosquitoes would instantly find him.

They walked for at least a mile before they were saved from the mosquitoes by the wind. It was a warm southeasterly wind that was both strong enough and steady enough to prevent the mosquitoes from flying. Ellsben raised his arms and faced the wind and said, "Thank you, wind."

Cal thought he saw something in the distance. There appeared to be something strung across the river. "What is that?" Cal pointed.

"I don't know," Ellsben said. "It looks like somebody strung some ropes across the river."

"Maybe we can use the ropes to get across," Cal said.

"Maybe." Ellsben sounded doubtful.

When they got closer to the ropes, it became apparent that the ropes were a part of an old bridge that someone had built. There were four main ropes: two base ropes, and two ropes that worked as handrails. The bottom of the bridge had wooden planks strapped to the main base ropes. The handrail ropes and the base ropes were attached to large oak trees on both sides of the river.

"Someone who used to live around here must have had to cross the river frequently," Ellsben said. "It had to have taken a lot of work to put this bridge together. Look at how long it is."

Mont grabbed the ropes that worked as handrails and pulled on them. "I bet if we go over one at a time the bridge will hold."

Ellsben put a hoof on one of the wooden planks and pressed down. The bridge creaked, but held firm. "I don't trust it," Ellsben said.

"I don't either," Cal said. "The ropes are starting to rot. It could be a lot worse on the other side."

"If we don't use this bridge, how are we going to get to the other side?" Mont asked.

Ellsben grunted and crossed his arms tightly against his chest. "I don't like this bridge, but maybe we should try it. The more we follow the river, the farther off course we'll end up. We're already a lot farther south than we should be." Ellsben stared at the bridge intently. "If we continue to follow the river, we're eventually going to come to a main road, and we've got to avoid any main roads, especially main roads that connect to bridges that cross this river. Like I said before, they'll be watching all the regular bridges all the time."

"Then let's cross here," Mont said. "I don't think this bridge is as bad as it looks. It can support our weight."

Cal looked down at the river's banks and saw several long, black snakes. "I don't trust this bridge," Cal said.

Ellsben put his front hooves on the bridge, and then he lifted his right front hoof and stomped it down. The bridge swayed and creaked. "If it can hold me, it definitely can hold each of you."

"What if it can't hold you?" Cal asked.

"Then..." Ellsben frowned. "Depending on where it breaks, I might be able to get out of the river without being bitten."

"Don't try it," Cal said.

"We've got to try it," Mont said. "We've got to get to the other side."

Ellsben stomped on the bridge again, and again all that happened was the bridge creaked and swayed. "All right," Ellsben said. "I'm going to do it." Ellsben backed up and stared at the bridge the way a soldier might stare at an enemy before going into battle, looking for strengths and weaknesses. He took several deep breaths and leaned his torso forward, clapped his hands once, and charged. As he galloped across the bridge, several of the wooden planks snapped under his hooves, leaving holes like teeth missing from a mouth, but the four main ropes held. When Ellsben reached the other side, he grinned and bucked and let out a happy yell. "I made it! Come on over."

Mont immediately began crossing the bridge. He put a hand on his hip and stuck his nose up in the air and said with the drawl of a Southern gentleman, "What a splendid day to go for a stroll." Cal laughed, and this encouraged Mont. "A splendid day," Mont said. He walked across the entire bridge with his hand on his hip and his nose in the air. When he reached the other side, he turned and looked at Cal. Mont smiled and waved and said, "Come on, slowpoke. Get over here."

Cal touched the rope handrails and looked down at the wooden planks. He had a bad feeling about the bridge. He didn't want to cross it. A bead of sweat ran down his forehead.

"What's the matter?" Ellsben called out.

"Nothing," Cal said.

Mont waved his arm. "Come on, slowpoke."

What if he decided not to cross? What if he decided to stay on this side of the river? Cal had to fight the urge to look back because he knew if he did he would go back. No. He wasn't going to turn back. That wasn't the choice he would embrace.

Cal walked on the bridge. With each step he took, he could feel the wooden planks under his feet gently bow from his weight, and he could feel the bridge casually sway like a dance partner each time he moved. The wind that was keeping the mosquitoes away seemed stronger now that he was on the bridge. Somehow he felt both afraid and overwhelmingly calm.

"Hurry up, slowpoke!" Mont shouted.

A beam of sunlight pushed through the clouds, and at the same moment Cal felt the planks disappear from under his feet, he felt himself being thrown to his right. One of the bridge's rope handrails had suddenly snapped, and this caused the bridge to violently twist to one side. Cal had the strangest sensation that he was flying. He felt as if he was ascending to the sky, not tumbling downward.

The water slapped him, stinging his face, and then quickly engulfed him. He was blinded by the water's murkiness; he could barely see the filtered light from above. His clothes absorbed the water and made him heavy. He felt as if invisible hands were reaching out in the darkness, grabbing his clothes, pulling him down. He was tempted to relax, to allow himself to sink. But no, he wasn't ready for the darkness. Cal kicked his legs, bringing himself up toward the light.

When his head broke through the surface of the water, he inhaled and blinked the dampness from his eyes. Ellsben was waving wildly at him and shouting, "Swim! Cal, swim, swim, swim!" Mont was running toward the river, but Ellsben grabbed him by the back of the shirt, stopping him. Mont screamed Cal's name.

Several long, black snakes slithered into the river. Once the snakes were in the water, Cal could no longer see them, but he knew they were coming toward him. On the other side of the river, behind him, he knew snakes were also slithering into the water.

Mont screamed Cal's name again.

He wasn't far from the river's bank. He could make it—he knew he could make it. Cal swam with every bit of strength he had. Water splashed his face, and he accidentally breathed some in. This made him cough, but he didn't slow. He continued swimming with all his strength. He thought he saw something black in the water to his right, but he couldn't let himself think about it, he had to keep his mind focused on swimming. Ellsben and Mont were both shouting Cal's name. Their voices conveyed an extra edge of panic; they could see how close the snakes were to Cal.

The river's bank wasn't far, he was almost there, but it seemed like it was taking him longer than it should to get there. He felt as if the water had turned into a thick syrup. Almost there. In a moment he would be on land, and Mont and Ellsben would clap him on the back, and Mont would probably let out a victorious whoop. He was almost there. He thought he felt his toe touch the river's muddy bottom; in a second he should be able to stand.

A black, triangular head popped out of the water next to Cal's face. The head was covered with tiny overlapping scales and had two narrow, cold golden eyes. The snake opened its mouth, and Cal could see its black forked tongue pressed against the pink flesh at the bottom of its mouth. A deep hissing sound came from the snake. It opened its mouth wider, making its long upper fangs seem even longer.

Cal dunked his head under the water and forced his body down as close to the bottom of the river as he could get. He hoped he was out of the snake's striking range. He propelled himself forward and soon found himself in water that was so shallow he could no longer keep his body completely submerged. Cal put his feet on the muddy riverbed, and as he was getting into a standing position, he felt a sudden burning pain in his right forearm. He looked down and saw the scaly triangular head of a huge snake clamped on his arm. The first thing he felt was disgust, and then the disgust was replaced by anger, not fear. With his left hand, Cal clasped the snake's neck and jerked its head away from his forearm. He felt its fangs slip out of his arm. The tip of the fangs scratched his skin, and the scratches burned as if they had tiny flames in them. A thick yellow fluid oozed out of the two deep punctures the snake's fangs had made in his arm. Cal squeezed the snake's neck, trying to strangle it. The snake's long body violently lashed back and forth, and then it tried to coil around his wrist. Cal lurched out of the water and whipped the snake's body three times against a large rock. The snake's muscles tensed, and then it abruptly went limp. Cal hurled it into the river.

Ellsben lifted Cal up and quickly carried him away from the river's bank. He set Cal down and said, "Stay calm. Try to stay calm. The faster your heart beats the quicker the poison will get into your system."

Mont's face was white, and he was staring at Cal with wide eyes. Cal had never seen Mont look so scared before; he hadn't thought Mont was capable of becoming as scared as he now appeared.

"Sit down," Ellsben said to Cal. Ellsben reached into his pack and removed his knife.

"I lost my pack," Cal said. "It's in the water."

"Don't worry about your pack," Ellsben said. "There's nothing in it that can't be replaced." Ellsben put a hand on Cal's shoulder and told him to lie on his back.

Cal did as he was told.

Ellsben gripped Cal's wrist. "This is going to hurt, but it has to be done."

"Yes," Cal said, even though he didn't know what Ellsben was talking about.

Gently, Ellsben placed the tip of the knife at the edge of one of the punctures in Cal's arm; the blade felt cool. With a swift, smooth motion, Ellsben stabbed the knife into Cal's arm and drew it across the distance between the two punctures, leaving a deep gash. A mixture of dark blood and thick yellow venom flowed out of the gash. Ellsben squeezed the flesh around the gash, forcing the fluids to flow out faster.

Cal's arm no longer burned; now it felt numb. "Did you get enough of the poison out?" Cal asked.

"I think so," Ellsben said. "You'll be fine."

Cal could tell that Ellsben didn't believe what he said. The numbness in Cal's arm traveled like roots from some fast-growing plant through his entire body. Even though he knew the air wasn't cold, he began to shiver. He couldn't stop shivering.

"Find some dried wood," Ellsben said to Mont. "We need to make a fire for Cal."

Mont nodded. He looked relieved to have something he could do to help.

Cal's trembling worsened. His stomach throbbed and then tensed, forcefully expelling its contents. Puke ran down the left side of Cal's face from the corner of his mouth. He wanted to reach up to wipe it away, but he couldn't make his arms move. His fingers curled and froze in place, making his hands appear as if they had turned into talons. He looked at Ellsben, and Ellsben's face was blurry. When he tried to speak, he wasn't sure if any words were coming out. He wanted to reach up and grab Ellsben's hand because he thought that if he held on to Ellsben, he wouldn't slip away. Ellsben wouldn't let him slip away.

But Cal couldn't reach up. He slipped into darkness.

TWELVE

KOZAL

Mont came back with a bundle of dried sticks and twigs clutched to his chest. He wasn't sure how long he'd been gone; he was too upset to be able to estimate the passage of time. He hoped he hadn't been gone long. Cal was lying on his back with his arms curled over his stomach. His eyes were closed, and he was shaking and muttering unintelligible words. Ellsben had knelt down beside Cal and was gently stroking his forehead. When Ellsben saw Mont, he quickly stood up and pointed to an area of the ground near Cal and said, "Bring that wood here. We need to get a fire going. He's wet from the river, and it's important that we make sure he's dry and warm."

Mont brought the sticks and twigs to the spot where Ellsben had indicated. He stacked them in a conical shape, which was the best for fires, and then ignited them. He burned the tip of his right finger because he was so worried about Cal he wasn't fully paying attention to what he was doing. Mont sucked the tip of his finger for a second and then promptly forgot about his burn.

"Is he going to be all right?" Mont asked.

"Yes, he's going to be..." Ellsben sighed. He made a face that seemed to express a combination of anger and hurt. "I don't know," Ellsben said. "That's the truth. I don't know if he's going to be all right or not, but the way he is right now sure makes it hard for me to think that he's going to be all right."

"He'll be all right." Mont gave Ellsben an angry look. "He'll be all right." Mont went to Cal and grabbed his hand. Cal's skin felt cold, and his fingers were twitching. "You're going to be all right," Mont whispered. "Don't worry."

Ellsben was pacing. His hooves hit the ground with such force that globs of mud splashed up and stuck to his legs. "This is my fault. I never should have said that it was OK to cross that bridge."

Cal muttered something and then twisted his head to his left and grimaced.

"What's wrong?" Mont asked. He put his ear next to Cal's mouth so that he could hear Cal in case all he could do was softly whisper. "What's wrong?" Mont asked again. Cal didn't, or probably couldn't, respond. Saliva foamed up at the corners of his mouth. Cal's hand tensed, and his fingernails dug into Mont's palm, and then his hand went limp and slipped out of Mont's grip.

"You fellows got any food you'd be willing to spare?" a deep, rough-sounding voice asked.

Mont turned around and saw a short, filthy man coming toward him. The man was skinny and had straight, greasy, gray hair that hung down, covering his shoulders. There was a shallow pit filled with scar tissue where his right eye should have been. A thick scar ran from the top of the man's forehead, into his empty eye socket, and reemerged at the bottom of the socket and continued down the man's cheek, ending at the edge of his chin. The man's clothes looked like they hadn't been washed in weeks. "Can you fellows spare me some food?"

"We don't have any food," Ellsben said. "Go away."

"You've got a campfire," the man said. "You must be getting ready to do some cooking."

"We're not cooking," Mont said. "Our friend is sick. We made this fire to keep him warm. Now leave us alone."

"What's wrong with your friend?" the man asked.

"He's sick," Ellsben said. "Now go—"

"I wasn't talking to you." The man narrowed his eye. "You quiet down, naggie. I was talking to the boy."

"Go away," Mont said.

"What happened to your friend?" The man was standing next to Mont and staring down at Cal.

"He got bit by a river snake," Mont said. He didn't look at the man.

"A river snake bit him?" The man started laughing and shook his head. "You mean that boy didn't know he shouldn't swim in the river?" The man continued laughing.

Mont stood up and faced the man. He was furious. "There's nothing funny about what happened. Now you better get out of here, or in about a second you're going to wish you'd left." Mont turned his hands into tight fists.

The man took a step backward. "There's a cure for those snakebites."

Mont didn't believe this man; he was certain the man was crazy. "And how do you think we can cure him?" Mont almost didn't ask the question because he didn't think the answer would be worth hearing, but at the same time he believed there was a slight chance this man might honestly know a cure, and it couldn't hurt to hear what he had to say.

"Did you drain the poison from the bite?"

"Of course we did," Ellsben said.

"I wasn't talking to you, naggie."

"Get out of here," Mont said. "We're not going to give you any food."

The man leaned close to Mont, and his stale body odor made Mont feel sick. "Don't you want to cure your friend?"

"We've already drained the poison," Mont said. "We didn't need you to tell us that."

A tiny smile appeared on the man's face. "That's just step one." The man leaned down and grabbed Cal's arm.

"Don't touch him!" Mont shouted. He caught the man's shoulders and forcefully pushed him back. The man stumbled and almost fell down. "Stay away from him," Mont said.

"Why don't you want to help your friend?"

"We are helping him," Mont said.

"You're not helping him," the man said. "You're letting him die."

"He's not going to die." Mont glared at the man, daring him to contradict him.

"He will die," the man said.

Mont shoved the man backward; he didn't want him anywhere near Cal. "Get out of here!" Mont shouted.

"If you don't help him, he's going to die."

"We are helping him," Mont said. "Now leave us alone."

"You need to get him some leaves from the cyntum plant," the man said. "Grind up the leaves and put them under his tongue. Those leaves will neutralize the poison."

Mont stared at the man. He didn't know if he should believe him or not. "I don't know what that plant is."

"I could find it for you, or I should say I think I can find it," the man said. "Cyntum grows around here. It's kind of rare, but I bet I could find it."

"You better not be lying," Mont said.

The man laughed and rolled his eye and shook his head. "The plant works. I'll find it, and it'll work. You'll see."

Cal let out a loud moan, and Mont ran to him. Cal's eyelids were twitching as if he was trying to open his eyes. Mont put his hand on Cal's forehead. Cal felt as if he had developed a fever. "He's too hot," Mont said to Ellsben. "Should we put out the fire?"

"No," Ellsben said. "His body's fighting the poison, that's why he's hot. We need the fire to dry his hair and clothes and to keep him dry when he sweats."

"The fire doesn't matter," the man said. "The only thing that matters is the cyntum leaves." The man shook his head and then wandered off into the woods.

Mont was sure he wouldn't see the man again, and he was glad. The man was crazy. Right now they had to take care of Cal; they couldn't be distracted by worrying about what that man was going to do.

"This is my fault," Ellsben said. "Crossing that bridge was stupid."

"It wasn't stupid," Mont said. "The bridge held you, and it held me. What happened was just bad luck."

"It wasn't bad luck," Ellsben said. "It was stupid, and it was my fault. He wouldn't be like this if I hadn't decided to cross that bridge."

"Don't blame yourself," Mont said. "If I'd thought the bridge wouldn't hold, I wouldn't have crossed it. All of us thought it was safe. What happened was honestly just bad luck."

Ellsben angrily stomped his hind hooves and hung his head.

A low groan escaped Cal, and his jaw began trembling so much that a rhythmic clacking sound came from his mouth each time his upper and lower teeth came together. Mont hoped Cal wouldn't bite his tongue. Thick white spit with dozens of tiny bubbles slipped over Cal's lower lip and slowly slid down the side of his face. Mont used his shirt-sleeve to wipe away the spit. Cal's face was flushed.

"Cal, you hang in there," Ellsben said. He came over and knelt down beside Cal and put his right hand on Cal's fore-head. "Hang in there. Don't let that poison win, Cal. Fight it."

The tips of Cal's fingers curled and pressed tightly into his palms, making his hands into fists. Was this just a reflex? Or was this Cal's way of signaling that he was fighting the poison?

"You hang in there, Cal." A tear ran down Ellsben's cheek. "Hang in there."

"I found it. Here."

Mont was startled by the sound of the man's voice. He was standing behind Mont. Both Mont and Ellsben had been so focused on Cal neither one of them had noticed the man until he spoke. This was dangerous. They had to pay attention to their surroundings; they couldn't ignore what was going on around them. What if the bounty hunters had shown up?

"It was easier to find them than I thought," the man said. "There was a small patch of cyntum growing near the base of an elm over there." The man turned and gestured toward the direction he'd walked.

"Let me see the leaves," Mont said.

The man opened his left hand. Three finger-sized, dark-green leaves rested in his palm. Mont leaned closer to get a better look at the leaves. They had smooth edges and appeared to have a thin coat of wax on them.

"Have you ever heard of this plant?" Mont asked Ellsben.

"No," Ellsben said.

"Of course he hasn't heard of it," the man said. "He's a naggie. What do naggies know about healing?"

"We don't need your stupid plant," Mont said. "Now get out of here."

The man's eye narrowed, and his forehead wrinkled. "When your little friend dies, remember that you could've saved him. It will eat at you all your life. If you'd given him the leaves, he would've lived."

"Get out of here!" Mont screamed.

The man spit and muttered something and started to leave.

"Give Cal the leaves," Ellsben said.

The man turned and looked at Ellsben and then at Mont.

"We can't give him the leaves," Mont said. "If we don't know what they are, they could make things worse."

"It can't get any worse," Ellsben said. "Maybe the leaves will help. If not..." Ellsben couldn't finish the sentence; he couldn't talk about Cal dying.

"Ah," the man said. "The naggie's being smart."

"Give him the leaves," Ellsben said.

The man ignored Ellsben. He stared at Mont, waiting for Mont to make a decision.

"Those leaves better not hurt him."

"Do you want me to give him the leaves or not?" The man raised his eyebrows.

"Yes," Mont said.

"Maybe you have more brains than I thought." The man took the leaves and began rubbing them between his thumb and fingers, breaking the leaves into tiny pieces. "Yes, good. The leaves are fresh. They're nice." The man went over to Cal, squatted down, and reached out and touched Cal's cheek. He held his fingers there for a moment and then jerked his hand back as if he'd burned his fingers. He shook his head and frowned, muttering something to himself.

"What's wrong?" Mont asked. He didn't trust the man, and seeing him near Cal made Mont nervous.

"The fever has him. The fever's bad." The skinny man pulled his lips back in a snarl and glared at Mont. The man's teeth were brown and rotten, and he had five scattered vacant slots were teeth should have been. "This is your fault. If you'd let me give him the leaves, if you hadn't wasted good time insulting me, the fever would never have gotten this bad."

The man grabbed Cal's chin and forced his mouth open, and then he quickly stuffed bits of leaves under Cal's tongue. Next, the man pushed Cal's mouth shut and held it closed so that Cal couldn't reflexively spit the leaves out.

What if the man was an assassin? Panic began to bubble in Mont's gut. What if the leaves were poisonous, and the man was using them to make sure Cal died? Mont looked at Ellsben to see if the same thought had occurred to him, but apparently it hadn't. Ellsben was watching the man and Cal as if he was expecting Cal to miraculously open his eyes and sit up and smile.

Cal's arms started flapping against his chest. The man continued to hold Cal's mouth shut. "You shouldn't have waited so long," the man said. "You let the poison take root." Cal's legs kicked; in another situation it would have been comical because it appeared as if Cal were attempting to do some kind of folk dance.

"Those leave are hurting him." Mont grabbed the man's hand and tried to pull it away from Cal's mouth.

"Get away, stupid boy!" The man was amazingly strong; Mont couldn't tear his hand away from Cal.

"Let go!" Mont shouted.

Cal's legs suddenly stopped kicking, and his arms went limp.

"Stupid boy! Get away, get away!"

"You killed him!" Mont swung his fist at the man, but he was able to move his head fast enough to avoid the punch. Mont grabbed the skinny man by the throat.

"No. Stop it," Ellsben called out. He hurried over to Mont and pulled him away from the man.

Mont dug his fingernails into Ellsben's forearms and tried to pry himself free from Ellsben's grasp. "Let go of me!"

The man took his hand away from Cal's mouth. He cocked his head and stared at Cal for a moment, and then he touched Cal's forehead. A smile slowly appeared on the man's face. He turned and looked at Mont and Ellsben and said, "The fever's leaving. It's leaving."

"Liar!" Mont shouted. "You killed him."

"*I* saved him. *You* almost killed him." The man walked toward Mont. His forehead was wrinkled, and his face was red. "*You* were the one who could have killed him." The man pointed a stubby, callused finger in Mont's face.

Mont lunged at the man, but Ellsben held him back. "Let go of me." Mont squirmed, but he couldn't break free from Ellsben's arms. "Let go."

The man scratched his chest. "Let him go. Let him see his friend." The man turned his head and spit. "Let him see."

Ellsben carried Mont over to Cal. He slowly released Mont, and as soon as Mont was free, he knelt down and touched Cal's throat. The right side of Cal's face twitched. "He's not hot anymore." Mont looked amazed.

"The cyntum works." The man nodded. "It works. I told you it works."

"Hey," Mont said. He squeezed Cal's shoulder. "Are you feeling better?"

There was no response from Cal.

"Ah," the man said. "You don't know anything about poison, do you? The cyntum will save him, it will. But it's not like a miracle from God. He's going to be sick for a long time."

"How long?" Mont asked.

"That depends on how strong he is."

Ellsben knelt down and touched Cal's forehead. It was difficult for Ellsben to believe that Cal's fever had completely disappeared, but it was true.

"Now," the man said. "Let's eat."

Mont started to get up, but Ellsben put a hand on his shoulder. "Stay with him," Ellsben said. Ellsben went over to his pack, got a sandwich, and offered it to the man.

"What is it?"

"It's a cheese sandwich," Ellsben said. "The bread is a bit stale, but it's the best I can offer."

"*This* is how you treat me?" The man made a disgusted face and scratched his chest. "*I* saved the boy. *I* saved him, and all you can offer me is filthy naggie food."

"I don't have anything better," Mont said.

"Filthy naggie food. That's how you thank me." The man scampered over to Mont and leaned close to him. The man's breath had an odor that reminded Mont of rotten onions. "I wish I'd never given him the cyntum." The man pointed at Cal. "I wish I'd let him die."

"Damn it." Mont stood up. He went to his pack, ripped it open, reached in, and pulled out a sandwich. He tossed the sandwich at the man. The man's arms shot out with astonishing speed, and he managed to catch it without the sandwich falling apart.

The man took a huge bite of the sandwich, and as he was chewing it, his face suddenly puckered as if he'd discovered he'd just taken a bite of a turd. "*This* is no good." The man looked at the sandwich as if he was considering tossing it away, but then he brought it up to his face and stuffed most of it in his mouth. "You saved the good food for yourself." Bits of the sandwich flew out of the skinny man's mouth when he said this. "You're saving the good food for yourself."

"I gave you the good food." Mont held his pack open. "Do you see anything better in there? I've got one more sandwich, and it's the same as the one you're eating."

The man jammed the rest of the sandwich in his mouth. "You're saving the best food. Keeping it for yourself."

Mont took the last sandwich from his pack and threw it at the man. The sandwich slapped the man's chest, and he grabbed it with his left hand, but a slice of cheese slipped out and landed on the muddy ground. The man looked down at the piece of cheese and swore with such conviction that it sounded as if he was the victim of some great tragedy. He snatched the cheese from the ground and spit on both sides of it, and then he wiped the cheese on his shirtsleeve, cleaning off the mud. Next, he inspected the cheese, making sure not even the tiniest bit of mud was still clinging to it. He wiped the cheese on his sleeve again, looked at it, and then his lips curled into a small smile. He pushed the cheese back in the sandwich and took a huge bite of it. "Ah," the man said. "Years ago I would have spit this out. Stale bread, cheap cheese. But it's better than what I've been able to find to eat lately."

"That's all I have," Mont said. "You can leave now."

"Leave?" The man's eye widened. "I saved your friend, and you don't even have the courtesy to introduce yourself. You can't even lower yourself enough to utter one thank-you to me."

"I'm sorry," Mont said. "I should have thanked you for your help. Thank you for getting that plant."

"I still don't know your name," the man said.

"My name is Cron Graton," Mont said. He wondered how he was going to get rid of the man.

"And what's your friend's name?"

"He's my brother. His name is Lang."

The man was silent for a moment; he seemed confused by what Mont had just said. The man muttered something to himself, and then he stuck out his hand and said, "My name is Kozal."

Mont didn't want to shake Kozal's hand, but there was no polite way to avoid it. Kozal's fingers and palm were callused, and his grip was surprisingly strong. "Thank you for your help," Mont said.

Kozal smiled. "Now we're being polite. That's good. Now we're showing we have manners."

Mont didn't say anything. He thought that maybe if he didn't show interest in conversation Kozal would become bored and would decide to go away.

"What are you boys doing with that naggie?"

"He's our naggie."

"But what are you doing with him? Why are you traveling with him?"

Mont wished he didn't have to tell the story; however, he hoped that once he told it Kozal's curiosity would be satisfied and he would leave. "We're taking our naggie to our uncle's farm."

"Why are you doing that?"

"Because we're going to live with our uncle now. Our daddy got killed in the war. Even though our farm isn't very big, Mama's selling it because she says it's too much to take care of without Daddy around."

Kozal started laughing. His laughter came out in deep spurts, sounding almost like a dog barking. "Your poor daddy died in the war."

"What in the hell is so funny about that?"

"Poor Daddy."

"Get out of here," Mont said. "Leave us alone."

"Poor boys with the poor dead father," Kozal said. "I suppose Daddy was a hero too? Sacrificed his life to save twenty men. Or was it more than twenty?"

"Go," Mont said. "Leave."

"You can stop your act," Kozal said. "I'm not stupid."

"Leave."

"You could almost pass as a Southern boy," Kozal said. "Your accent is good. But I'm not stupid. You can't fool me."

"Leave us alone."

"And he's not your brother."

"He is my brother."

Kozal's face reddened, except for his scar. Kozal's scar stayed white; it looked as if someone had painted a white stripe against his red face. "You're a liar. A liar."

"You better leave." Mont was trying to control his anger.

"His name isn't Lang."

"Leave."

"I heard the naggie call him Cal."

"What do you want from us?"

"Admit that you're a liar."

"OK," Mont said. "We're liars. We lied to you."

"Now tell me the truth."

"It's time for you to leave," Ellsben said.

"Tell your naggie to show some respect."

"You need to leave," Mont said.

"After you tell me the truth," Kozal said.

"Leave now or I'll take you away from here." Ellsben walked toward Kozal.

"Don't touch me, you filthy naggie." Kozal was angry, but he also appeared to be afraid of Ellsben. He took several steps backward.

"Leave now." Ellsben kept moving toward Kozal.

"Leave," Mont said.

"Tell me the truth. Who are you?" Kozal leaned toward Mont.

Ellsben stomped one of his front hooves, and Kozal jumped back. "Leave now," Ellsben said. "I won't warn you again."

"Filthy naggie doesn't know his place." Kozal glared at Ellsben. "We wouldn't have had all these troubles if it wasn't for naggies. Naggies belong in Zana where they came from. Naggies never should have been brought here."

Swiftly, Ellsben lunged forward and reached out, trying to grab Kozal. But Kozal, moving with the agility of a hunted rodent, managed to evade Ellsben. Kozal let out a disgusted hissing sound and said, "The naggie will learn respect." Then Kozal scampered off into the woods.

Mont stared in the direction Kozal had gone. He half expected to see Kozal come slinking back. "Do you think he'll give us any more trouble?" Mont asked.

"I hope not," Ellsben said.

Mont went over to Cal and found a mosquito feeding on the side of Cal's face. Carefully, trying not to hurt Cal, Mont swatted the mosquito. A small blot of blood squirted on Cal's cheek from the mosquito's crushed body. Mont flicked the mosquito's body away, and then he licked his thumb and used his moist thumb to wipe off the small blot of blood. Cal mumbled something.

"Can you hear me, Cal?" Mont put his ear close to Cal's mouth. There was no response, only the soft sound of Cal's breaths.

After the sun went down, Ellsben started yawning. He needed to rest. Mont told Ellsben that he would watch Cal for the night. "I know I'm not going to be able to fall asleep," Mont said. "You might as well get some sleep if you can."

"Thanks," Ellsben said. "I'm exhausted. But if you get tired or if anything happens, you be sure to wake me up."

"I will."

THIRTEEN

KOZAL'S STORY

Cal felt a terrible pounding in his head. It was as if his heart had somehow managed to travel up and was thumping against the inside of his skull. He attempted to open his eyes, but his eyelids seemed to be glued shut. His right forearm burned. Was his arm draped over something hot? Cal tried to move his arm, but couldn't.

He wondered where he was. He remembered seeing snakes, but he wasn't sure if what he remembered was real or if it had been a nightmare. He remembered being in the water and then seeing the narrow, golden eyes of a snake. He remembered the snake opening its mouth, and he remembered hearing a deep hissing, and then his memory stopped. He wondered if these were real memories. If they were real, what happened?

He became aware of the sounds of crickets chirping. He also became aware of the scent of smoke from a campfire. He listened for the sounds of voices. He wanted to hear Mont or Ellsben, but he only heard the crickets. Could the bounty hunters or a group of Congressers have captured him? What if Mont and Ellsben had been killed?

His eyes still would not open. Panic began to erupt from the pit of his gut. He had to open his eyes. He had to know where he was. He had to find out what had happened to him. Cal concentrated on his eyes. At first nothing happened, and this caused him to consider the terrible possibility that he might be permanently paralyzed. Maybe he was dying, and his body was shutting down. The erupting panic intensified, and this caused the pounding in his head to worsen. *Concentrate,* Cal told himself. He had to fight the panic and concentrate on his eyes. He had to see. Trying to open his eyes felt the same as trying to lift an incredibly heavy object.

Suddenly it happened. His eyelids popped open, and a sharp pain stabbed deep into his eye sockets, causing thick tears to drool down his cheeks. All he could see was a smeared mixture of dull colors. He wanted to blink away the thick tears, but his eyelids still resisted obeying him. It seemed to take forever to make his eyelids blink. With the first blink, his vision worsened. The second time he managed to blink, the dull colors began to solidify. It was not as difficult to blink the third time, and after the fourth blink his blinking became effortless, and the dull colors bloomed into sharp focus.

Far above him was the branch of a tree. A slight breeze moved the branch's leaves, causing them to dance in and out of the flickering light from a campfire. Cal heard the sounds of what he thought was somebody quietly moving around. Was it Mont or Ellsben? He tried to move his head, but he couldn't make the muscles in his neck work. He managed to open his mouth, but he couldn't speak. Out of the corner of his eye, he saw a shadow move, and he was certain that the shadow was from a person. The panic he'd felt earlier came back. He sensed the person who cast the shadow wasn't Mont, and the shape and size of the shadow was definitely too small to be from Ellsben.

Cal fought to make his body move, but all he could manage to do was move his fingers. He desperately tried to turn his head so that he could see who had cast the shadow. In his mind he saw the bounty hunter with the thin red beard slowly walking toward him. He imagined the bounty hunter raising the crossbow that he'd been holding at his side. He imagined feeling the bolt from the crossbow slamming deep into his chest.

Using every bit of concentration he could muster, Cal managed to turn his head, and as he moved his head he felt a deep pain in the muscles of his neck that reminded him of a rag being ripped. He winced and bit down on his lower lip. Fortunately, the pain quickly subsided to a tolerable level.

Mont was sleeping beside him. Cal smiled. He was happy to see that Mont was here, that Mont was unhurt. About twenty feet away from the campfire, near a patch of bushes, Ellsben was sprawled on the ground, sleeping. Good. Both Mont and Ellsben were here.

The shadow Cal had seen earlier briefly appeared and slid across Ellsben's flanks. It was the bounty hunter. The flames from the campfire were keeping the bounty hunter hidden from Cal. He opened his mouth to shout out a warning, but his throat was dry and his voice refused to work. He concentrated on his left arm. His fingers twitched rapidly as if he were attempting to play a wild tune on a piano, and then his arm began trembling as his muscles started to respond to his mind. With more force than he had intended, Cal's arm shot out, and his hand slapped Mont's shoulder, causing a loud *whack* sound.

Mont instantly sat up, his eyes wide, his hands clenched into fists, ready to fight. When he saw that Cal was awake, a huge smile appeared on Mont's face. "Hey," Mont said. "How are you—"

"Look there," Cal managed to croak. He pointed toward where he thought the bounty hunter was.

Mont looked in the direction Cal was pointing. Cal expected Mont to become frightened, but instead of becoming frightened, Mont got angry. He stood up and rushed toward the bounty hunter.

"No," Cal said. His voice was returning.

There was no possible way Mont could fight the bounty hunter and win. Mont would be quickly killed. Cal couldn't see Mont anymore. He heard Mont swearing, and he heard another voice shriek, and then he heard what sounded like two bodies wrestling on the ground. Ellsben abruptly woke up and stood up. He stomped a hoof and then charged forward to help Mont.

Another shriek. Then someone shouted, "Get your hands off me, you dirty naggie. Get your smalta-picking hands off me!"

Looking over the top of the campfire's flames, Cal saw Ellsben pick up a small, skinny man. The man had a large scar across his face, and he appeared to be missing his right eye. When Ellsben lifted the man up, he pinned his arms against his side. The man squirmed and kicked his legs wildly, but the way Ellsben was holding him made it impossible for the man to be able to kick Ellsben. The man swore in frustration and said, "Put me down. Dirty naggie."

"You're a thief," Mont said.

"I'm not a thief." The man appeared offended and shocked that such an accusation would be aimed at him.

Mont pointed at the man. "If you're not a thief, what were you doing going through our packs?"

"I was curious. I wanted to know who you really are."

Cal felt the muscles in his back begin twitching, coming to life. The muscles in his thighs and calves contracted and then slowly relaxed. Cal clenched and unclenched his hands several times. He looked at his right forearm to see why it felt as if it was being burned. A white piece of cloth, which looked like it had been torn from a shirt, was wrapped around Cal's forearm. Blood had soaked through the white cloth and had dried, leaving a large, brown splotch. Cal took in a deep breath. He pushed his chin down against his chest and forced himself to sit up. At first the muscles in his back were so tense he felt as if an invisible force was trying to pull him backward, to the ground. Then a warmth flowed though his back as his muscles relaxed.

The man saw Cal and grinned. "See. Your friend is better. The cyntum I gave him worked. I saved him."

Mont looked at Cal, and then he looked at the man. Now Mont appeared confused rather than angry.

"I saved your friend. If I hadn't given him the cyntum, you'd be burying him right now."

Cal leaned forward and drew his knees to his chest. When he moved his legs, the muscles in his calves and thighs twitched for a moment; his muscles were still weak, but he felt strength creeping into his legs. He touched the ground with his hands and breathed in deeply. Now he was confident he had the strength to stand. The muscles around his knees tensed as Cal slowly brought himself up. At first he felt as if the world was pitching and rolling, and he had to stumble forward several steps to prevent himself from falling. He closed his eyes, and this made the dizziness lessen.

Suddenly, in his mind, Cal saw Ellsben holding a knife. Ellsben put the tip of the knife's blade on Cal's forearm, and Cal remembered the blade felt cool. Ellsben made a deep slice across a small part of Cal's forearm. Dark blood and a thick yellow fluid wept out.

Why would Ellsben cut him? Cal opened his eyes.

"I saved you." The man was staring at Cal; his one eye was opened wide. "I saved you."

Cal remembered seeing the head of a snake. Its mouth was open, and its black, forked tongue was pressed against the pink flesh at the bottom of its mouth. It had long fangs. It had cold, golden eyes.

"I saved you," the man said.

An old rope bridge. Cal remembered walking across an old rope bridge.

"I saved you."

Part of the bridge broke. Cal remembered being in the water and swimming with all his strength, he remembered Mont and Ellsben shouting to him. A burning pain in his right forearm. Cal remembered looking at his arm and seeing the black, scaly, triangular head of a river snake clamped on his arm. He remembered feeling anger, not fear. He remembered grabbing the snake by the neck, pulling its fangs from his arm, and then killing it by whipping its body against a rock.

Ellsben had cut his arm to drain the poison. Ellsben saved him.

Cal stared at the man. Who was he? Why was the man claiming to have saved him? Why hadn't Ellsben or Mont disputed this man's claim?

"I saved you." The man nodded his head. "I saved you."

Slowly, Cal walked toward Ellsben and the man. "Put him down," Cal told Ellsben.

Ellsben dropped the man, and he landed on his hands and knees in front of Cal. He looked back at Ellsben with a horrible scowl and said, "Filthy naggie." Then he looked at Cal and smiled. He stood up, extended his hand, and said, "My name's Kozal."

Cal shook the man's hand and said, "Hello."

"Who are you?" Kozal asked.

"I told you our names," Mont said.

"You lied," Kozal said. His eye narrowed to a slit. "I want the truth."

"What does it matter to you who we are?" Cal asked.

"The naggie cut you and drained some of the poison from your arm, but there was already enough poison flowing through you to kill you. I gave you some cyntum leaves. The naggie didn't even know what cyntum was. If I hadn't given you the cyntum, you'd have died." Kozal nodded his head. "I saved you, so you owe me the truth."

"Leave my brother alone," Mont said. He was afraid that right now, after being unconscious for so long, Cal could be confused and might reveal who he was. Mont wanted to redirect the conversation to prevent Cal from mistakenly telling

Kozal something he shouldn't. "You may have saved him, but that doesn't make you a hero. You're a common thief."

"He's not your brother," Kozal said, his face turning a deep red. "And I'm not a thief."

"You are a thief," Mont said. "I caught you going through our packs. What did you steal?"

"I stole nothing." The deep red color of Kozal's face was metamorphosing into a dark purple. He scowled, revealing his rotten teeth. "I was looking in your packs to find out who you really are."

"What did you steal?"

"*Nothing.*"

Mont lunged at Kozal and thrust his hand into the breast pocket of Kozal's shirt. Kozal shoved Mont away.

"What's this?" Mont asked. He held up a small brooch that he'd gotten from Kozal's pocket.

Kozal tensed, and he stood up straight, looking almost like a soldier standing at attention. "That's mine," Kozal said. His voice was much deeper than it had been. He was acting unnaturally calm. He held out his hand and said, "Give it back to me."

Mont curled his fingers around the brooch. "No. You can't have it until you give us back whatever you stole from our packs."

"I stole nothing from your packs." Kozal's calmness was eerie. "That brooch belonged to my mother. Now give it back to me."

"No." Mont raised his arm up and pulled it back. "Tell me what you took from our packs, or I'll throw your brooch in the fire."

"I'll kill you." Kozal said this in the same tone of voice a person would use when saying that it looks like it's going to rain. However, Cal sensed that Kozal's outward lack of emotion was only a mask hiding an intense anger that was bubbling up inside. If that brooch was harmed, Kozal would become extremely dangerous.

"Give him back the brooch," Cal said.

"Not until he tells us what he stole."

"Give it back to him now."

Mont looked at Cal to see if Cal was serious. When he saw that Cal was serious, he hesitated; he wasn't sure what he should do. "We need to find out what he stole," Mont said.

"It doesn't matter," Cal said. "Give it back to him."

Mont frowned. Then, suddenly, he threw it at Kozal.

A scared squeal escaped Kozal as his hand shot out and captured the flying brooch. He held the brooch against his chest and muttered something that sounded like a prayer. He brought the brooch up to his face and stared at it, inspecting it for damage. Gently, with a forefinger, he wiped the brooch. Then he affectionately kissed it and stuffed it deep into his breast pocket.

"You're a good boy," Kozal said to Cal. "I'm glad I saved you."

"Are you a thief?" Cal asked.

"No." Kozal shook his head. "I've stolen nothing from you."

"Why were you going through our packs?" Cal asked.

"I was curious. I wanted to know who you really are." Kozal smiled. "Now I know."

"Who are we?" Mont asked. There was a slight smirk on his face because he expected Kozal's answer wouldn't be anywhere close to the truth.

Kozal gave Mont a nasty look. Then he smiled at Cal and said, "You're the prince. You're the one they're looking for."

Mont laughed. "You think he's a prince? If he was a prince, he sure as heck wouldn't be walking around here with a naggie."

"You're a good liar," Kozal said to Mont. "But not good enough to fool me."

"You're insane," Mont said.

"Liar," Kozal mumbled and turned his back to Mont.

"What makes you think I'm a prince?" Cal asked.

"That story he told me didn't make sense." Kozal glanced back at Mont, and then he looked at Cal and shook his head. "He said you were delivering this naggie to your uncle. Why would the naggie stay with you? We've just about lost the war. There's no longer any central authority to enforce the laws. The naggies are almost all running off now." Kozal leaned toward Cal. "Besides, your accents give you away. I could tell from the first words he spoke that your friend's accent was fake. I'm not easy to fool. And your accent is even more obvious. You were raised as a member of the Northern upper class."

"Even if what you said is true, why does that make you think I'm a prince?"

"Not *a* prince. *The* prince." Kozal nodded his head and leaned even closer to Cal. "You're Prince Lanshire."

"And you're completely insane," Mont said. He tapped his temple and made a goofy expression.

Kozal ignored Mont. "I know the truth," Kozal said to Cal. "Don't bother me with lies."

Cal stared at Kozal for a long moment. "Tell me about yourself," Cal said.

"Yes." Kozal grinned. He put a hand on Cal's shoulder and nodded. "You didn't lie. You're a good boy. A good boy." Kozal slid his hand down from Cal's shoulder and stepped back a couple of steps. "I don't talk about myself. My business is my business. But I know who you are, and you didn't lie to me, so you deserve to know about me." Kozal walked over to the dying campfire and sat down near it. He motioned for Cal to join him.

Cal sat down next to Kozal. His injured arm was throbbing. He rested his forearm across his thighs, and then he placed his left hand on the white cloth that was wrapped around his forearm, covering his wound. Gently, he squeezed his arm and rubbed the area around the wound with his thumb, attempting to massage away the throbbing. This helped, but the throbbing refused to completely go away.

"You're a good boy." Kozal smiled.

"Where do you live?" Cal asked.

"Right now I don't live in one spot. I travel. I can't go back to my home."

"Why?"

"Because they're hunting me."

"Who's hunting you?"

"The Congressers."

"What did you do?"

Kozal looked down at the ground. He seemed embarrassed. "I'll tell you, but not right now." Kozal looked at Cal. "Do you want to know where I grew up?"

"Yes."

"Have you ever heard of the village called Forat?"

"No."

Kozal smiled. "I didn't think so. Forat's a tiny village. It's south of here. On foot it would take you about two days to get there."

"That's where you grew up?"

"Yes. That's where I was born. That's where I grew up. That was my home."

Cal listened intently as Kozal told his story.

———

Kozal was born in a small house on the outskirts of Forat. He had an older sister named Jana. He and his sister were raised by their mother because their father had died a month before Kozal was born. Their father was harvesting apples, and he fell out of an apple tree and broke his neck. It was not easy raising two children by herself, but somehow Mother always managed to get by. She was the hardest working person Kozal had ever known. He loved his mother. She always took care of him; she always made sure he was all right. Always. No matter what.

When Kozal was a child, he was sickly. He was born too early, and because of this his lungs didn't develop properly. Especially when he was a young child, there were many days when his chest felt as if it had filled with liquid, and this caused him to wheeze and gasp for breath if he walked more than several steps. When this happened, Kozal had to stay in bed, sitting up with several pillows between his back and the bed's headboard. Sometimes he had to stay in bed for many days. Even though he didn't feel well, he was always happy when he was bedridden and Mother was around to care for him. She was so kind. She loved him so much. She always knew how to make him feel better. Always.

There were many times Mother wasn't able to take care of him. She had to work to support them. She harvested apples in the fall, she baked and sold bread, and she did many chores for their more affluent neighbors. Mother was such a hard worker.

Kozal hated when he was sick and Mother had to work because that meant Jana was supposed to take care of him. Jana was full of smiles and was kind and helpful when Mother was around; however, the moment Mother left Jana would start taunting him, trying her best to upset him so that his breathing would get worse. Oh, she thought she was smart. But she wasn't anywhere near as smart as she thought she was. Even though Kozal was years younger than her, he could easily outsmart her. He learned quickly how to force himself to ignore her taunts. He showed her that he was her superior. He made it clear.

After she finally got it through her thick skull that her taunts weren't working and were never going to work again, she tried to make his breathing worse by sneaking up on him and suddenly yelling or dropping something that would make a loud noise, trying to startle him. But this didn't work either. He learned to listen for her, to expect her, and he was able to stay calm no matter what she did. He was her superior. And never once did he tell Mother about what Jana was doing because he wanted to prove to Jana that he could outsmart her by himself; he didn't need Mother to protect him from her.

By the time Kozal reached his tenth birthday, he began helping Mother work. He started out by helping her harvest apples, and then he went to work for their neighbors, help-ing them take care of their crops. Shortly after he turned thirteen, he helped a neighbor build a barn, and by doing this he learned carpentry skills and how to repair tools. With these new skills he was able to do more work, and the more work he did the less work Mother had to do. Helping her made him so proud. He would have worked even harder if he could, but he had to be careful because if he pushed himself too hard his breathing trouble would come back.

Jana hated to work. She never did any more work than she absolutely had to, and because of this the neighbors stopped hiring her to do chores. Mother made Jana help her bake the bread that she sold, and Mother made Jana keep their small house and yard clean. Frequently Jana would pretend that she was sick, but Mother always saw through Jana's little act. Mother never let Jana get away with pre-tending to be ill; she always forced Jana to work. Mother was smart; no one could fool her.

Kozal was fifteen when Mother was hurt. It was hor-rible. Mother was in so much pain Kozal couldn't stand it. He wanted to cry, but he didn't because he had to show her that he was strong; he had to show her that he would be able to take care of her. Poor Mother. It shouldn't have happened to her; she didn't even remotely deserve what happened. If it was possible, Kozal would have gladly switched places with Mother. He would have gladly let the accident happen to him instead of her.

Mother had walked to a neighbor's house to deliver bread, and he insisted on giving her a ride home. The neigh-bor knew how hard Mother worked. He was a good man; it wasn't his fault. His horse spooked and ran, then stumbled and fell, and the wagon Mother was riding in flipped over. The neighbor was thrown from the wagon and broke his wrist, but poor Mother was pinned under the wagon. The back edge of the wagon smashed Mother's legs. It was terrible. The neighbor ran to get help, but it took more than an hour before he could find four strong men to lift the wagon. Poor Mother had to suffer under the weight of the wagon for over an hour, but she was brave. She was so brave. She didn't let the pain consume her.

Both of her femurs were broken. The doctor tried to set the bones, but they never healed properly. Mother had to stay in bed for almost a year. During the time Mother was bedridden, Kozal worked during the day and took care of Mother in the evening. Jana was supposed to take care of Mother during the day, but Jana frequently left Mother alone because she had become infatuated with a neighbor boy. He lived two miles down the road with his mother and father and two brothers in a dirty shack. The boy was a thief. His whole family was nothing but a group of thieves; no one who knew them would have anything to do with them. The sheriff had arrested the boy and everyone in the boy's family more than once. They would steal anything they could get their dirty hands on.

Mother told Jana to stay away from the boy. She told Jana that the boy was good for nothing except trouble, but Jana wouldn't listen. Mother always gave excellent advice, but that didn't matter to Jana—she wanted to show Mother that Mother couldn't control her. Jana was very, very disrespectful to Mother. Finally Mother had enough, and she ordered Jana to stay away from that dirty boy. Jana told Mother that she couldn't stop her, that she was going to spend every moment she could with the boy. Poor Mother. If she could've gotten out of bed, she would have grabbed Jana and knocked her down, and Jana would have remembered the respect for Mother that she'd forgotten. Since Mother couldn't get out of bed, she did the only thing she was able to. She told Jana that she had to make a choice: stay away from that boy and remain with her family, or go with that dirty boy and leave her family and home forever.

Jana chose the boy. She swore at poor Mother and told her that she was nothing but a useless invalid and that every breath of air that Mother breathed was a waste of air that could be used for people who weren't going to be stuck in a bed for the rest of their lives. Jana told Mother that she should do the world a favor and die, and this was more than poor Mother could take. Mother lunged at Jana, and when she did this, she tumbled out of bed and hit the floor hard, twisting her crippled legs. Mother screamed from the pain, but Jana did nothing to help her. Jana went to her bedroom and put her clothes in a sack, and then she walked out of the house. She left poor Mother on the floor.

Mother was on the floor for the entire afternoon. Kozal was out working, repairing the roof on a barn, and he didn't get home until evening. He knew before he even entered the house that something was wrong; he sensed that Mother needed him. He cursed himself for not having sensed this sooner. Kozal ran into the house, and when he saw Mother on the floor, he almost panicked. But he didn't let himself panic because he knew that if he panicked he wouldn't be able to help Mother, and Mother desperately needed his help. He gently lifted her up and placed her on the bed and stroked her hair. He told her that he would get the doctor, but she said no, she didn't want the doctor—she wanted to talk to him. Kozal sat on the edge of the bed and leaned his head close to Mother so that she could speak softly to him. He wanted her to save her strength.

The expression that appeared on Mother's face when she began telling him what Jana had done scared Kozal; he had never seen such intense anger in Mother before. The more Mother told him, the more Kozal absorbed her anger. He stood up; every muscle in his body was tense, and his face felt hot. Kozal told Mother that Jana was garbage, that it was best that Jana was gone. He started to tell Mother that he was going to find Jana and make her suffer for what she'd done to Mother, but she stopped him. Mother reached out her hand and motioned for Kozal to come close to her. He sat down on the edge of the bed again, and she placed her hand over his mouth and said, "Don't ever say Jana's name again. I never want to hear it. Don't ever mention her again. Ever. She doesn't exist. She never existed."

Kozal promised Mother that he would never again mention Jana. Then he went through the house and gathered up Jana's belongings that she'd left behind and anything else in the house that reminded him of her and threw them in a pile in front of the house and burned them. Later he shoveled the ashes into a ditch and spit on them as they floated away on top of the scummy water that was flowing in the ditch. Jana and the boy must have gone someplace far away because Kozal was unable to find her. He never told Mother, but he went out many times searching for Jana. She was lucky he never found her because if he had, he would have made her suffer. He would have made her wish she'd never treated Mother the way she had. Oh, he would have done things that would have made her sorry. Yes, he would have made her sorry for hurting poor Mother.

Because Mother's crippled legs kept her from being able to easily move around, she frequently became ill. This was terrible. Mother never used to get sick. Kozal only remembered her having two slight colds before her legs were injured. After the wagon accident, Mother frequently got horrible stomach pains, and sometimes she also got headaches that were so bad she couldn't open her eyes. Kozal was always there for her when she was ill. He fed her, gave her healing herbs, held her, and talked to her. He did everything he could for her. He would have cut off his arm if it would have helped her. He loved Mother so much.

The war killed Mother. It made her so angry she couldn't sleep or think about anything else, and this was too much for her fragile health. She needed lots of rest, and she needed to stay calm, but the war took all that away from her. She hated the thought of so many people fighting, killing, maiming each other over naggies. She said naggies were dirty, violent, smelly creatures, and they never should have been brought to this continent. They'd done nothing but cause trouble for the kingdom. Mother said that if anyone in power had any brains, instead of fighting a war, they would have put the naggies, every last one of them, on ships and sent them to Zana, back to the continent where they came from. If they knew back three hundred years ago, when they'd captured and brought over the first group of naggies, how much trouble the naggies would end up causing, they never would have brought over even one naggie.

Kozal tried to get Mother to think about something other than the war and the naggies, but it was impossible to distract her. She talked about the war and the naggies until her voice was hoarse. She had almost no sleep for three days, and by the end of the third day she started feeling sharp pains in her chest. Mother said that if she was able to she would join the army and fight those Northern naggie lovers. She said the king had gone insane. He wanted to set all the naggies free and let them run wild through the kingdom. If the king had his way, eventually the naggies would take over the kingdom, and the people would be the naggies' slaves. The king and all the Northern naggie lovers had to be stopped. Kozal grabbed Mother's hand and kissed it and told her that he wouldn't let the naggies take over. He told Mother that he would join the army and fight those Northern naggie lovers. When he said this Mother started crying, and he held her and told her she needed to rest. He told her she needed to stop thinking about the naggies. He told her that if she didn't rest and stop thinking about the naggies, she was going to make herself very sick.

Mother's chest pains worsened. Kozal did everything he could think of to help her relax, but she couldn't get the naggies and the war out of her mind. She became delirious, and even in a delirious state she couldn't escape thoughts of the naggies and the war. At one point she shook her fist and mumbled something about the dirty naggies. Kozal knew he was losing her, and this frightened him. He had never been so scared in his entire life. What would he do without Mother? He grabbed her hands and kissed them and begged her not to die. He spread her silver hair out on her pillow and gently brushed it and told her how beautiful she was. He kissed her forehead and told her she couldn't leave him, she had to stay with him. Mother opened her eyes and looked at him, and he was sure she was coming back, he was sure she was going to get better. Kozal carefully laid his head on her stomach and looked at her, and she managed to reach up and stroke his neck. She smiled and whispered to him that he was a good boy. Then her eyes lost the ability to see, and a long sigh escaped her, and Kozal knew she had left him. He lifted up her torso from the bed and hugged her and told her he loved her.

That evening Kozal dug a grave for Mother behind the apple orchard, next to Father's grave. He was in a trance when he buried her because if he allowed himself to think about what he was doing he'd never be able to do it. After Mother's grave was filled, Kozal dropped down and curled up on top of the dirt that covered the grave and fell asleep. He went into a deep sleep, almost as if his body temporarily died, and when he woke up the next morning he was still in a trance. It felt as if he was not in control of what he was doing, as if somebody else other than his own mind was directing his actions. He went into the house and changed his clothes and combed his hair, and then he left the house and began walking down the road that led to the village. When he arrived at the village, he couldn't remember walking the four miles he had to walk to get there. In the village every house was prominently flying the new flag the Congressional government had recently adopted. Kozal found where the military had set up a station for volunteers. About a dozen sullen men were standing in line, waiting their turn to speak with the recruitment officer.

The recruitment officer looked at Kozal and laughed. The officer had a fat face and a small nose, and he reminded Kozal of a pig. "We're looking for men, not little boys," the officer told Kozal. This was almost more than Kozal could take; he had to fight the urge to lunge forward and smash his fist against that officer's face. Even though Kozal was small, he certainly didn't look like a child. That pig officer was trying to humiliate him. Kozal glared at the officer. The men who had been in line in front of Kozal took the pig's side and laughed at Kozal and told him to go home. They said this war would be fought and won by men—they didn't need any little boys hanging around. Kozal spit at them, and when they came after him, he scurried away.

Kozal rushed home, talking loudly to himself, swearing all the way. Once he was home, he immediately went to Mother's grave and sat down on the ground beside the grave. He told Mother what had happened, and then he asked her what he should do. What happened next brought a huge smile to Kozal's face. Mother answered him. He heard her not with his ears, but in his mind. She told him not to be upset; she told him to wait and that eventually they would need him. She told him that they would beg him to join them. She told him to be patient.

The first year of the war went well for the Congressers. They won all the major battles, and for a while it looked as if they might win the war. During this time Kozal lived at home, and he only left his property when he absolutely had to. He did just enough work to survive. He rarely saw anybody. He tried to be patient because Mother had told him to be, but he had to admit that he was possessed by many doubts. What if Mother had been wrong? What if Mother had been confused? What if they never needed him? Kozal frequently thought about the pig officer. He hoped the pig would get captured by Northern soldiers, and he hoped those Northerners would turn the pig over to some naggies. Kozal had to smile every time he thought about what a group of naggies would do to the pig.

The second year of the war started out well for the Congressers, but in July of that year the Congressers lost their first major battle. This was because in July the king dismissed General Macton and replaced him with General Grintar. Macton was afraid to fight, but not Grintar. He wouldn't back down. Grintar went on the offensive, and he stayed on the offensive. The Northern provinces had a much greater population than the South, and this meant they had far more troops. And because they had many more troops, they could afford to lose more men than the Congressers could. Grintar knew this, and that's why he kept attacking and attacking. Grintar was going to wear the Congressers down until they had almost no troops left.

Mother was right; he should have never doubted Mother. By the end of the second year of the war, the Congressers were desperate for volunteers. But Kozal didn't volunteer, not right away. He wanted them to be even more desperate. Although he wanted the Congressers to win—there was no way he could ever for even an instant hope that the naggie-loving Northerners would win—he had to admit he was enjoying hearing about how many battles the Congressers were losing. Kozal enjoyed hearing about the losses the Congressers were suffering because this proved how wrong that pig officer and those stupid men were. They wouldn't turn him away and make fun of him now.

Kozal waited until March of the third year of the war before he went back to the village to volunteer again. He only went back because he'd promised Mother he'd fight the naggie lovers; otherwise, he'd have never considered going back and offering to help the people who had humiliated him. Never.

The pig wasn't there. Kozal had wanted the pig to be there because he wanted to make the pig grovel; he wanted to make the pig beg him to volunteer. He wanted to hear the pig tell him what a good soldier he'd make. Kozal imagined the pig telling him that his small size would actually be an advantage in a battle because he would be a smaller target and could get into places where bigger men couldn't.

A thin man with a broken arm was the new recruitment officer for the village. His eyes were a pale blue, and he had a difficult time maintaining eye contact. He kept nervously looking down at the papers on his desk and randomly shuffling them. Kozal asked the officer what had happened to his arm, and the officer told him that he broke it during a battle two weeks ago. He'd stumbled, and a horse trampled him. He said his arm was the only reason he was here. He said if his superior officer hadn't ordered him here, he would still be out there fighting those Northerners. He said his broken arm wasn't enough to keep him from being able to fight. Those Northerners want to set all the naggies free. The man's cheeks turned red, and he said he'd rather die than live to see all the naggies running around free. "Naggies are born criminals," the officer told Kozal. "It's part of their nature. They'd rather steal than work for something." The officer leaned close to Kozal and whispered, "Male naggies like our women. If they think they can get away with it, male naggies will force themselves on our women."

Kozal nodded. He told the recruitment officer that he agreed with him and that's why he'd come to volunteer.

Kozal said that the naggie lovers had to be stopped. The recruitment officer grabbed Kozal's hand and firmly shook it. "Thank God for men like you who are willing to step forward and fight for what is right," the officer said. "I wish there were a million more men like you out there." The officer started blinking rapidly; he appeared as if he was about to start crying. "We need more men if we're going to be able to keep fighting. Too many of our men have been killed."

"We'll keep fighting," Kozal said to the officer. "We'll win."

Hearing this seemed to give the officer strength. He straightened his posture and said, "Yes, we will win."

Kozal filled out several forms that the officer gave him, and then he signed his name at the bottom of the page of the last form. He was now a part of the Congresser army.

The officer sent Kozal to a village located several miles to the north. That's where Kozal would receive his uniform and weapons and would be assigned to a unit. Kozal walked rapidly to this village; although it wasn't far, he'd never been there before. It was a small village; Kozal was able to walk from one side of the village to the other side in less than two minutes. The Congressers had converted a barn into a warehouse. Kozal's uniform and sword in a scabbard were brought out of this barn and given to him by a soldier who had lost both of his hands. This soldier didn't speak. He dropped the sword and scabbard at Kozal's feet, shoved the uniform against Kozal's chest, and then turned away from Kozal and quickly disappeared into the barn.

When Kozal put the uniform on, he discovered that it was too big and that it wasn't new. The pants were several inches too long for him, and so were the sleeves on the shirt.

On the breast of the shirt there was a tear that had been repaired with tight black stitching. Across the belly of the shirt there was another tear that had been repaired with black stitching, but surrounding this tear was a faint brown stain. Someone had tried to scrub this stain out of the cloth, but it had refused to completely disappear. Blood. Kozal wondered where the man who had first worn this uniform was buried.

Kozal picked up the sword and scabbard that had been dropped at his feet. He attached the scabbard to his belt. He held the sword up and studied its double-edged blade. This was the first time he'd ever held a sword. A tall man suddenly appeared, grabbed Kozal by the upper arm, and dragged him into an open space behind the barn. The man had a thick neck and muscular arms. He had narrow, mean eyes, and he wore a broad, drooping mustache that made his face appear to have a deep, perpetual frown. The man quickly showed Kozal how to properly hold the sword, and then he rapidly demonstrated how to fight with a sword. He told Kozal that the enemy could attack from any side, and so he should never assume his back was safe. "Always know what's going on behind you," the man said. Then he told Kozal not to worry about all the bolts and arrows that would be flying through the air during a battle because if he thought about them he'd lose his concentration and wouldn't be able to fight. The man told him that if a bolt or arrow was meant for him, God would deliver it, so there was no point worrying about them. "If it's your time to die, you'll die," he said. "If it's not your time, you'll be fine."

That was the only training Kozal received. How could they expect him to fight properly when this was the only training they gave him? He'd never been a soldier; he didn't know how to fight in a battle. They were wrong to send him into battle without properly training him.

The other men in the unit he was assigned to didn't like him. They had been fighting together for over a year, and they didn't like having a new man, a man who'd never fought, put with them. Kozal kept to himself. The men in his unit wouldn't speak to him unless they had to, and then they wouldn't say one word more than necessary.

Kozal was with this unit for three days without anything happening. They moved close to territory controlled by the Northerners, but they didn't make any plans to attack. At least they didn't make any plans that Kozal was aware of. The men were always whispering to each other. Kozal hated sitting around doing nothing. He needed to do something; he needed to keep his mind occupied. He began to feel nervous and agitated.

On the morning of the fourth day that he was with the unit, Kozal was woken by someone who kicked him just below his ribs. He sat up and clutched his side. The kick had been strong enough to cause a sharp pain. It was still dark; the eastern sky was starting to turn pink, hinting that the sun would soon peek over the horizon. "Get up and get ready," a voice said to Kozal. He could see the silhouettes of many men; other Congresser units had come to his unit's camp. Excitement fluttered in Kozal's belly. Finally, they were going to attack the Northerners.

A man grabbed Kozal's arm and pointed, showing him the direction he was supposed to go. Kozal moved quickly. There were men in front of him, there were men behind him, and there was a small group of men to his left side and to his right side. Soon Kozal could smell the combination of smoke and food cooking. They were close to the Northerners. Kozal smiled. The Northerners were getting ready to have breakfast. They weren't prepared to fight; they were going to be completely taken by surprise. Those naggie lovers were going to get a whipping they'd never forget.

The Northerners were camped in a large field. There were enough tents to make the camp look like a small village. Kozal only saw about a dozen men moving around the camp. The rest of the men must still be asleep. This was a good thing because Kozal guessed from the size of the camp the Northerners must have at least four times more men than the attacking group of Congressers had. They had to take the Northerners by surprise; otherwise, they would need a miracle to be able to defeat all those Northerners.

Suddenly the men in front of Kozal let out a shrieking war cry and charged into the Northern camp. The men behind Kozal were archers, and they began rapidly shooting flaming arrows into the camp. The flaming arrows hit the tents, and the tents quickly burned. Soon the camp was filled with thick smoke and the sounds of screaming men. Only a few Northerners engaged the attackers, and they were killed before Kozal reached the camp. The Congressers let out a victorious yell, and Kozal yelled with them and waved his sword over his head.

What happened next took Kozal completely by surprise. Hundreds of Northerners suddenly appeared. They hadn't been asleep in their tents. They'd left a score of men in the camp to make the camp appear occupied while the rest of the men hid in the nearby woods. While the Congressers were focusing their attention on attacking the camp, the

Northerners were swiftly and silently surrounding the Congressers. Kozal had never experienced anything even vaguely similar to the situation he found himself in. Men were running in every direction. Kozal didn't know which way he should go or what he should do. Men were falling everywhere, some screaming, their chests or backs or abdomens pierced by crossbow bolts or arrows.

A group of Northerners on horseback galloped into the chaos, swinging their swords wildly. A Congresser from Kozal's unit was slammed on the throat by a sword, and his head snapped back, coming almost completely off. Blood sprayed out of the man's neck, hitting Kozal's face, getting into his eyes. The blood blinded him, but he kept moving because he was too afraid to stand still. He stumbled over a corpse and fell flat on the ground. He heard and felt the thunder of a horse galloping over him; somehow its hooves missed him.

Kozal rubbed his eyes, and his vision, blurry at first, came back. A man was lying beside Kozal. He had an arrow sticking out of his chest, and he was gripping the arrow with one hand, probably trying to pull it out. The man looked over at Kozal and opened his mouth, and blood came out instead of words. Kozal stood up and looked around and saw to his left there was an opening, an area where no men were currently fighting. If he ran through the opening, he could escape into the woods.

Kozal ran. As he entered the woods, he thought he heard his commanding officer calling his name, ordering him to come back. Kozal ignored him and kept running. He ran without knowing where he was going. He was in a daze. As he was running, he realized that he was still holding his sword. When he saw his hand clenching the sword, he felt like tossing it away, but before he tossed the sword away, the logical part of his mind took over and told him that the sword could be useful, and it would be foolish to get rid of it. He stuffed the sword back into its scabbard.

After running several miles, Kozal had to stop and rest. He looked over his shoulder and was surprised to find that no one was behind him. He hadn't thought he could escape from the battle so easily; while he was running he'd imagined several Northerners chasing after him. When he stopped to rest, he was expecting to hear voices demanding he surrender. Kozal had no intention of fighting because he knew he couldn't win. He didn't know how to fight. The best he could hope for was a chance to get away at some point after they made him a prisoner.

But there were no Northerners pursuing him. Unless they were following him at a distance, hoping he'd lead them to a secret Congresser camp. Kozal closed his eyes and listened for several minutes, but he heard nothing that would indicate men were nearby. He opened his eyes. There was no one nearby; if someone was, he was sure he would have sensed their presence by now.

Kozal wasn't sure what he should do. He'd promised Mother he would fight the naggie lovers, but he didn't know if he should keep his promise. If he went back and fought, he would be killed, and his fighting and death would accomplish nothing. The Congressers hadn't given him the training he needed to be able to effectively fight in a battle. It was their fault he'd had to run away. Kozal was certain that if Mother had known how they would throw him into a battle without proper training she would never have accepted his promise to fight the naggie lovers. Mother didn't know what it would be like. Still, Kozal didn't want to break his promise without Mother's permission. He needed to go back to Mother. He needed her advice.

It took Kozal four days to get home. It should have only taken him three days, but he had to travel slower than usual because he had to make sure he stayed out of sight. He was wearing a Congresser uniform, and this meant he had to make sure he didn't run into any Northerners. He also had to make sure he didn't run into any Congressers because now he was a deserter, and the punishment for deserting was death. Kozal was worried about running into naggies too because while he was with his unit he'd heard quite a few stories about bands of runaway naggies roaming around in the woods. He knew a naggie would slit his throat just for fun, but now he was in even more danger because of his Congresser uniform. If some naggies caught him while he was wearing the uniform, they would torture him before they killed him, and the thought of being tortured by naggies scared him more than anything. Naggies knew many horrible ways to torture; they were violent creatures by nature, and they had no compassion.

When Kozal finally made it home, he immediately went to Mother's grave. He knelt down beside her grave and asked her what he should do. He told her he didn't know what he should do; he told her he would do anything she wanted him to. But Mother didn't answer him. Was she angry with him for running away? Kozal kissed the dirt over Mother's grave and stroked it and begged her not to be angry at him. He told her he'd gotten scared, that they hadn't properly trained him; he told her if he'd stayed he'd have been killed. He told her he hadn't even come close to killing a naggie lover. They hadn't taught him to fight. He told her it was pointless going into battle and being killed unless he could kill at least several naggie lovers. Kozal kissed the dirt over Mother's grave again and asked her to forgive him for running away. He told Mother he needed her help, needed her to tell him what he should do. But Mother still wouldn't answer him.

Tears ran down Kozal's cheeks. He stroked the dirt over Mother's grave and pleaded with her to help him, to tell him what he should do.

"Get up, boy," a voice said.

Kozal turned his head and saw two men walking toward him. They were coming from the direction of the house; they'd probably been looking for him in the house. Kozal became angry when he thought about those strangers snooping around in Mother's house. Mother would have never let men like them into her home. Kozal stood up.

"We've caught us a deserter," one of the men said. The other man smiled and nodded. These men were dirty, smelly, nasty, barely better than animals.

"We might as well kill him now since we get paid the same whether we bring him in alive or dead," one of the men said. They both drew their swords. Kozal tensed. He wasn't going to let them kill him in front of Mother. He had to protect Mother from that.

One of the men charged toward Kozal, and Kozal, feeling as if someone else had taken control of his body, moved swiftly. He dodged the man's sword, while at the same time he managed to jerk his own sword from its scabbard. And with the smooth motion of an expert who'd performed this action hundreds of times, he thrust the blade upward, deep into the man's gut. The man's eyes opened wide; he'd been taken completely by surprise. A hissing sound came from the man's mouth, and Kozal wasn't sure if it was the sound of air being forcefully expelled or inhaled. The man dropped to his knees and immediately fell on his right side.

Kozal pulled his sword out of the man. This was difficult; it felt as if the man's abdominal muscles had contracted and were gripping the sword. The moment the sword's blade came out of the man, a dark mixture of blood and abdominal fluids spilled out of the wound, soaking the man's shirt. His right hand moved as if it was going to clasp the wound, but the hand abruptly went limp and flopped to the ground.

A noise that sounded like a grunt made Kozal quickly look over his shoulder. He saw the second man lunging at him, swinging his sword. Kozal tried to leap backward, out of range of the sword's downward arch, but he wasn't quick enough. The sword slashed across his face, and its sharp tip slit open his right eye, blinding him. Kozal howled and scrambled backward. He felt blood streaming down his face and dripping from his chin and the edge of his jaw. If this had happened somewhere else, Kozal probably would have given up, he probably wouldn't have had the will to fight back, but there was no way he was going to allow this man to kill him in front of Mother. It would have destroyed Mother to have her only son killed in front of her. Finding strength he didn't know he had, Kozal let out a screech and lunged at the man. He swung his sword at Kozal, but Kozal was able to duck under the sword. He grabbed the man's legs, knocking him down, and then before the man could regain his bearings, Kozal jumped on his back. The man tried to flip Kozal off his back, but Kozal's grip was too tight. Kozal brought the edge of his sword's blade up, under the man's chin, and then with all his strength he pushed the blade into the man's throat and pulled it across, causing a long, deep cut. Next, Kozal flung himself off of the man's back. The man somehow managed to stand up. He turned toward Kozal. Blood gushed out of what looked like a huge mouth on the man's neck. His face had turned an unnatural white. He took two steps forward and then collapsed.

Kozal apologized to Mother. He told her he was sorry he'd caused so much trouble; he told her that if he'd had any idea that this was going to happen, he would have never come home. Mother didn't answer him, and he was sure she was angry at him. Kozal grabbed the first man and dragged him into the woods, far away from Mother, and then he went back and got the second man. He dumped the second man on top of the first man.

Suddenly it felt as if the world was wobbling. Kozal stumbled to the house. He wanted to lie down, he wanted to rest, but he couldn't because there was a strong chance that those two men weren't the only men sent to look for him. They would look for him here. He had to leave and never come back.

When Kozal entered the house, what he saw made him angry, and this gave him a burst of strength that he needed. The men had demolished the inside of the house. Mother's mattress was shredded, her bureau had been smashed to pieces, and her clothes were scattered everywhere. There was a strong odor of urine; one of the men had pissed on the floor of Mother's bedroom. Kozal couldn't stand it; he rushed from Mother's bedroom. His bedroom was in the same condition as Mother's bedroom, but he didn't care. They were after him, so he understood why they'd destroyed his belongings, but they shouldn't have destroyed Mother's things. She was innocent. They had no decency; they were as bad as naggies.

Kozal picked up a pair of his pants and one of his shirts from the floor. He took off his Congresser uniform and threw it in a corner. He put on his shirt and pants. Next he went into his closet and got down on his knees and felt the floor with his hands, searching for the floorboard that was loose. When he found the loose floorboard, he dug his fingernails into the crack and pried it up. He tossed the floorboard aside and quickly thrust his hand into the hole in the floor. For a moment he was afraid that what he'd hidden under the floor had disappeared, and his fingers wildly searched for the object. Where was it? When his fingers found the tiny wooden box, he quickly pulled it out of the hole. The box, especially the top, was covered with dust. He blew the dust off the box and then carefully opened it. Inside was Mother's brooch. Kozal kissed it and held it tightly against his chest.

The sound of rustling leaves made Kozal quickly stand up. He listened. The sound of the leaves had probably been caused by a gust of wind, but Kozal didn't feel fully confident of this explanation. Someone could be outside. Kozal thrust the brooch deep into his pocket. He couldn't fight anymore; he didn't have the strength. He was going to have to run. Kozal crawled to the front door so that if anyone was outside they wouldn't be able to see him walking past the windows to the door. He listened. He was prepared to hear the sounds of whispering voices or footsteps, but all he heard was the chirping of a bird.

Slowly, he stood up and put his hand on the doorknob. His fingers twitched, and the doorknob rattled, which scared him. Kozal gripped the doorknob and quickly turned it, and then he pulled the door open and ran out of the house and into the woods. It was difficult to run; he kept tripping because his vision was different with only one eye.

After Kozal had gotten almost a mile from the house, he stopped and listened and looked for any signs that he was being followed. He didn't hear or see anyone. The world wobbled, and Kozal had to grab a tree to keep himself from tumbling over. He needed help. He reached in his pocket and grabbed Mother's brooch, and this immediately made him feel stronger.

Kozal went to the doctor's house. This was the doctor who had helped Mother after her legs were broken in the wagon accident. The doctor was a smart man and a kind man, and Kozal knew that the doctor would help him. Kozal almost didn't make it to the doctor's house because the world kept wobbling, making it almost impossible to walk. When the world wobbled too much, he would grab Mother's brooch and hold it, and this would make him feel better; it gave him the strength to stay on his feet.

The doctor didn't want anything to do with Kozal. He said that if he was caught helping Kozal, he would be guilty of helping a deserter, and they would hang him. The doctor said men had already been here looking for Kozal. But the doctor was too kindhearted to be able to turn Kozal away. He cleaned the tissue in the area where Kozal's right eye used to be and bandaged it. He wrapped up a dozen bandages and gave them to Kozal and told him to keep the wound clean and to change the bandage every day. Then he gave Kozal a small jar filled with healing herbs and instructed him in how to take them. The doctor escorted Kozal to the back door and told him to leave and to never return to the area again. Kozal thanked the doctor and promised him that if he got caught, he would deny that the doctor had helped him. He would say he'd stolen the bandages and healing herbs.

Injured and carrying his meager supplies, Kozal stumbled off into the night.

———

Cal looked up from the campfire as Kozal finished telling his story. Kozal told him that the Congressers weren't actively looking for him anymore because they didn't have the men or resources to search for deserters. However, his name and description was on a list of wanted deserters that the Congressional Military Headquarters printed and sent out to all towns and villages in the South. This meant it was impossible for Kozal to establish himself in a new community.

"I have to make sure very few people see me, and I have to keep moving because if I stay in one place for too long my chances of getting caught are much greater," Kozal said. "I've had to live like this for two years."

"We've been living like that, but only for a short time. It's very difficult. I'm impressed you've been able to survive on your own for so long," Cal said.

"It is difficult," Kozal said. "But I've been able to manage because I'm clever, and because sometimes Mother helps me, gives me advice." Kozal took out the brooch and looked at it, and then he put it back in his pocket and said, "She doesn't like to give me advice; she wants me to figure things out on my own. But if I get into real trouble, she helps me."

Cal felt his energy fading. He put his face in his hands. Kozal leaned close to him and asked him if he was feeling sick again.

"No," Cal answered. "I don't feel sick. I just feel very tired all of a sudden."

"You need to keep your strength," Kozal said. "Your body still has the poison in it. You can't let yourself get weak. I'll make you some tea that will help you." Kozal stood up and looked at Mont and said, "Boil some water. I'll go find the herbs to make the tea."

The tea helped. Cal felt much better a few minutes after he drank it. Kozal sat down beside Cal and told him that even though he felt better he should rest. Cal agreed and thanked Kozal for the tea.

"Where are you traveling to?" Kozal asked.

"That doesn't concern you," Ellsben said.

"Quiet, naggie." Kozal glared at Ellsben. "I wasn't speaking to you."

"I can't tell you exactly where we're going. That has to be kept a secret," Cal said. "All I can tell you is that we're headed west."

When Cal said west, Kozal became agitated and shook his head. "No. West is not good. Don't go west. Go any direction except west."

"Why?" Cal asked.

"It's rumored that General Grintar has moved his men to the Western territories. General Lan has ordered most of what's left of the Congresser army to the western border.

General Lan is convinced Grintar is planning on attacking from the west. If you go west, you'll almost certainly be captured by Congressers. The border is being heavily patrolled."

"We have to go west," Cal said. "We don't have a choice."

Kozal looked as if he'd felt a sudden pain. He reached in his pocket and grabbed the brooch and muttered something. He turned his back to Cal, Mont, and Ellsben. He muttered some more, and Cal realized that Kozal was having a conversation with the brooch. After a minute, Kozal put the brooch back in his pocket and turned toward Cal. "I'll help you," Kozal said. "I can guide you past the Congressers. I know the territory."

"Why do you want to help us?" Cal asked. "What would you get out of helping us?"

"If I help you, maybe you could help me."

"How do you want me to help you?"

"Perhaps when you take the throne, you might—"

"I never said I was the prince."

"Well, *if* you were the prince, perhaps maybe after you take the throne you could issue a pardon, get rid of the bounty that's on my head. I mean, you could issue the pardon after you bring the Southern provinces back into the kingdom."

"I'm a naggie lover. Are you sure you want to help me?"

"No, I don't *want* to help you," Kozal said. "But I'm willing to help you as long as you promise to help me."

"If I was the prince, I would issue a pardon for you as soon as the Southern provinces are brought back into the kingdom. Besides, once the Southern provinces are brought back into the kingdom, all laws or orders passed by the

Congresser government will be reviewed, and most will be rescinded."

Kozal smiled and nodded. "You will make a good king."

"If you can guide us safely past the Congressers, there will be a financial reward for you as well as a pardon."

Kozal's smile broadened.

"We don't need your services," Ellsben said. "I know how to get to where we're going."

"Don't listen to the naggie," Kozal said to Cal. "He may know how to get there, but he doesn't know where the Congressers are or how to avoid them. He'll get you captured."

"We don't need him," Ellsben said.

"Quiet, naggie." Kozal glared at Ellsben.

"We don't need him," Ellsben repeated.

"I think he can help us," Cal said.

Ellsben wanted to argue, but he saw that Cal had firmly made up his mind. Ellsben shook his head and shrugged and turned away.

"Let's go," Cal said. "We've got at least an hour before dark."

"No," Kozal said. "You need to rest. The tea is making you feel stronger than you really are right now. Rest. By the time you wake up tomorrow, most of the poison will be out of your system."

Cal nodded. "But I want to get up early and leave as soon as the sun starts to rise."

FOURTEEN

BOUNTY HUNTERS

Cal felt a hand grab his shoulder. He slowly opened his eyes and turned his head and saw Mont sitting next to him. "How are you feeling?" Mont asked.

"Exhausted." Cal sat up, and his right forearm began to throb around the area where the snake had bitten him. He put his left hand on the bandage that was covering the wound and pressed down, hoping to make the throbbing stop, but when he pressed down a deep pain flared in his forearm and traveled all the way up to his shoulder. Cal winced and jerked his hand away.

"How is your arm?" Mont asked.

"It hurts a lot more than it did yesterday."

"This will help," Kozal said. He was holding a metal cup over the campfire, gently stirring whatever was in the cup with a fat stick. "I'm making a paste with some herbs.

Mother taught me the recipe. This paste will numb the pain, and it will help keep your arm from getting infected."

Mont leaned close to Cal and whispered, "I don't like him."

"Try not to insult him," Cal said.

"Will you really grant him a pardon?" Mont asked.

"Yes. He saved my life."

"I don't trust him," Mont whispered. "Do you trust him?"

"Not completely," Cal whispered back.

Ellsben brought Cal a thick slice of bread. "We don't have much food left," Ellsben said. "We barely have enough to get us through two days."

Cal looked for his pack, because he had several sandwiches in it, and then he remembered that he'd lost his pack in the river. "Here," Cal said. He ripped the piece of bread in half and offered half of it to Ellsben.

"No," Ellsben said. "You need to eat the bread. It's important that you get your strength back."

"The naggie's right," Kozal said. "You need to eat, even if you're not hungry. If you don't at least get that whole piece of bread in your belly, you'll be too weak to travel the distance we need to go today." Kozal walked over and sat down next to Cal. "Eat," he said, pointing at the bread Cal was still holding. "Eat."

Cal wasn't hungry, but he knew Ellsben and Kozal were right, he needed to eat. He took a bite of the bread, but his mouth was dry, and this made it difficult to chew. After he chewed for a while, his saliva began to flow and he was able to swallow the bread.

Cal finished eating, and then Kozal grabbed his wrist and said, "Let me take care of your arm." Kozal removed the piece of cloth that had been used as a bandage from Cal's forearm. The cloth had a large brown stain of dried blood on it, and when Kozal pulled the bandage away from Cal's arm, there came a faint rotten odor. Kozal tossed the cloth in the fire.

"You're starting to get an infection," Kozal said.

Cal looked at his wound. It was covered with a rough, dark scab, and at the edge of the scab a thick yellow pus was oozing out.

"Naggie," Kozal called out. "Bring me a fresh piece of cloth."

Anger started to show on Ellsben's face, but he quickly hid it behind a neutral expression. He reached in his pack and removed another piece of cloth and brought it to Kozal. Quickly, making sure his hand didn't touch Ellsben, Kozal grabbed the piece of cloth. "First I must clean the nastiness away," Kozal said. He put his finger on the scab and pushed down, forcing the pus out. Then he wiped up the pus with the cloth. The throbbing in Cal's arm worsened. Kozal smiled and stirred whatever was in the cup with the fat stick. Next, Kozal brought the cup up to his face and sniffed. "Good," he said. He set the cup down and then stuck his first two fingers into it and scooped out a glob of bright green paste. Kozal smeared the green paste over Cal's wound.

At first the paste burned, and Cal instinctively started to shake his arm, causing the paste to come off, but Kozal grabbed his arm and held it still. "Wait," Kozal said. "Wait."

The burning sensation began to change, and soon Cal felt as if a small block of ice was being pressed on his wound. This cold sensation felt good. The throbbing began to slowly lessen.

"Naggie," Kozal said. "Bring me another piece of cloth."

Ellsben brought a piece of cloth, and Kozal wrapped the cloth around Cal's forearm, covering the wound. "The paste should keep most of the pain away," Kozal said. "And it will fight the infection."

Cal thanked Kozal.

"We need to go," Kozal said. "Follow me." He led them into some brush that was difficult to push through, but after a while the brush thinned, and they found themselves on a narrow path. "This is a path made by deer," Kozal said. "We can't use any of the regular trails because there's a large camp of Congressers about a mile from here. They will be patrolling the area. We need to stay alert."

A mosquito buzzed near Cal's ear; he swatted at it, and it flew away. His arm felt almost normal now. The cool numbness had disappeared without the pain returning. Only a faint, barely noticeable throbbing remained.

By midmorning it had gotten hot. There were no clouds, and the sunlight was strong. Cal had to keep wiping away the sweat that was beading up on his forehead. Cal's canteen was in his pack, so it had been lost with his pack in the river. Ellsben offered to share his water with Cal. When Kozal saw Cal drinking out of Ellsben's canteen, Kozal looked as if he'd just witnessed one of the most disgusting things he'd ever seen. Kozal mumbled something and shook his head.

"How do you feel?" Mont asked.

"Hot," Cal said.

"That means you feel fine," Mont said. "Because it is hot."

Cal smiled.

"How does your arm feel?" Mont asked.

"Not bad," Cal said. He lifted his arm up. "That paste worked. Most of the pain is gone."

"I want you to tell us if you start to feel tired or need to rest," Ellsben said. "Don't push yourself too hard."

"I'll let you know if I get tired," Cal said. "Right now I'm fine."

"All right," Ellsben said. "Just make sure—"

"*Quiet.*" Kozal suddenly stopped and hunched down. He pressed a finger over his lips. His eye was wide and moving rapidly back and forth, observing everything it could. Kozal leaned forward as if trying to get closer to a sound he was hearing.

"What is it?" Mont whispered.

"Hide," Kozal said. "Hide." Kozal dove to the ground and rapidly burrowed into some thick brush.

Mont looked around and shrugged. "He's crazy. I don't see anything or hear anything. Do you?"

"No, I don't," Cal said. "But I think we should hide. It's better to hide for no reason than to stand here and risk getting killed."

"Cal's right," Ellsben said. He quickly looked around. "There's no place right here where I can hide—I'm too big. I'm going to go back in the direction we came from. I remember a spot where the brush is tall. It's not too far from here." Ellsben turned and quietly trotted down the path, leaning forward to keep his torso low.

Cal and Mont pushed their way into the brush on the other side of the path from where Kozal was hiding. They remained still and listened. The only thing Cal heard was a crow squawking somewhere off in the distance. The branches from the brush were poking against Cal's sides and the back of his neck. He was lying on his belly and was uncomfortable, but he couldn't change the position he was in without making the brush shake, so all he could do was try his best to ignore his physical discomfort. Mont leaned toward Cal and put his mouth near Cal's ear and whispered, "There's nobody nearby. That Kozal's crazy. Let's go find Ellsben."

"No, we need to wait for a while," Cal whispered back.

"I don't want to wait too much longer," Mont whispered. "I need to stand up. I'm getting a cramp in my leg."

Someone coughed. A quick, soft cough. Was it Kozal?

Mont raised his eyebrows.

Cal turned his head, trying to see in between the many leaves that surrounded them. He thought he saw someone slowly moving down the path, coming from the direction that they had been going. The crow abruptly stopped squawking, and now there was complete silence. This unnerved Cal. He worried that the silence would cause any sound he might inadvertently make to seem magnified, as loud as a shout. He wanted to close his eyes, to shut the world out, but he didn't because he knew he had to stay alert. The motion he'd seen on the path was a man. Cal could now see a pair of dusty, dark leather boots. The boots came close to the brush where Cal and Mont were hiding and stopped. Another pair of boots, older and starting to tear at the seams, appeared and stopped next to the first pair. Cal very slowly turned his head so that he could see the faces of the boots' owners.

It was the bounty hunters. The red-haired man was holding his crossbow up, and his finger was wrapped around the trigger. The man with the curly black hair had his hand on his sword's handle, ready to quickly withdraw it from its scabbard.

"I smell a naggie," the red-haired man said.

"There's a naggie track over there," the black-haired man said. "Do you think it's from the naggie they're traveling with?"

"It's possible," the red-haired man said. "I know we saw them with a naggie, and we've seen naggie tracks with their tracks, but I'm still having a hard time believing that they're actually traveling with a naggie. Naggies are unpredictable; they have no loyalty. It doesn't make any sense for them to be traveling with a naggie."

The black-haired man nodded in agreement.

Cal was certain that at any moment the red-haired man would see them. He considered getting up and running away, but he quickly rejected this idea because he knew he wouldn't get far before a bolt from the crossbow would slam into his back. All he could do was continue hiding, and if it became necessary, he would fight. It would be a fight he almost certainly would lose, but fighting back and losing would be better than giving up. The red-haired man turned his head and now seemed to be staring right at them. Mont looked at the ground; he was too scared to look at the red-haired man. Cal forced himself to keep his gaze on the red-haired man because he knew he might have to react at any second. The red-haired man's eyes narrowed almost imperceptibly, and he brought the crossbow up and aimed it at the brush where Cal and Mont were hiding. Cal felt suddenly cold, and he readied himself to fight. He knew there was almost no chance of winning or getting away, but he wasn't about to give up.

The red-haired man leaned close to the brush, and for a moment Cal was certain that the man was making eye contact with him. But then the red-haired man suddenly turned away. He looked up, scanning the upper branches of all the nearby trees.

"They're not here," the black-haired man said.

"Maybe not," the red-haired man said. "But they're close."

"How do you know?"

"I can feel it. Right here." The red-haired man pressed a fist against the top of his belly. "When I feel something in my gut, the feeling is always true. I know they're close."

The black-haired man's fingers slowly released their grip on the sword's handle. He put his hands on his hips and said, "Let's keep moving. We're wasting our time here."

The red-haired man carefully looked all around, searching for any signs he might have initially overlooked. "I'm going to find them. Today." The red-haired man sounded both determined and frustrated. He spit and then turned and pushed his way into the brush not far from where Kozal was hiding. The black-haired man followed him.

Cal listened to the sounds of the men moving away. About a minute after the sounds of the men had disappeared, Mont whispered, "Do you think they're gone?"

"I think they're gone," Cal said. "But let's wait here for a while in case they come back."

Mont nodded. He agreed.

There was a noise. Cal held his breath and listened. It sounded like someone had stepped on some of the dried leaves that were scattered on the ground. Had the men secretly circled back to this area? Another sound. Brush rustling. Had the men found them?

"Stay where you are," they heard Kozal say. "Don't move."

Cal immediately felt relieved. The sounds that they had just heard had come from Kozal.

Carefully, Kozal pushed his way into the brush where Cal and Mont were hiding. He lay down as close to Cal as was possible. "Those men are hunters," Kozal said. His breath had a terrible odor that reminded Cal of a rotting carcass. "They're hunting you," Kozal said. He brought his face closer to Cal, so that now their noses were almost touching. "They're hunting you, and if they catch you they'll do terrible things to you. Things you don't even want to think about." The odor of Kozal's breath was making Cal feel sick. "Don't let them catch you."

"I won't let them catch me," Cal said.

"Good." Kozal smiled. His cheek suddenly twitched, and he reached up and scratched it. "I'm going to track those men. We need to know where they're going. You two wait here until I get back." Kozal didn't wait for a response. He quickly got up and scurried off in the direction the bounty hunters had gone.

Cal waved a hand in front of his face, trying to fan away the lingering odor from Kozal's breath.

Mont sat up. "I don't trust that guy."

"I know," Cal said. "I don't completely trust him either."

"What if he tells the bounty hunters where we are so that he can get a reward?"

"I don't think he will," Cal said. "He wants to get a royal pardon. I think that will keep him honest."

Mont frowned. "I wish there was a way to get rid of him."

"He won't be with us much longer," Cal said. "We're close to the Western territories. Once we find General Grintar, Kozal won't have to be with us anymore. We'll only have to be with him for another day or two."

"I wish we were in the Western territories right now," Mont said.

"So do I."

They waited for what Cal guessed was about half an hour. He started to get worried because he didn't think Kozal should have been gone for so long. Had the bounty hunters captured Kozal? If they had, would Kozal be able to convince them that he didn't know anything about the boy they were looking for? Kozal was clever and might be able to convince the hunters of anything, but Kozal would almost certainly give in and reveal the truth if he believed they were about to hurt or kill him. Cal decided that it would be crazy to continue hiding where they were. If the bounty hunters had captured Kozal, and if Kozal told the hunters everything, Cal and Mont would be dead if they stayed where they were. They needed to hide somewhere else, quickly. Kozal could be leading the hunters to them right now.

Cal looked at Mont and said, "Let's get out of here."

"Why?" Mont nervously looked all around. He thought Cal had heard or seen something that he hadn't.

"If those hunters caught Kozal, he might bring them back here to us," Cal said.

Mont stood up quickly. "You're right. That little bastard could tell them exactly where we are. We need to get away from here."

"But we can't go too far."

"Why not?"

"Because of Ellsben," Cal said. "He's expecting to find us here. We need to hide someplace where we can see this area in case he comes back. If we leave here and he comes back and doesn't find us, he might run off looking for us in another direction. If we don't know where he is and he doesn't know where we are, we might not be able to find each other."

Cal and Mont pushed their way out of the brush. Cal felt nervous the moment he came out; he felt naked, exposed, vulnerable. He scanned his surroundings for someplace where they could hide. About twenty feet to his left the ground sloped up, and at the top of the slope was a small patch of brush. From up there they would have a good view of this area, but the brush was thin and wouldn't hide them very well. Cal glanced around some more and didn't see anyplace better. Even though the brush wouldn't give them much cover, they would be able to see much farther from the top of the slope and could escape to another place if they spotted the hunters returning. Cal tapped Mont's arm and pointed to the slope, and then he headed toward it and Mont followed him.

Not more than a minute after they reached the top of the slope and settled into the brush, they heard a voice. The voice came from far away, and Cal couldn't figure out what the voice had said. He listened, but didn't hear the voice again. "Get ready to run," Cal said to Mont. "If those hunters get too close, one of them will spot us up here."

"Let's go now," Mont said.

"No," Cal said. "We need to wait. They might not be coming this way, and if we start running, they'll hear us and come after us. Let's see if we can figure out what they're doing before we react."

Very faintly they heard the sounds of someone walking—feet crunching the dried leaves and twigs that covered the ground. Cal was lying flat. He decided it would be smart to get into a crouch so that his legs would be ready to propel him forward at any second. He was sure that soon he was going to have to run as fast as he could. His heart was thumping rapidly in anticipation.

"Where are they?" a voice said. When Cal and Mont heard the voice, they looked at each other and smiled.

"Quiet, naggie," Kozal said.

Soon Ellsben's head and torso came into view. He appeared annoyed. Several seconds later Kozal came into view; he was walking about ten feet in front of Ellsben, and he kept glancing over his shoulder as if he was worried that Ellsben might suddenly attack him.

Cal stood up and waved at Ellsben. When Ellsben saw Cal, a giant, relieved grin appeared on his face. He waved back at Cal, and Cal ran to him. Ellsben reached down and gave Cal's shoulder a friendly squeeze. "I'm glad you're all right," Ellsben said. "I was worried."

"I was worried too," Mont said. "Those men were standing right next to where we were hiding. I was sure they were going to find us."

"The hunters are heading east," Kozal said. "But they could change direction at any minute. They could be circling back this way now. We need to move away from here."

"I saw a couple of Congressers when I was looking for a place to hide," Ellsben said. "They had their backs to me and didn't see me."

"It's very dangerous now," Kozal said. "There are Congressers all around, and those hunters are close. We can't travel on the paths I was planning on using." Kozal let out an angry, grunting noise. Then he said, "This way will be difficult and will take much longer, but it should be safer. Come. Follow me."

Kozal led them through thick brush that, at times, was almost impossible to move through. Branches kept snagging their clothes and hooking their legs, causing them to periodically stumble. After what Cal guessed was about a mile and a half, the brush thinned, but the ground became rocky, and they had to walk slowly because it was difficult to walk over the rocks without slipping. The rocky ground was especially difficult for Ellsben to walk over; his hooves weren't flexible like feet.

By the time the sun started to go down, Cal felt as if he'd hiked twenty miles from the area where they'd hidden, but he knew that at best they had only traveled three miles. They found an area surrounded by tall pine trees that would keep them hidden, and they decided that this spot under the trees would be a good place to spend the night. "We're very close to the border of the Western territories," Kozal said. "Depending on the route we have to take, we should make it to the territories in less than two hours."

"I want to leave as soon as the sun starts to come up," Cal said. "It's important that we get to the territories as quickly as possible."

Kozal nodded.

Cal was hungry, but there were only three pieces of bread and one slice of cheese left. Mont divided the bread and cheese into four equal portions. Eating the small piece of cheese and bread awakened Cal's stomach, and he felt even hungrier than before he ate. His stomach gurgled, and he did his best to ignore the hunger pangs. Kozal kept eyeing them as if he suspected that there was more food that they were keeping hidden for themselves. Kozal muttered something and then sat down with his back resting against the trunk of one of the pine trees. He scratched the side of his face, yawned, closed his eye, and let his head droop.

Ellsben volunteered to stay awake to keep watch, and Mont said he'd take the second watch. Mont told Ellsben to wake him as soon as he got tired. Cal said he would take over after Mont. "Don't force yourself to stay up all night," Cal told Mont. "I don't want you exhausted tomorrow. Wake me up when you start to feel sleepy." Mont promised Cal he would.

Cal lay down. The ground smelled like pine needles. He tried to ignore his hunger and the faint throbbing that he felt in his injured arm. He was uncomfortable and didn't think he was going to be able to fall asleep, but eventually, without even realizing that it was happening, he sank into a deep sleep.

FIFTEEN

CAPTURED

"Cal, wake up."

Slowly, Cal opened his eyes. It was dark, but there was enough light from the stars for Cal to be able to see the silhouettes of his surroundings. Mont was leaning over him. "Wake up," Mont whispered. Cal could tell by the tone of Mont's voice that he was worried about something. "Wake up." Mont tapped Cal's shoulder.

"I'm up," Cal said. He sat up, rubbed his eyes, yawned, and stretched his arms. The muscles in his neck and back were stiff from sleeping on the hard, lumpy ground. There was a faint but steady throbbing in his forearm where the snake had bitten him. Gently, he rubbed the injured area of his arm with his thumb, and this made the throbbing almost disappear. "What's the matter?" Cal asked.

"Kozal's gone," Mont said.

"How long has he been gone?"

"At least three hours," Mont said. "Probably longer. He left while Ellsben was still on watch."

"Did he tell Ellsben where he was going?"

"He told Ellsben he had to pee."

"Was Ellsben worried about Kozal not coming back?"

"No." Mont shook his head. "But Kozal had only been gone for about fifteen minutes when I took over the watch. Ellsben's been asleep for most of the time Kozal's been gone."

"We need to wake Ellsben up," Cal said.

They woke Ellsben and explained the situation to him. Ellsben frowned, thought for a moment, and then said, "He isn't just out wandering around. Something's wrong."

"That's what I think," Cal said.

"Do you think those hunters or some Congressers caught him?" Mont asked.

"Probably," Ellsben said.

"I think we should leave here now," Cal said. "I don't want to wait until the sun comes up."

Ellsben and Mont agreed with Cal. They grabbed their packs, and then Ellsben looked up and studied the stars to figure out which way was west. The piece of cloth that Kozal had used to bandage Cal's forearm was loose. Cal untied the piece of cloth and removed it from his arm. In the dim light he couldn't see much, but it appeared that his wound had healed in one day as much as what would normally take a week or more. Cal touched the wound with his left index finger. The scab had mostly flaked away; there were only small, scattered pieces of the scab still on his arm. Cal could feel a thick line where scar tissue was forming.

"How is your arm?" Ellsben asked.

"Much better," Cal said. "That paste Kozal rubbed on it is amazing. It's healing faster than I can believe."

"You still need to keep it covered," Ellsben said. "You don't want to get dirt in it." Ellsben reached into his pack and removed a piece of cloth. He wrapped the cloth around Cal's arm and then tied it together so that it would stay in place.

"Which way do we need to go?" Mont asked.

"Follow me," Ellsben said. "And stay alert. If we're not careful, we could walk right into a camp of Congressers."

Cal and Mont walked side by side. It was silent, and the silence made Cal feel uneasy. He wished he could hear crickets chirping or the hooting of an owl or the yapping of a coyote. Any normal sounds from nature would have made him feel that everything was all right; the silence made him feel as if something was wrong.

Ellsben abruptly stopped, and Mont almost walked into him. "What is it?" Mont whispered. Ellsben put a finger over his lips, warning Cal and Mont not to say another word. Then Ellsben pointed at his right ear, indicating that he thought he'd heard something.

Cal listened, but he heard nothing. He wondered what it was that Ellsben had heard, if Ellsben had actually heard anything. Cal suddenly had the feeling that somebody was staring at him, and he turned around. Nothing. As far as he could see there was nothing around them except for several trees clumped together about twenty feet to their right. If there was somebody nearby, the darkness was hiding them.

"I think someone is following us," Ellsben said.

"What did you hear?" Mont asked.

"I'm not sure," Ellsben said. "I heard some kind of noise—it could have been anything. But I've got a gut feeling that we're being followed."

"I've got the same feeling," Cal said.

"Do you think it's the hunters?" Mont asked.

Ellsben shook his head. "The hunters wouldn't follow us. If they found us, they'd attack us."

"We need to keep moving," Cal said. "We need to get to the Western territories and General Grintar as fast as we can."

"Make sure both of you stay close to me," Ellsben said. "There's a good chance we might have to run, and if that becomes necessary, I want both of you to get on my back."

The horizon turned pink. Cal kept looking back at the eastern horizon as he walked, waiting for the moment when the edge of the sun would suddenly appear. Now, as it was getting lighter, Cal could see farther. He stopped several times and quickly looked all around, hoping to catch sight of whoever was following them, but he never saw anyone.

When the sun finally showed itself, causing the sky to change from black to light blue, several columns of rising smoke became apparent. The smoke was from campfires, probably from a camp of Congressers. Although Cal couldn't be sure, because the drifting smoke made it difficult to tell exactly where it was originating from, he guessed that the camps were probably about a mile away.

They walked across a large field, and Cal didn't like doing this. He hated being out in the open. Ellsben said he didn't like being out in the open either, but there wasn't any choice. He said the undergrowth was too thick for them to head in a northwest direction, and he didn't want to go southwest because that would bring them too close to those campfires.

"We should be in the Western territories pretty soon," Mont said.

"I don't know where the border is exactly," Ellsben said. "But I know we're close."

"I wish we were there now," Mont said.

"It won't make any difference," Ellsben said.

"What do you mean?" Mont asked.

"We won't be safe just because we're in the Western territories," Ellsben said.

"The Western territories are neutral," Mont said. "The Congressers can't follow us there."

"Legally the Congressers can't follow us there, but that won't stop them," Ellsben said. "And those hunters sure aren't going to turn back just because we've crossed a border."

Mont nodded. "I know," he said. "But I'll still feel better once we're in the territories."

"How far away do you think General Grintar is?" Cal asked.

"Zinn told me that once we cross into the Western territories, it should take us about half a day to reach General Grintar."

Cal was glad that they were now in a forest. The trees would make it difficult for anyone to see them from a distance, and the scattered patches of brush would give them places to hide. He didn't want to have to cross any more fields in the daylight.

A fly landed on Cal's cheek, but it managed to quickly get away before Cal could swat it. The temperature was rising. It was getting hot, and it was only midmorning. By this afternoon it was probably going to be unbearably hot. Cal could feel his shirt sticking to the damp skin under his arms.

A shrill, metallic whistle suddenly screamed. Another whistle, coming from another direction, screamed back. Then another whistle screamed from another direction and appeared to be answered by the original whistle.

Cal, Mont, and Ellsben looked all around. There was no direction that appeared safe—the whistles had come from every direction. They were surrounded.

"Let's go straight," Cal said. "We've got to move. We can't wait for them to get here. We might be able to get past them."

"On my back," Ellsben said. "Quick."

Cal put his hands on Ellsben's back and was getting ready to pull himself up when a deep voice shouted, "Halt!"

Cal turned toward the voice. A uniformed Congresser officer, on horseback, was approaching them. The officer had long, curly blond hair and a thick mustache. He was holding his sword in his right hand and was pointing it at Cal. "Don't move," the officer ordered.

Five more Congressers appeared. These Congressers were on foot and were not officers. Their uniforms were dirty and threadbare, and their lean faces gave the impression that they hadn't eaten a decent meal or had a proper night's rest in a long time. Three of the Congressers had crossbows, and they had their crossbows aimed at Cal, Mont, and Ellsben. The other two Congressers were holding swords.

"I'll fight them," Ellsben whispered to Cal. "If I fight them, I might be able to buy enough time for you and Mont to get away."

"No," Cal said. "Let them take us. We'll find a way to escape later."

"Gentlemen," the officer said to Cal and Mont. "Come over here. I want to speak with you. The naggie needs to stay right where he is."

Cal and Mont walked over to the officer. He studied them for a moment, and then he put his sword in the scabbard that was attached to his belt. "I'm Major Fost."

"Hello," Cal said.

"What's wrong, Major?" Mont asked, using a Southern accent. "If you're looking for a naggie that's been stirring up trouble or something, I want you to know that that naggie is our naggie, and he's been good. He couldn't have done anything wrong, at least not recently, because he's been with us."

A smile slowly appeared on the major's face. "That's pretty good. Under other circumstances I might have believed you."

"It's the truth, sir," Mont said. "Our naggie's been good."

"You can stop pretending," the major said. "I know who you gentlemen are."

"No sir," Mont said. "I'm sure you don't know us. We haven't been into any trouble."

The smile left the major's face. "Gentlemen, I wish I didn't have to do this," the major said. "But I have to place you under arrest. You are now prisoners of the Congressional government."

Cal nodded.

"Now I'm going to have your naggie's hands bound," the major said. "Tell him not to resist. Otherwise..."

Cal made eye contact with Ellsben, and Ellsben crossed his wrists and held his arms out. One of the Congressers put down his crossbow and went up to Ellsben and quickly tied his wrists together. It was obvious that the Congresser was afraid of Ellsben; as soon as he tied Ellsben's wrists, he quickly moved away and grabbed his crossbow.

"Take their packs and search them," the major ordered. Then he looked at Cal and Mont and said, "I'm sorry, but I have to do this."

"I understand," Cal said.

Mont's and Ellsben's packs were opened up, and their contents were dumped on the ground and spread out. There wasn't much left in the packs, just some clothes, a knife, and some paper that their bread had been wrapped in. The major dismounted and walked over to the clothes and pushed them around with the tip of his boot, and then he shrugged and turned away.

"Why are there only two packs?" the major asked.

"I fell in a river and lost my pack in the water," Cal said.

The major nodded, accepting this explanation. He then reached down and grabbed Ellsben's pack and inspected it, looking to see if it had any hidden pockets. When he was done with Ellsben's pack he dropped it, and then he inspected Mont's pack. After he was finished with Mont's pack, he had his men put all the stuff back in the packs. "Gentlemen," he said to Cal and Mont. "Please follow me." The major got on his horse. He led them back in the direction they had come from. When they were close to the spot where they'd spent the night, the major turned south.

Ellsben followed behind. He was told by one of the Congressers not to follow too close, so he kept about twenty feet back from Cal and Mont. The three Congressers with crossbows kept them constantly aimed at Ellsben. One crossbow carrier stayed to the right of Ellsben, the second stayed to his left, and the third stayed behind him. The crossbow carriers all kept far enough away from Ellsben so that he couldn't kick them; it was apparent from the way they watched Ellsben that they were afraid of him, even though they pretended not to be.

The major led them down a wide path that eventually brought them to a clearing where the major and his men had made a camp. The camp consisted of half a dozen tattered tents, two fire pits, a small wagon, and three horses. Two of the major's men had stayed at the camp. When they saw the major they saluted, and he crisply saluted back.

All of a sudden there came a shriek, which startled Cal. He turned toward the direction the shriek had come from. At the edge of a clearing, tightly tied to a tree, was Kozal. "I told you, Major!" Kozal shouted. His mouth was twisted in a wild, ecstatic smile. "I told you!"

The major frowned and stared at Kozal.

"You see." Kozal's twisted smile broadened, and he opened his eye as wide as possible. "I told you!"

Quickly, gracefully, the major dismounted.

"You can untie me now," Kozal said. "Yes."

The major walked over to Kozal and stood in front of him. He put his hands on his hips and looked at Kozal with an expression that could only be interpreted as disgust.

"That's the prince," Kozal said. "You didn't believe me when I came to you, but now you see I wasn't lying."

Mont leaned close to Cal and whispered, "Did you hear that? He wasn't captured. That piece of garbage went to them and told them about us."

"I really didn't think he'd do this," Cal whispered back. "I thought a royal pardon would be worth more to him than a reward from the Congressers."

"That's the prince," Kozal said. "If you torture the prince, his friend, and their naggie, they'll admit the truth. You'll see."

"I don't need to torture them," the major said. "I know that's the prince."

Kozal let out a happy sigh. "Now Macton will be the king, and the war will be over."

The major stared at Kozal. There wasn't even a hint of a smile on the major's face.

"I ended the war," Kozal said. He wasn't looking at anyone when he said this; he appeared to be talking to himself. "Mother will be so proud. I stopped the naggie lovers."

"You've done nothing to be proud of," the major said.

"The prince," Kozal said. "I gave you the prince."

"You betrayed them," the major said. "Like you betrayed our men when you ran away from the battle. You're a deceitful coward."

Kozal flinched his head and grimaced as if he'd been unexpectedly slapped. "The prince. I gave you the prince. Now set me free."

"You will not be granted clemency," the major said.

"But I gave you the prince."

"You're a deserter," the major said. "The punishment for desertion is death. You will be executed today."

Kozal stared at the major as if he expected him to suddenly start laughing and say that he was only joking. When Kozal realized that the major was serious, his face turned a dark red and he strained against the ropes that were binding him to the tree. Kozal swore, foaming at the mouth and vehemently calling the major every disgusting word he could think of. He flapped his head from side to side as he swore.

The major turned toward one of his men. "Gag the prisoner," he ordered.

A deep, growling sound gurgled up from Kozal's throat. A Congresser, holding a wad of cloth that was to be used as a gag, walked up to Kozal. When the Congresser brought the cloth close to Kozal's mouth, Kozal snapped at him like a rabid animal. The Congresser jumped back. "Mother!" Kozal screamed.

The Congresser abruptly lurched forward and stuffed the cloth in Kozal's mouth. Kozal squirmed and tried to force the cloth out of his mouth. The Congresser took a thick rope and strapped it around the lower half of Kozal's head, tying the gag in place. Kozal moaned and squirmed and vigorously shook his head, and then he suddenly stopped. He relaxed and rested the back of his head against the tree and closed his eye. Several strands of his stringy hair hung over his face.

"You never should have trusted that lunatic," the major said to Cal.

"I didn't trust him," Cal said. "I misjudged him. He helped us, and I believed he'd continue helping us because I'd agreed to grant him a pardon after the war. Also, I promised him a financial reward."

The major nodded. "That should have kept him on your side, but he decided he'd get a better deal by turning you over to us. He thought that would make him a hero. He was wrong."

Kozal opened his eye and looked at the major for a moment, and then he closed his eye. Otherwise, he remained motionless.

"I want this centaur hobbled," the major said to his men. "I also want him tethered to that tree over there."

Ellsben frowned deeply, but he didn't resist. He allowed the Congressers to hobble and tether him.

"Please follow me," the major said to Cal and Mont. He led them to his tent.

Inside the tent there was a small, round table that was surrounded by four stools. In a corner of the tent there was a cot that was covered with a blanket, and beside the cot there was an oil lamp. At the foot of the cot there was a wooden trunk.

The major motioned for them to sit down. After Cal and Mont were seated, the major sat on a stool and leaned forward, resting his forearms on the table. He appeared sad. "Gentlemen," he said. "This war is no good. We went to war because a lot of powerful people who should have known better decided to feed their egos and dig their heels in and refuse to give an iota even when it was obvious that without compromise there would be a disaster. That's what this war is, a disaster. It's a war for the centaurs. For freeing the centaurs, for keeping the centaurs enslaved." The major slowly shook his head. "Do you know how many men have died in this war? More than your mind will let you imagine. I've seen thousands of bodies lying on the battlefield, and I've seen hundreds of men with missing limbs or with their guts hanging out, screaming, crying, praying. Just the thought of it makes me sick."

Suddenly the major stood up and started pacing. "The war for the centaurs wasn't worth fighting. Not one man should have had to die."

"I wish the war had never happened," Cal said.

The major looked at Cal and attempted to give him a smile, but he was unable to. He sat down and crossed his arms. "This war has made men do things they didn't want to do. I've had to do things I never dreamed I'd have to do. Things that will haunt me the rest of my life." The major gazed silently down at the table for a minute, and then he looked up at Cal and said, "General Lan is about twenty miles from here. I'm going to go to him and report to him that I have you. I'm certain he'll send a message to President Dengon, asking the president what he wants us to do with you."

"What do you think the president will want you to do?" Cal asked, even though he was pretty sure he already knew the answer.

The major didn't respond, and his silence confirmed what Cal suspected. President Dengon would give an order to have Cal executed.

Slowly, the major stood up. He smoothed the front of his uniform with his hand, cleared his throat, looked at Cal, and said, "I can only leave three of my men here to guard you. I have to travel with the rest of my men because there are several groups of runaway naggies living near the area where General Lan and his men are currently located. The runaways hate anyone in a Congressional military uniform; they would kill us in a second if they get a chance. So I need to travel with at least four men for protection."

Cal nodded.

"Because I can only leave three of my men here to guard you, I'm going to have to have you gentlemen bound. I apologize. I honestly wish I didn't have to do it, but I can't risk leaving you free with only three guards to watch you. It's my responsibility to make sure you don't escape."

"I understand," Cal said.

"Again, I apologize." The major stepped outside of his tent and made several hand gestures to his men. After a minute he came back in the tent and was soon followed by one of his men. The man was holding a small tray, and on the tray were two sandwiches and two metal cups. The major motioned for the man to put the tray on the table. The man set the tray on the table and then, without saying a word, quickly left the tent.

"I noticed you gentlemen didn't have any food with you," the major said. "I thought you might be hungry."

"Yes," Cal said. "We are hungry. Thank you."

"You're welcome," the major said. "Your centaur is being fed now too."

Cal picked up his sandwich and took a huge bite of it. In between the slices of bread was a dry chunk of cheese and some stringy meat that tasted like wild turkey. The bread was stale, and normally Cal would have thought the sandwich tasted awful, but right now he was so hungry the sandwich tasted just about as good as the best meal he'd ever eaten. Mont was obviously hungry too; he ate his sandwich so fast he barely had time to chew. The metal cups were filled with fresh water.

While they were eating, the major stepped outside of the tent. The moment the major was out, Cal leaned close to Mont and whispered, "We have to escape after the major leaves. I'm going to pretend to get very sick, and hopefully they'll untie me."

"Then what?" Mont asked.

"I'll figure a way to get Ellsben free first because we're going to have to fight, and he's got the most strength."

"I can probably slip out of the ropes," Mont said.

"How?"

"I've read that if you tense your muscles when you're getting tied up the ropes will become a little bit loose when you relax, and then you can slowly work yourself free."

"Be careful," Cal said. "Don't try to get free until you're sure the major and his men are far enough away so that they can't be called back with a whistle. There's no way we'll be able to escape if the major and his men are here."

Suddenly the major came back into the tent. He looked at Cal and Mont as if he had heard a word or two from their whispered conversation, and he was now trying to figure out from their expressions what they had been saying. After looking at them for a moment, he frowned and nodded his head once; he guessed that they had been making escape plans, but this didn't upset him because that's exactly what anyone rational in their position would do. "Gentlemen," the major said. "Please follow me."

The major brought them to a pair of tall beech trees that one of his men had picked out. They were at the opposite end of the clearing from where Kozal was tied. Ellsben was tethered to a tree about thirty feet from them, and his back was facing them. The way Ellsben was tethered made it impossible for him to face Cal or to even be able to look back at Cal; there was no way Cal would be able to subtly communicate with Ellsben. The major grabbed one of the trees and pushed against it to make sure the trunk was sturdy and free of rot. Satisfied with the first tree, he tested the other tree. "Good," he said. Then he faced Cal and Mont and said, "Gentlemen, you're not going to be comfortable. I'm sorry that I have to do this, but I don't have any options."

Mont was tied first. His arms were brought behind his back and around the trunk of the tree. His wrists were bound together, and his ankles were tied together, and then they were tied to the tree's trunk. Cal was tied up the same way. As Cal's wrists were being bound, he made his hands into tight fists, tensing up the muscles in his forearms. After the man who had bound Cal stepped away, Cal relaxed and found that what Mont had read was true. The ropes around his wrists were a bit loose.

"Gentlemen," the major said. "I will return as soon as possible. While I'm away, Sergeant Bast will be in charge." The major went into his tent and came out with some papers. He rolled these papers up and put them in a saddlebag. The men he would be traveling with surrounded him, and he quietly gave them orders, which Cal couldn't hear. Then the major went to Sergeant Bast and whispered something to him. Sergeant Bast nodded once, indicating that he agreed with whatever it was the major had whispered. Cal wished he knew what the major had said.

Soon after the major departed, Sergeant Bast started staring at Cal. Bast's face was expressionless, cold, and this unnerved Cal. He looked away, gazing at the ground, but he could sense that Bast's stare was continuing.

Cal closed his eyes and mentally prepared himself to pretend to be sick. He hoped he would be able to convince Bast to untie him. Once he was untied, he wasn't sure exactly what he would do because he knew he couldn't win a fight with a man who'd been fighting in battles for years. If he was going to fight, he was going to have to take Bast completely by surprise—that was the only way he'd be able to win. The only other option he had was to somehow get Ellsben free before Bast or his men were aware of what he was doing, but this option seemed very unlikely to succeed. There was almost no way he would be able to get to Ellsben without being noticed.

"Open your eyes, boy," a raspy voice said. The voice was loud, and it startled Cal. "Open your eyes." The voice was almost shouting now.

Cal opened his eyes.

Bast had his face close to Cal's. His eyes were cold and gray, and his cheeks were marred by many deep pockmarks. Long, straight, greasy blond hair framed his face. He smiled, and this smiled scared Cal.

"What's the matter, boy?"

"I-I don't feel good," Cal said.

"That's a shame." Bast pretended to look concerned.

"My stomach is getting cramps," Cal said. He puffed his cheeks out and made his lower lip tremble as if he was about to vomit. "I need to lie down."

Cal's head suddenly snapped toward his left shoulder, and a painful tingling exploded across the right side of his face, causing his eyes to water. Bast had slapped him. Cal hadn't expected to be slapped, and because he was taken completely off guard, he now felt disoriented. He tried to blink away the tears.

"Don't whine to me that you don't feel good," Bast said. "Because I don't care."

Cal let his head hang; he was certain that if he raised his head and made eye contact with Bast, Bast would slap him again. Maybe even punch him.

"My brother was killed, murdered, because of your father," Bast said. His face was so close to Cal that he could smell the faint odor of onions on his breath. "Your father sent troops down here to fight us. We didn't invade the Northern provinces. All we wanted was our independence. But you Northern naggie lovers had to force your beliefs and your way of life on us. You called us barbarians because we use naggies to work our fields, and yet you let thousands of men and women in your cities work for wages that keep them in filthy poverty. You are more concerned with how we treat our naggies, our animals, than how you treat the poverty-stricken men and women in your cities."

"Naggies are not animals," Cal said, not looking up. "They have the same brains as people, only their bodies are different. Their intelligence, their feelings are the same."

"They are animals," Bast said. "And your father is a criminal. He's a murderer. He's responsible for every person who's died or was maimed in this war. Your father caused more suffering, more hurt, more pain than can be imagined. I'm sorry that when he was killed he didn't suffer longer, although I'm sure the demons in the afterlife are making him suffer. I hope the demons make him feel twice the pain that he's caused."

Cal looked up at Bast. "My father acted honorably. He did what he had to do to keep the kingdom together."

Bast spit, and Cal felt the warm, sticky saliva oozing down his cheek. "My brother died, my brother had his guts ripped out of his body, because your father decided to keep the kingdom together."

It was almost impossible, but Cal managed to stay silent. He desperately wanted to defend his father, but he knew that if he opened his mouth he would make Bast even angrier, and that would make his situation worse. Although it was going to take all of his willpower, Cal knew the smartest thing he could do right now was to not say another word. He was going to have to force himself to ignore Bast and concentrate on trying to slip his hands free from the ropes that were twisted around his wrists.

Bast reached down and pulled a dagger out of a leather sheath that was attached to his belt. He pushed the tip of the blade against the right side of Cal's throat; he pushed hard enough to cause pain, but not hard enough to penetrate the soft flesh. "President Dengon is probably going to order your execution, but I don't think I want to wait for that order. I'd like to kill you right now."

Cal folded the fingers of his right hand tightly together to make his hand as narrow as possible. He pulled his arm upward, against the rope, and he felt the rope slip over his wrist, but the rope got stuck at the fat part of his hand, at the area right below the base of his thumb.

"I want to slit your throat," Bast said. "My brother was murdered, my family's home was burned to the ground, and many of my friends, people I've known all my life, have been murdered or crippled for the rest of their lives because of your father's war. I'm not going to wait for President Dengon's orders. What if he decides to spare your life? I'm not going to wait for his decision. I condemn you, and I'm going to execute you."

One of the two soldiers who had been left at the camp under Bast's command suddenly came running up to Bast. He had been watching and listening to what Bast had been saying to Cal. The soldier had short blond hair and large, crooked front teeth. He grabbed Bast's arm and pulled it back so that Bast was no longer holding the dagger up to Cal's throat. "You can't touch him," the soldier said. "If you kill the prisoner, there will be hell to pay. They'll hang you." The soldier spit on the ground. "They'll hang *me* if I let you harm the prisoner."

Cal was afraid his hand was starting to swell from the pressure of the rope. If his hand did swell up, there would be no way he'd be able to slip it free from the rope's coil.

Bast slid his dagger back into its sheath. He put a hand on the soldier's shoulder and said, "If the prisoner tries to escape and I kill him while trying to stop him, they wouldn't hang me for that."

The soldier spit on the ground again, and then he shook his head. "I don't want any part of this. They'll question me, and I don't want to have to sit there and look at them and tell them a pack of lies. No sir."

"You won't be lying to them if you don't see anything," Bast said. "If you don't see anything, you can honestly tell them that you don't know what happened."

"How can I not see anything?" The soldier frowned. "I'm sure as hell not going to tell them I fell asleep while I was on duty."

"You and Frand won't be here when it happens," Bast said.

Cal twisted his hand, and the rope was dragged down to his knuckles. He grabbed the rope with his fingers, keeping it in place so that Bast and the soldier wouldn't notice that his hand had slipped free from the rope.

"Frand and I can't leave here, Sergeant," the soldier said. "Major Fost ordered us to stay here."

Cal wondered if Mont had managed to get his hands free. He wanted to look at Mont, but he didn't because he suspected Bast would be able to figure out what they were thinking by their expressions. He had to keep his eyes down and his expression neutral.

"I'm in command here," Bast said. "I'm ordering you and Frand to leave. Check out that western path. I thought I heard horses. Some of General Grintar's soldiers might be on patrol, looking for this prisoner. Find out if they're headed this way."

Cal used the thumb of his right hand to pull at the rope that was coiled around his left wrist. He bunched the fingers of his left hand closely together and managed to easily slip his left hand through the coiled rope.

"You heard horses?" The soldier gave an alarmed expression, but this expression was quickly extinguished. "Horses," the soldier muttered. He nodded his head, understanding that this was just an excuse to get him and Frand to leave.

"That's right. I heard horses," Bast said. "Now I want you and Frand to find out if some of Grintar's men are in the area. That's an order."

"Yes sir," the soldier said. He looked as if it wouldn't take much to convince him to disobey this order.

Cal knew that as soon as the two soldiers left he was going to have to quickly act, and he couldn't make a mistake because he would only have the element of surprise on his side for three or four seconds at best, and he could only defeat Bast by taking him completely by surprise. To keep himself calm, Cal forced himself to breathe slowly, taking in deep breaths.

The two soldiers were standing near the front of Major Fost's tent. They were talking, and they looked about as happy as a pair of wet cats. Bast crossed his arms and narrowed his eyes. "Get moving!" Bast suddenly shouted. The soldiers nervously glanced at Bast, and then they picked up their crossbows and quickly disappeared into the forest.

Bast turned toward Cal and smiled.

Cal's heart began thumping wildly. He told himself to calm down. He had to stay calm; he had to be able to think clearly. He couldn't make any mistakes.

"This is quite an opportunity," Bast said as he walked toward Cal. "I believe in God, and I believe this opportunity is a gift from God."

Cal raised his head and made eye contact with Bast. By keeping Bast's attention focused on his face, Cal would gain maybe a second when he went after Bast with his hands, and a second might be exactly what would determine whether he succeeded or failed.

"I'm grateful for being given this opportunity," Bast said. He was standing close to Cal. "God is delivering his justice through me." Bast slowly wrapped his right hand around the handle of his sword.

The leather sheath that housed Bast's dagger was attached to Bast's belt near the area where his sword's scabbard was fastened. Cal couldn't glance at the dagger; he had to keep eye contact with Bast, had to keep Bast's attention focused on his face. Since he couldn't glance down at the dagger, he was going to have to use his memory to direct him to it.

"I will deliver God's justice," Bast whispered.

Cal let the ropes that he was holding with his fingers drop, and without breaking eye contact with Bast, he swiftly brought his arms forward from behind the tree's trunk. With his right hand he grabbed the dagger's handle and jerked it from its sheath. Then, with a violent upward thrust, he jammed the dagger deep into the center of Bast's belly, just below his sternum. Bast's eyes widened, and his jaw flopped open. Cal yanked the dagger out—it was now covered with dark blood—and used it to cut the rope that was binding his legs to the tree.

Mont let out a victorious yell, and Cal looked over at him and saw that Mont had managed to get his hands free. "I was able to slip out of that rope right away," Mont said. He leaned down and began to untie his legs.

Bast staggered like a drunk trying to stay on his feet. Cal rushed over to Ellsben and used the dagger to cut the rope that was binding his wrists together. As he cut through the rope, the dagger slipped and sliced the meaty part of

Ellsben's right hand, just below the thumb. A thin stream of blood trickled out of the cut. Ellsben wiped the blood away; luckily the cut wasn't very deep.

"Sorry," Cal said.

"It's nothing," Ellsben said. He took the dagger from Cal and cut the rope that had been used to tether him to a tree, and then he cut the leather straps that had been used to hobble him.

A shrill whistle suddenly sounded. Cal spun around and saw that Bast had a small metal whistle pressed between his lips, and he was frantically blowing it. He was calling for help.

Ellsben charged at Bast, and somehow Bast managed to find the strength to draw his sword. He clenched both of his hands around the sword's handle and stood ready to fight Ellsben.

With amazing speed, Ellsben whirled around and kicked Bast with his hind legs. Ellsben's hooves hit Bast's chest, and there was a sharp cracking sound as Bast's ribs broke. The whistle flew out of Bast's mouth as he was thrown backward, and the sword clumsily tumbled out of his hands. He let out an *oomph* sound when he hit the ground, and before he could raise his hands to protect himself, Ellsben had scooped up the sword and thrust the blade down into Bast's chest. Bast's body stiffened, and then he began trembling. After a minute, his trembling abruptly stopped and his body went limp. Ellsben pulled the sword from Bast's chest and cleaned the blood from its blade by wiping it across Bast's left shoulder.

There came the sounds of men running; their feet made crunching noises as they rapidly stepped on the dried leaves that blanketed the forest's ground. Cal looked and saw the two men Bast had sent away. The men's faces revealed panic the moment they saw that the prisoners were free. One of the men stopped and crouched down and aimed his crossbow at Ellsben and pulled the trigger. Fortunately, the bolt missed Ellsben, although it passed so close to his neck he could feel the wind the bolt created as it cut through the air.

Cal grabbed a rock and threw it at the man who'd shot at Ellsben. The rock hit the man's upper lip and the bottom of his nose. The man jerked his head back and almost dropped his crossbow. Blood flowed from his nostrils.

Mont threw a rock at the second man, hitting his chest. The second man stumbled backward a step, and Mont threw another rock, hitting the man's right shoulder. Before Mont could throw another rock, the second man turned and ran back into the forest and began furiously blowing a whistle.

The first man aimed his crossbow at Ellsben again, but before he could shoot, Ellsben charged at him and swung the sword, and the sword's blade caught the man under his chin. The man's head instantly snapped back, and the sword's blade almost completely took the man's head from his body.

The whistle in the woods was now being answered by other whistles, from all directions.

"Fost is coming back," Mont said.

"It's not just Fost," Ellsben said. "I hear a lot of whistles. There must be groups of Congressers all around us. We have to get moving. We have to try to find a spot to hide."

After Ellsben had used the dagger to cut himself free from the hobbles, he had dropped the dagger on the ground. Cal grabbed the dagger and said, "Before we go I'm going to set him free." Cal pointed at Kozal.

"Are you crazy?" Mont's eyes widened. "He turned us over to the Congressers."

"If I leave him here, they'll kill him," Cal said.

"Good," Mont said. "Let them kill him. He didn't care if they killed us."

"He saved my life," Cal said. "I'm going to save his life, and that will make us even."

"Yeah, he saved your life, but he also turned you over to the Congressers, and he knew they'd most likely kill you," Mont said. "You don't owe him anything."

"Leave him," Ellsben said. "Let's go."

The whistles were getting louder.

"I'm going to set him free." Cal ran over to Kozal and quickly cut the ropes that were binding him. As soon as his arms were free, Kozal reached up and tore off the gag.

"Now we're even," Cal said to Kozal. "You saved my life, and now I've saved your life."

"We're not even," Kozal said. "I saved your life, and then I gave you to the people who want you dead. Now I owe you."

"Forget it," Cal said. "Just get out of here and don't try to follow us."

The whistles were getting closer. Ellsben looked all around, trying to figure out which would be the best direction to go. It didn't seem to matter—the whistles were coming from everywhere.

"There are Congressers all over this area," Kozal said. "You're in the middle of a hornet's nest." Kozal shook his head. "They are staying in small camps so that they can keep an eye on a larger amount of territory. They've been watching for you, and watching for Grintar to return from the Western territories."

"We've got to leave now," Ellsben said. Although Ellsben was doing his best to sound calm, Cal could hear fear in his voice. He pointed west and said, "We'll go this way. Hurry."

"No." Kozal grabbed Cal's arm. "You'll get caught if you run that way. You can't run—there's too many of them. You have to hide."

"Come on," Mont said.

"There's a cave nearby," Kozal said. "I've hidden in it, and they don't know about it. The entrance is covered by a thick bush. That's where I'm going. Follow me."

"We're going to his cave," Cal told Mont and Ellsben.

Mont's forehead wrinkled; he couldn't believe what he'd just heard. "We can't trust him. You know that. We can find our own spot to hide."

"He won't go to the Congressers again," Cal said. "He knows they'll hang him if they get their hands on him."

Kozal abruptly darted into one of the tents. He was in the tent for less than a minute. When he came out of the tent, he had a cloth bag slung over his shoulder. "Food," Kozal said. "I've got food for us."

The whistles were so loud now the men who were blowing them had to be almost within sight.

"Follow me," Kozal said. He ran into the forest and led them down a steep slope. At the bottom of the slope there was a large oak tree that had fallen over and died, and behind the tree was a large bush that had many thick vines tangled up in its branches.

Cal saw a Congresser moving in between the trees. The Congresser wasn't moving toward them, and Cal was pretty sure he hadn't seen them; however, there certainly were more Congressers nearby, and if they didn't hide quickly they would be spotted.

Kozal got on his hands and knees and pushed his way into the bush, pulling the bag of food behind him. Cal followed Kozal. About two feet into the bush there was a hole. Kozal was already in it; only his head was sticking out of the hole. "Be careful," Kozal said. "Try not to slide. It goes down sharply at first."

"This hole isn't big enough for Ellsben to get through," Cal said.

"It won't be easy, but he'll be able to squeeze in," Kozal said. "Now get in. Quick." Kozal's head disappeared into the darkness.

Cal backed out of the bush. "There's a hole, but I don't think it's big enough for Ellsben to get through. We're going to have to find another hiding spot."

"No," Ellsben said. "We won't be able to find another spot. You and Mont get into that hole. I'll try to follow, but if I can't, don't worry about me."

"We're not going to leave you," Cal said.

"Go," Ellsben said. "I can probably outrun them, but even if I can't it doesn't matter. They're not looking for me."

Cal hesitated.

"Go," Ellsben said.

Cal went back into the bush and looked at the hole. He couldn't see Kozal, but he could hear him whispering his name and telling him to hurry. Cal stuck his head into the hole, and then decided he'd rather enter feetfirst, so he turned around and dropped his legs into the hole and felt for sturdy ground to place his feet. The ground at the mouth of the hole went down steeply. Cal carefully crawled backward. He could hear Kozal calling him. After about twenty feet the ground became flat.

The mouth of the hole was the only source of light, and its oval shape reminded Cal of an eye and made him feel as if he was being watched. He moved into the darkness, out of the light that was spilling in from the hole, because being in the darkness made the feeling of being watched less intense.

Mont's head abruptly appeared at the mouth of the hole. "Cal?"

"Be careful," Cal said. "The ground is steep."

Mont entered the hole headfirst and quickly crawled down until he was near Cal.

"Is Ellsben coming?" Cal asked.

"He said he would follow me," Mont said.

They looked up at the hole. Cal wondered if Ellsben had decided he couldn't fit down the hole, or if some Congresser had gotten too close, and Ellsben had thought it best to run away. Cal wondered when he'd see Ellsben again.

"Where's your naggie?" Kozal said from somewhere in the darkness.

"Shut up," Mont said.

"Did your naggie run off? They do that."

"I said, shut up." Mont sounded as if he was close to losing his temper.

Kozal muttered something. Cal guessed that Kozal had probably sworn, or had made some insulting remark about Mont.

"Hello." It was Ellsben. He was kneeling on his front legs, looking into the hole. "I don't think I can get through the hole."

Kozal made a disgusted grunting noise. "Tell your naggie that he can squeeze though the opening. Then tell him that there's much more room down here."

"Try," Cal called up to Ellsben. "Try to get through."

Ellsben leaned his torso as far forward as he could and stretched his arms out in front of him like a diver. He dug his fingers into the ground and pulled. He had to stretched his front legs out straight, and this was awkward and painful. Cal rushed up to Ellsben and grabbed his wrists and pulled. Ellsben's hindquarters were stuck in the opening of the hole. Ellsben pushed his eyes shut and grimaced and forced his hind legs backward, as straight as he could make them. Cal pulled with all his strength. Ellsben grunted and tried to drag himself forward by pressing on the ground with his front hooves.

Suddenly there was a loud crumbling sound of dirt breaking free. Ellsben's hindquarters had gotten through the mouth of the hole, and now he was sliding down the steep ground, trying unsuccessfully to stop himself. Cal attempted to get out of the way, but he couldn't. Ellsben's chest slammed against Cal's right shoulder, sending Cal tumbling down. Dirt sprayed in Cal's face, and some of the dirt got in his nose and mouth, causing him to cough and feel as if he was choking. When they reached the bottom of the slope, one of Ellsben's front hooves smacked the right side of Cal's face. Luckily the hoof bounced off his cheek and caused no more damage than a stinging slap. The left side of Ellsben's torso landed on Cal's chest, and Ellsben scrambled to get his weight off Cal. "Are you all right?" Ellsben asked.

Cal sat up and coughed. He could taste the dirt that had gotten in his mouth. He spit several times, trying to get rid of the dirt taste. "I'm all right," Cal said. He spit a couple more times. "Are you OK?"

"I think so." Ellsben stood up. "It's huge in here. I didn't think I'd be able to stand up straight, but I can. I can't even feel the top when I reach up."

"Tell your naggie to be careful." Kozal had positioned himself next to Cal. "There are places in here where the top is low."

"What are we going to do now?" Mont asked.

"This cave has many tunnels, and the tunnels go in just about every direction," Kozal said. "Most are dead ends, and it's easy to get lost. But I know the tunnels. I can get you to the Western territories."

"Let's go," Mont said.

"Not all the way," Kozal said. "They're looking for us. It's too dangerous to leave here now. We'll spend the night here. Early tomorrow morning there will be fewer patrols; then we can leave."

"I agree," Cal said. "We have to stay in here today. It will be much safer to leave tomorrow morning. But I want to be close to the opening that leads to the Western territories."

"I will take you there now," Kozal said. "We'll get close, and then we can rest and eat."

"You can't get us there in this darkness," Mont said. "We need to figure out a way to make a torch."

"Bah!" Kozal let out an exasperated sigh. "I don't need to be able to see. I know this cave better than I know the lines on my hands."

"Since we can't see, we're going to have to hold on to each other," Cal said. "I'll put my hands on Kozal's shoulders, Mont will put his hands on my shoulders, and Ellsben will put his hands on Mont."

Everyone agreed with Cal.

"Let's go," Kozal grumbled. "I want to get there."

Cal placed his hands on Kozal's shoulders. Kozal's muscles were thin, but the muscles felt firm, and Cal was certain Kozal had a lot more strength than he appeared to have. Mont put his hands on Cal's shoulders and said, "Ellsben's got a hold of me. We're ready."

They walked slowly. The ground was smooth except for an occasional rock that needed to be stepped over and an occasional shallow hole that needed to be circumnavigated or gently stepped into to prevent an ankle from being twisted. Kozal had the bag of food slung over his right shoulder, and every now and then Kozal would stop abruptly and Cal would walk into the bag of food, squishing it between his chest and Kozal's back. If there was a loaf of bread in the bag, the bread was going to be as flat as a cracker by the time they got to the spot where they were going to stay until morning.

After they had been walking about half an hour, Mont asked, "We're not lost, are we?"

"No." Kozal was offended by this question. "Didn't you hear what I told you, boy? I said I know this cave better than I know the lines on my hands."

"Fine," Mont said. "But if you do get lost, admit it. Don't lead us all over the place while you try to figure out where you are."

"Boy, if you're so smart, why don't you lead your friends out of here?" Kozal lunged forward, away from Cal. Cal reached out, trying to find Kozal, but his hands found nothing but air and the side of the cave.

"I knew we should have figured out a way to make a torch," Mont said. "There's got to be a way we can start a fire. We could burn my shirt. We could wrap pieces of my shirt around something and burn it, and that might give us enough light to be able to find our way out."

"No," Cal said. "Kozal is going to take us to the place near the opening that leads to the Western territories. That's what we agreed to."

"We can't trust him," Mont said. "We're better off without him. I know we can find our way out of here."

"No," Cal said. "We're not going to wander around guessing which way to go. We could be down here forever."

"I know we can find our way out," Mont said.

"Kozal is going to lead us," Cal said. "I don't want to walk around guessing which way to go."

"Fine," Mont said. He wasn't happy that he'd been overruled, and the anger he felt slipped into his tone of voice. "If that's what you want to do, that's what we'll do. But I think it's crazy to trust him."

"Kozal," Cal called out. "Where are you?"

"I'm not going to help you anymore." Kozal sounded like he was a good distance ahead of them. "I'm tired of being insulted."

"Kozal," Cal said. "I want you to lead us."

"And I want to be treated like a human being," Kozal said. "I want respect."

Mont started to say something, but Cal stopped him.

"I'm not going to help," Kozal said. "Mother didn't raise me to be a guide dog. Mother would be very angry if she saw how her boy was being treated."

"Kozal," Cal said. "You promised to lead us to the Western territories. Now you need to keep your promise."

"No!" Kozal shouted. "That promise is dead. The boy's insults killed that promise."

"I let you free," Cal said. "I could have left you tied to that tree."

There was no verbal response from Kozal. Cal waited for a minute, and when he still heard no response, he began to worry that Kozal had left them. "Kozal," Cal called out. "If I hadn't set you free, you'd still be tied to that tree. Or maybe, by now, you'd be hanging from one of the tree's branches."

Silence. Cal wondered if Kozal had left, or if Kozal was ignoring him. He was about to call out again when he heard Kozal whisper, "I'll keep my promise."

"Thank you," Cal said.

"But I will not tolerate any more insults." Kozal made a strange noise that reminded Cal of a dog growling.

"You won't be insulted," Cal said. "Now lead us to that spot like you promised."

Cal waited, and eventually he felt Kozal's hand on his arm. Without saying a word, Kozal pulled his hand away from Cal's arm, and Cal immediately reached out and found Kozal's shoulders. Kozal was tense as if he was ready to abruptly run away or fight. Cal knew he was going to have to pay close attention to Kozal because he was certain it wouldn't take much to make Kozal run off in anger, and it might not take much to make Kozal attack them. Ellsben knew enough to keep quiet; Cal hoped Mont would remember not to say anything to or about Kozal.

"We're ready," Cal said.

Mont put his hands on Cal's shoulders, and Ellsben leaned forward and put his hands on Mont's shoulders. This time Kozal moved much faster than he did before.

After they had been walking for a while, Cal began to hear an occasional high-pitched noise, but he couldn't tell which direction the noise was coming from. The noise echoed and seemed to be coming from every direction. Kozal started muttering unhappily to himself. The hard ground now felt soft, as if they were walking on a thin carpet. The high-pitched noise was becoming more frequent and seemed to overlap as if it was coming from different sources.

"What is that?" Cal asked.

"They make such a nasty mess," Kozal grumbled. "We're stepping in filth."

"What are they?" Cal asked. "Where are they?"

"They're above us," Kozal said. "Many of them. We're in their home, and they're not happy. They're not used to visitors."

Cal was about to ask Kozal if the creatures he was talking about were dangerous when there was an explosion that sounded as if the top of the cave was coming down. Cal let go of Kozal's shoulders and instinctively threw his arms over his head and crouched low to protect himself from whatever was falling from above. The high-pitched noises were incredibly loud now, but the high-pitched noises were being drowned out by what sounded like hundreds of leather coats flapping in the wind. Cal felt something briefly touch the side of his face, and then something slapped the top of his head. He tried to crouch lower and fell forward, and when he thrust his hands out to break his fall his hands slid because the ground was covered with a thick, slimy substance.

"Bats!" Mont called out. He sounded excited. This was a new experience, and he was enjoying it; he didn't sound the least bit afraid. "There must be thousands of them," Mont said. "Listen to them flying. Isn't this great?"

Ellsben let out a loud, disgusted grunt. He definitely didn't think the bats were great.

"They're dirty creatures," Kozal said. "They leave filth everywhere."

The high-pitched sounds and the flapping noises were rapidly diminishing; the bats were almost gone. Cal stood up. His hands were gooey from what he now knew was bat crap that he'd touched on the ground. He wiped his hands on his pants, but even after he did that his hands still felt slightly gooey. He spit on his hands and vigorously rubbed them together, and then he wiped them on his pants again. This time his hands no longer felt sticky.

"When do you think the bats will come back?" Mont asked.

"Soon," Kozal said. "This part of the cave is their home, and it's too early for them to go outside now. They're angry at being disturbed; they're not used to having visitors."

"Let's keep moving," Cal said. "I don't want to be here when they come back."

"I thought it was amazing having them flying all around us like that," Mont said.

"You can stay here and wait for them," Kozal said.

Mont started to say something, but he stopped himself before he completed saying the first word of whatever it was he was about to say. Although it wasn't going to be easy, Mont knew that at least for as long as they were in this cave he had to refrain from insulting Kozal.

Cal put his hands on Kozal's shoulders. "Let's go," Cal said.

They had walked for almost an hour when Cal noticed that he could see Kozal's silhouette. They were close to an opening. The light was diffuse, and Cal couldn't tell where it was coming from, but it was gradually getting brighter as they walked. Kozal began muttering to himself, and then he suddenly stopped.

"Here," Kozal said. "We can stay right here until tomorrow morning. To our right is a tunnel that leads to an opening. When we go out, we will be in the Western territories."

SIXTEEN

THE HILLS

Kozal handed out food from the bag that he'd been carrying. He gave Cal a hunk of bread, a piece of cheese, and a strip of dried beef.

"Let's sit down," Mont said. "I hate to eat standing up."

Cal moved his feet across the ground, feeling for bat crap. The ground was flat and felt hard and dry; the bats apparently didn't spend much time in this area of the cave. Carefully, making sure he didn't drop any of the food he was holding, Cal crouched down close to the ground. He held the food against his chest with one hand, and he touched the ground with his other hand, using it to steady himself as he sat down. The ground was hard, but surprisingly warm.

"Thank you for bringing us to this cave," Cal said. "If you hadn't brought us here, we would have been in a lot of trouble."

"If you hadn't untied me, I would have been in a lot of trouble," Kozal said. "We're even now. We're even."

Cal wrapped the bread around the cheese and the strip of dried beef, and took a bite of this improvised sandwich. It was good. Both the bread and the cheese were fresh.

"This is great," Mont said with a mouthful of food. "I was starving, and this hits the spot." Cal and Ellsben agreed with Mont.

Kozal chewed loudly and smacked his lips as he ate. He ate quickly, finishing before Cal, Mont, and Ellsben were even halfway done eating. As soon as Kozal was finished eating, he started to mutter to himself, a deep, angry sound. Eventually, some of the words became clear, and then everything he was saying became clear.

"Mother would be furious," Kozal said. "If Mother had seen how they treated her boy, she would be furious. Her boy gave them what they wanted. The war could have ended in their favor because of what her boy did. But they showed him no respect, no appreciation for what he did for them because they wanted to take all the credit for finding the prince. Fost wanted all the credit for finding the prince."

Mont leaned close to Cal and put his lips next to Cal's ear and whispered, "I don't like this. He's lost the little bit of sanity that he had."

Cal whispered in Mont's ear, "I don't like this either. Hopefully he just needs to get this out of his system, and after he talks for a while he'll calm down."

"What if he doesn't calm down?" Mont asked.

"We'll see what he does," Cal whispered. "I don't think he'll do any more than talk to himself for a while, but if he does we can subdue him."

Suddenly Kozal began giggling, and eventually the giggling evolved into a full belly laugh. "Fost thought he was going to hang me. That's what he thought. Now he's the one they're going to hang. He had the prince, but he didn't guard the prince properly, and the prince escaped. The prince is gone. They'll hang him for that, and Mother will be happy when that happens."

"Kozal," Cal said. He thought that if he talked to him, Kozal might calm down and his mind might focus back on reality. "Have you decided where you'd like to live?"

Kozal didn't answer him. He was silent. Maybe his mind had been brought back to reality, and now he was confused. His mind might not have properly processed what Cal had just said.

"Have you decided where you'd like to live?" Cal repeated.

"Live?" Kozal asked.

"Yes," Cal said. "Are you going to stay in the Southern provinces, or are you going to go someplace else where you won't have to hide all the time?"

"I'm done with the Southern provinces. I hope they put the naggies in charge of the Southern provinces." Kozal let out a low, satisfied grunt. "That would serve all of them right. See how they like taking orders from naggies."

"Where do you want to live?" Cal asked.

"I'm going to go to the Western territories," Kozal said. "I'm going to travel west until I reach the coast. When I reach the coast I'm going to build a home."

"That sounds nice," Cal said.

"I only wish I could bring Mother with me."

"How far into the Western territories do you think Grintar is?" Cal asked. He wanted to change the subject; he didn't want Kozal to start talking about Mother and getting himself all worked up again.

"Not far," Kozal said. "Grintar and his army are near the border. He's moved close to the border because he's been told that you're traveling to him."

"How do you know this?" Cal asked.

"I know that he's near the border because I heard Fost talking about it," Kozal said. "I know that he moved close to the border to wait for you because that's the most reasonable explanation. Unless he's given up on you and is going to attack Macton and put himself in charge of the kingdom."

"If Grintar's about to attack Macton, we have to reach him before he begins moving toward Enara," Cal said. "It'll be a real mess if he attacks Macton."

"Don't worry," Kozal said. "I'm sure he hasn't left the Western territories yet."

"What if he has?" Cal asked.

"It doesn't matter," Kozal said. "You could catch up with him before he reaches Enara."

After a while Cal began to feel sleepy. He yawned and stretched and tried to fight the fatigue that had seeped into him, but it was a fight he soon lost. "I'm exhausted," Cal said. "I'm going to take a nap."

Mont gave Cal a shirt from his pack to use as a pillow. Cal lay down on his side, and the dagger that he'd taken from Bast pressed uncomfortably against his thigh. He had the dagger in its sheath, and the sheath was attached to his belt. Cal rolled over on his back and reached down and loosened his belt and removed the sheath with the dagger. He rolled over on his side again and clutched the dagger close to his chest. As he fell asleep, he thought he faintly heard the squeaking of a bat flying somewhere nearby.

A hand grabbed Cal's right forearm, and somebody whispered his name. Cal was too sleepy to speak; all he could do was let out an unhappy mumble. He heard his name whispered again, and now he became more alert. He opened his eyes, but it was too dark to see anything.

"Wake up." It was Kozal.

Cal sat up and yawned. "What do you want?" Cal asked. He felt like he'd just fallen asleep, and he was irritated at Kozal for disturbing him.

"It's morning," Kozal said.

"Morning?" Cal couldn't believe it.

"Yes," Kozal said. "You've slept a long time. The others are asleep, and we need to wake them."

"How do you know it's morning?" Cal asked. He couldn't believe that he'd slept so long.

"I can sense it. The sun will be up soon," Kozal said.

Cal stood up and stretched. His back was stiff from sleeping on the hard ground, and his neck was stiff too. He wanted to find Mont or Ellsben, but he had no idea which direction to walk. Besides, he was afraid if he started walking he might trip over one of them.

Sensing what was on Cal's mind, Kozal grabbed Cal's arm and said, "Here, I'll show you where your friend is." Kozal led Cal to Mont.

Mont was sitting with his back against the side of the cave, and was softly snoring. Cal put his hands on Mont's shoulders, and Mont instantly woke up. Unsure who had touched him and what was going on, Mont shoved Cal away from him.

"Mont," Cal said. "It's me."

"Cal?" Mont sounded confused.

"I'm in front of you," Cal said.

"Sorry," Mont said. "I was trying to stay awake in case anything happened."

"Everything's fine," Cal said.

"I don't think I was asleep for long."

"I didn't think I'd been asleep for long either," Cal said.

"What time do you think it is?" Mont asked.

"It's morning," Cal said. "Kozal told me the sun is about to come up."

"I slept a lot longer than I thought," Mont said. "I'm sorry, I shouldn't have sat down. If I'd stayed on my feet, I wouldn't have fallen asleep."

"It's all right," Cal said. "There was no reason for you to stay awake."

"One of us should have been awake," Mont said. "I still don't trust him."

"Don't trust me," Kozal called out. "You should now. If I'd wanted to, I could have easily slit your throat while you were sleeping. But I didn't."

"If you'd tried, I would've—" Mont started to say, but Cal stopped him.

"Let's not start arguing," Cal said. "Please."

Although he sounded reluctant, Mont agreed.

Kozal made a grunting noise that expressed his disgust.

Cal woke up Ellsben, and Kozal handed out some chunks of bread and cheese for breakfast. After they finished eating, Kozal told them to follow him. There was now enough light for them to see silhouettes, and they followed Kozal's silhouette until they reached a small opening. Kozal slipped through the opening, and Cal followed him. Mont came out next. Ellsben managed to get his torso and front legs through the opening, but then he got stuck. Cal grabbed one of Ellsben's wrists, and Mont grabbed his other wrist. They pulled with every bit of strength they had. Suddenly, part of the opening crumbled away, and Ellsben was able to move forward.

In the distance, to the west, there were two tightly packed rows of hills. The golden rays of the sun reached out from the eastern horizon and illuminated the hills. Kozal said that General Grintar and his men were on the other side. Mont asked how long it would take to get to the hills, and Kozal said it would take about an hour to get there.

"Well," Kozal said. "I guess I'll go now. Good luck."

"I'd like you to stay with us," Cal said.

"No." Mont looked at Cal with an incredulous expression. "It's time for him to go. We don't need him."

Kozal wasn't looking at Cal, and Cal used this opportunity to silently mouth these words to Mont: *If he's with us, we can keep an eye on him.* Mont nodded his head once; he understood and agreed with Cal.

"I'll go," Kozal said. "I don't want to get too close to the Northern army."

"Stay with us," Cal said.

"Why should I?" Kozal sounded hostile.

"If you come with us to General Grintar, I'll make sure you're given enough food and supplies to get you to the coast of the Western territories," Cal said.

Kozal began muttering to himself. He was unsure what to do.

"I promise that you won't be made a prisoner, or bothered in any way."

Kozal frowned and scratched the back of his head. "You're sure they'll give me food and supplies?"

"Yes," Cal said. "I promise. You'll be given as much as you can carry."

A half a minute passed while Kozal considered this. He stared at the ground and mumbled to himself, and then he looked up at Cal and said, "I'll go with you. But I don't want to be around them for very long. I want to be given the food and supplies right away so that I can leave right away."

Cal agreed to this.

On the way to the hills they had to walk for about a mile through a field, and this made Cal anxious. He didn't like traveling in the open because he didn't like being exposed; he wanted to have the cover of trees and brush. Cal sensed that he was being watched, but he was pretty sure this was just a symptom of his unease in the open field. He tried to ignore the feeling of being watched, but it kept nagging him. Even when they finally entered a thin forest, Cal still suffered from the disconcerting sensation of being watched. None of the others seemed the least bit nervous, and Cal told himself that he was being paranoid. If someone was watching them, Cal was sure Kozal would sense it.

When they got close to the base of the hills, they began to see many trails of smoke drifting up from the other side of the hills. Kozal smiled and pointed at the smoke. "See," Kozal said. "Grintar and his men are over there."

"What if it's not Grintar?" Mont asked.

"Who do you think is over there?"

"There could be a camp of Congressers over there," Mont said.

"Congressers?" Kozal shook his head and frowned. "Look at all that smoke. Do you actually think that there are that many Congressers here in the Western territories?"

"There could be," Mont said.

"You're a fool," Kozal said.

"I'll go look," Mont said. "I'll go over there and see who it is."

"That's a good idea," Ellsben said.

"Be careful," Cal said.

"I will." Mont nodded. "I'll stay out of sight."

"How long do you think it will take for him to reach the top of one of those hills?" Cal asked.

"It shouldn't take more than half an hour before he's in a position to see Grintar and his men," Kozal said.

"*If* it's Grintar," Mont said.

Kozal shot him a disgusted look.

"We'll give you an hour," Ellsben said. "If we don't see you after an hour, we'll know...that the Congressers caught you."

"If they see me, I'll start yelling," Mont said. "If I yell I'm sure it will echo, and you'll probably be able to hear it."

"Do your best to stay out of sight," Cal said.

"I will," Mont promised. He smiled, and then he turned and went to the hills and quickly climbed one of them, and he soon disappeared from sight.

Cal still felt uneasy. He glanced around, half expecting to see a group of Congressers suddenly appear. If there was a large group of Congressers on the other side of the hills, it wouldn't be easy going around them because there were not many trees in this area, and that meant they couldn't expect much cover. To keep out of sight, they would have to travel a long distance out of their way, probably adding at least a day, maybe two days, to their journey, and this was time they couldn't afford. It was important that they get to Grintar as soon as possible.

"I sure hope that's Grintar and his men over there," Ellsben said.

"Stupid naggie." Kozal glared at Ellsben. "I told you Grintar's over there. It's Grintar."

"I'm tired of your mouth," Ellsben said. "If you call me a naggie again, you'll wish you hadn't."

"You are a naggie," Kozal said. "That's what you are. What do you want me to call you? A toad? A mouse?"

"I've had to listen to enough garbage from your mouth," Ellsben said. "I don't have to listen to it anymore."

Kozal sneered at Ellsben. "I'm not speaking garbage—I'm speaking the truth. You *are* a stupid naggie."

Ellsben's cheeks flushed, and he clenched his hands into fists and moved toward Kozal. Kozal's face twisted into an expression that showed both anger and fear.

"Filthy naggie." Kozal's voice was softer; it no longer projected a confident resonance.

"Keep saying *naggie*," Ellsben told Kozal as he moved toward him. "Because in a minute you're not going to be able to say *naggie* or anything else for a long time."

"Ellsben, stop," Cal said. "Don't touch him."

"Listen to your prince," Kozal said, the confidence creeping back into his voice. "Be a good naggie."

"Shut up," Cal told Kozal.

"The naggie needs to know his place." Kozal glanced at Cal and then glanced at Ellsben. "You need to know your place."

Ellsben suddenly bolted toward Kozal, and Kozal lurched backward, almost falling. Kozal swore at Ellsben and then scampered up the side of the closest hill, quickly disappearing behind a group of boulders.

"Kozal!" Cal called out. "Kozal, come back here."

There was no response from Kozal.

"Kozal," Cal called out again. "Don't run off now. Remember that I'm going to have Grintar give you the food and supplies you need to help get you to the west coast."

Still no response. Kozal didn't even bother to shout a rejection of what Cal had called out.

"I'm glad to be rid of him," Ellsben said. "I've honestly had enough of listening to all the racist garbage that kept pouring out of his mouth."

"I know," Cal said. "But I wish you hadn't chased him off. I wanted to keep him with us until we reached Grintar so that we could keep an eye on him. I don't think he'll try anything against us again, but I can't say I completely trust him. I don't like the idea of not knowing where he is and what he's up to."

Ellsben hung his head and didn't say a word. Cal couldn't tell if Ellsben agreed or disagreed with him.

"If he comes back," Cal said, "please don't fight with him again. I know it's not easy, but try to ignore the garbage he spits out."

"I will," Ellsben said. "I shouldn't have let him get to me like that."

Cal was about to say something to Ellsben when he saw movement out of the corner of his right eye. He snapped his head to his right and saw the red-haired bounty hunter standing about forty feet away, half hidden behind the trunk of a large tree. The red-haired man was aiming his crossbow at them.

"Look out!" Cal shouted as he dove to the ground.

Ellsben saw the red-haired man. He let out a deep yell and charged toward the bounty hunter. He ran in a zigzag pattern, which made it difficult for the man to aim his crossbow. The man shot a bolt, but it missed Ellsben. Bast's sword was in its scabbard, and the scabbard was attached to a leather belt that Ellsben had wrapped around his waist. Ellsben jerked the sword from its scabbard and let out another deep yell. The red-haired man managed to reload his crossbow, and he fired another bolt. This bolt sank into the upper part of Ellsben's right hind leg. Ellsben stumbled when the bolt hit him, but he somehow managed to keep charging forward. Frantically, the red-haired man tried to reload his crossbow, but he was unable to get another bolt in place before Ellsben reached him.

Swiftly, and with all his strength, Ellsben swung the flat part of the sword's blade down, smashing it against the red-haired man's forearms. There was a loud cracking sound that sent a chill up Cal's spine. The red-haired man let out a loud scream. The trigger of the crossbow was caught on his index finger, and the crossbow was dangling down below his limp, broken forearms. He grimaced, and his hands twitched as if he was trying to grasp the crossbow again. Ellsben thrust the sword into the man's chest, and the man somehow managed to find enough energy to lung at Ellsben.

Surprised by this, Ellsben jumped back, and the sword's handle slipped from his hand. The man tried to reach up, as if he thought he could make his hands pull the sword from his chest, but he couldn't even raise his forearms up. The man's face blanched, and his eyelids started fluttering rapidly, and then he let out a loud gasping sound and fell forward. The impact of hitting the ground drove the sword's blade through the man's body.

Ellsben stared at the red-haired man's body for a moment, and then he looked back at the bolt that was stuck in his hind leg. His face appeared surprised, as if he'd just become aware that he'd been shot. He reached back and grabbed the base of the bolt and quickly jerked it from his leg. Blood gushed from the wound. Ellsben pressed a hand against the wound, trying to stop the flow of blood, and then he stumbled forward, his eyes closed, and collapsed.

Cal shouted out Ellsben's name and started to run toward him, but just as he started running, he sensed someone behind him. Quickly, he stopped and spun around and saw the black-haired bounty hunter rushing toward him. The black-haired man was holding a sword over his head, ready to strike Cal down. Cal grabbed the dagger that he'd taken from Bast. He knew he couldn't block the sword with the dagger, but maybe, if he was lucky, he would be able to get close enough to the black-haired man to be able to stab him.

The black-haired man grinned; he knew he was about to accomplish what he'd been sent to do. He swung the sword down, and Cal jumped away. The sword hit the ground, causing a loud, metallic ringing and sending up a cloud of dust. Cal lunged at the man, intending to stab him in the chest with the dagger, but the man managed to swoop his sword up from the ground and expertly hit the dagger with the tip of the sword's blade, ripping the dagger from Cal's grip. Then he swung the sword at Cal's neck, and Cal jumped back. Cal felt the sword's blade pass under his chin, almost slashing his throat. The man moved toward him, and Cal stepped backward and tripped, landing on his rear. The man swung his sword down, and Cal threw himself out of the way. The dagger was close, and Cal wondered if he would be able to get to it. He knew the dagger would be almost useless, but without it he wouldn't even have a remote chance of being able to stop the black-haired man.

Cal lunged toward the dagger, but the black-haired man stopped him from reaching it by slamming his boot into Cal's gut. The air in Cal's lungs rushed out, and Cal curled up on the ground, unable to breathe in. With the tip of his boot, the man pushed Cal onto his back and held him in place by pressing the heel of his boot against Cal's chest. Cal gasped for air, but was only able to breathe in a tiny amount. A small, satisfied smile appeared on the man's face. He raised his sword up and mumbled what sounded like a prayer, but before he could bring the sword down into Cal's chest, there suddenly came a wild screech, and something crashed against the man.

It was Kozal. He had vaulted on the black-haired man's back. The man violently twisted his body, trying to throw Kozal off his back, but Kozal held on. Kozal had one arm wrapped tightly around the man's neck, and his other arm encircled the man's chest. Kozal's legs hugged the man's waist. The man reached back and grabbed Kozal's hair, and Kozal leaned forward and sank his teeth into the man's cheek. An angry howl erupted from the man's throat.

Moving as fast as he could, Cal stood up and ran to the dagger. Now Cal was able to breathe deeply, and the sudden rush of air in his chest gave him strength. He scooped up the dagger and charged at the man.

Before Cal was able to reach the man, he managed to flip Kozal off his back. Kozal lunged at the man, and the man thrust his sword into Kozal's chest. A large spot of blood blossomed on Kozal's shirt, circling the area where the sword had entered his chest.

Cal jammed the dagger's blade deep into the man's back, just below his neck. The man shouted out obscenities and dropped his sword and reached back with both hands, trying to grab the dagger. Kozal snatched the sword from the ground and began swinging it wildly, slashing the man's stomach and chest. The man fell to his knees, and Kozal slashed the side of the man's face, ripping a large hole in the man's right cheek. The man reached out, trying to catch the sword's blade, trying to stop Kozal, but when he grabbed the blade his hands were not able to hold on to it, and the blade slipped out of his grasp, leaving deep cuts across his fingers and palms. Kozal swung the sword with all his strength, and the blade hit the man's neck, slicing through his throat. Blood poured down his neck, and air whistled from his open throat each time he inhaled and exhaled. He swayed back and forth for a moment, and then he tumbled forward, his face smacking the ground.

Kozal dropped the sword. His face was pale, and the front of his shirt was now saturated with blood. Cal went to Kozal, and Kozal reached out as if he was about to shake Cal's hand, and then Kozal fell forward. Cal grabbed Kozal, wrapped his arms around him, and then slowly knelt down.

Kozal threw an arm around Cal's neck, and a small smile appeared on his face. "This is the second time I've saved you," Kozal whispered. He coughed, and blood began leaking out of the corner of his mouth.

"Yes, you saved me," Cal said. "You saved me. Thank you."

"Now you have to pardon me when you become the king." Kozal coughed again, and more blood leaked out of his mouth. "Now you have to pardon me like we agreed before."

"I will," Cal said. "I'll grant you a full, unconditional pardon, and I'll give you a large patch of land anywhere you want to live."

Kozal smiled. Then he sighed, and his eye lost its focus, and his muscles went limp. The arm that Kozal had thrown around Cal's neck slid down, flopping to the ground.

Gently, Cal laid Kozal down. Cal touched Kozal's neck, searching for a heartbeat, but there was no heartbeat. Kozal was dead.

SEVENTEEN

SHADOWS

E llsben moaned and opened his eyes. He looked around, and when he saw Cal he smiled, relived that Cal was all right. Ellsben forced himself to stand up, and by doing this he caused the wound in his leg to bleed rapidly. He held his right hind hoof up, unable to put pressure on his injured leg.

The amount of blood that was cascading out of the wound scared Cal. The bleeding had to be stopped quickly. Ellsben's pack was lying on the ground, and Cal ran to it and opened it and reached in, frantically searching for something he could use to stanch the bleeding. He found Ellsben's blanket. He unrolled the blanket and quickly tore it into four large strips. He folded one of the strips into a square and pressed the square against Ellsben's wound. It didn't take long before the square patch of blanket was saturated with blood. Cal made another square and used it to replace the first square. He tied the new square in place by wrapping the other two strips of the blanket around Ellsben's leg. A small stream of blood trickled out from under the patch and dripped off the tip of Ellsben's hoof. The stream of blood began to lessen, and after a while it finally stopped.

"You should lie down," Cal said.

"No." Ellsben shook his head. "There's less pain when I stand."

Cal's hands were sticky from Ellsben's blood. He wiped his hands on the back of his pants and managed to get most of the blood off. Now that everything was quiet, Cal suddenly felt exhausted. He wanted to sit down and close his eyes and rest for a while, but he fought this desire because he knew right now he had to stay alert. Cal took in a deep breath and shook his head, trying to force the exhaustion to dissipate.

"Cal! Ellsben!" Mont called.

Cal looked up and saw Mont rapidly climbing down the side of the nearest hill. Mont called out their names again. When Mont saw Cal looking at him, he started waving enthusiastically. Then, abruptly, Mont stopped waving. He saw the bodies of the bounty hunters and Kozal. He looked all around; he was confused. Cal and Ellsben appeared to be fine, but Mont was afraid there was more happening than what he could see. Mont climbed the rest of the way down the hill as quickly as he could.

"Cal," Mont said, out of breath. "What happened? Are you all right?"

"I'm fine," Cal said. "Ellsben's hurt, but he should be all right." Cal told Mont everything that had happened while Mont was away.

"I should have been here." Mont kicked the ground. "I should have stayed with you."

"There was nothing you could have done," Cal said.

"I could have helped." Mont looked at Cal. "If I'd been here, maybe Ellsben wouldn't have been shot, and maybe Kozal wouldn't have been killed."

Cal put a hand on Mont's shoulder. "And maybe if you'd been here you'd have been killed. You can't know what would have happened."

Mont frowned and looked down.

"Don't think about it," Cal said.

Mont glanced up at Cal, and then he looked down again.

"What did you find on the other side of the hills?" Cal asked. "Is Grintar over there?"

"Yes." Mont nodded. "It is Grintar. You won't believe how many men he has with him. There are tents everywhere. It's amazing."

"Did you talk to anybody from the camp?"

Mont shook his head. "I didn't know what I could say. I was pretty sure that if I went down there and told them the truth, they'd think I was crazy. I thought it would be better to come back here and get you."

"It's still dangerous here," Cal said. "There could be Congressers around or more bounty hunters. We need to get to Grintar right away."

"I agree," Mont said.

"Let me have your blanket," Cal said. "I want to cover Kozal before we leave."

Mont took his blanket from his pack and handed it to Cal. While Cal was covering Kozal with the blanket, Mont went to Ellsben and asked him how he was feeling.

"The leg hurts," Ellsben said. "It's throbbing like crazy. I can't stand on it, but at least I've still got three other legs to walk on."

"I wrapped the blanket around him," Cal said to Mont and Ellsben. "But as soon as we reach General Grintar, I'm going to ask that they send some men back here to bury him. Kozal deserves to be buried properly."

Ellsben moved forward, his gait much shorter than usual. "I'm sorry," Ellsben said. "I can't move very fast. I'm going to slow you down."

"Stay here and rest your leg," Cal said. "I think climbing those hills will be too difficult for you right now."

"I'm going to stay with you," Ellsben said.

"You don't have to," Cal told him.

"Yes, I do," Ellsben said. "I need to be with you in case you run into a patrol of Congressers, or some other trouble. I'd go crazy from worry if I stayed here."

Cal considered ordering Ellsben to stay here, because he was afraid that if Ellsben climbed those hills it would cause his leg to begin bleeding again, but Cal decided against it because he was sure Ellsben would feel insulted if he was ordered to stay behind. "If your leg starts to hurt too much, I want you to promise you'll stop," Cal said.

Ellsben nodded. "If it gets to be too much for me, I promise I'll stop."

They walked slowly. Ellsben tried not to, but every once in a while he winced from the pain. Cal asked him how bad his leg hurt, and Ellsben said the pain wasn't too bad, but it was obvious he was lying. Cal suggested they stop and rest. Ellsben said he didn't need to rest, but he looked relieved when Cal insisted that they stop for a while.

It took them an hour to reach the spot Mont had found where they could look down from the top of a hill into General Grintar's camp. If Ellsben's leg hadn't been injured, they could have reached this spot in less than half an hour. Ellsben apologized for slowing them down, and Cal told him there was no reason to apologize because the extra time didn't make a difference.

The size of General Grintar's camp amazed Cal. There were hundreds of tents, and the tents were set up in columns, creating a grid-like pattern of roads between the tents, making the camp look like a city. The men moved about the camp, giving the impression of a sense of purpose. There was nothing about what was going on in the camp that appeared sloppy or out of order. There were quite a few centaurs in the camp, and the centaurs were moving freely about, but it appeared that they had their own segregated area where they resided.

"Do you want to go down there and meet General Grintar now?" Mont asked.

"Yes," Cal said. "Let's go."

It was more difficult for Ellsben to climb down than it was for him to climb up, so they had to move extra slow. As Cal moved down the hill toward the camp, he realized that he was leaving his life as he'd known it behind, and this both excited and frightened him.

When they reached the bottom of the hill, two soldiers rushed over to meet them. The soldiers' dark blue uniforms were clean and crisp, their boots were freshly polished, and their hair was cut short and neatly combed. They stood with their backs straight and stared at Cal, Mont, and Ellsben. After a moment, one of the soldiers said, "This camp is off-limits. We can't take you in. We aren't allowed to give you food. If you are traveling west, we'll escort you around the camp."

"We're here to see General Grintar," Cal said.

"The general is busy," the soldier said.

"It's important that I see him immediately," Cal said.

"That's not possible." The soldier sounded annoyed. "Now I'm going to have to ask you to move on."

"The general's expecting me," Cal said. "I'm the prince."

The two soldiers looked at each other and were barely able to hold back smirks. "Move on," one of the soldiers said, making a brushing motion with his hand.

Cal took a step forward. "My name is Calton Lanshire. I am the prince of the Kingdom of United Provinces."

"If you don't move on, we'll have to arrest you." The soldier glared at Cal so that Cal would know he was serious.

"I'm ordering you to bring me to General Grintar," Cal said, doing his best to sound authoritative.

One of the soldiers started to say something, but he suddenly stopped. Both of the soldiers now appeared unsure of what they should do. One of the soldiers leaned over and whispered in the other soldier's ear, and the listening soldier nodded, agreeing with whatever had been whispered to him. The soldier who had whispered turned and quickly went back to the camp and disappeared behind a group of tents. The soldier who stayed behind put a hand on the handle of his sword and said, "Stay where you are. Don't try to run away."

"We won't run," Cal said.

They waited for what felt like forever. Nobody spoke or made eye contact. The soldier appeared nervous, as if he expected them to attack him at any second. He tightened his fingers around the handle of his sword. There were no clouds, and the sun was strong, so the air became uncomfortably warm. Several beads of sweat rolled down Cal's forehead, and he reached up and wiped the sweat away with the back of his hand. Sweat slid down the solder's face, but he ignored it. Ellsben tried to put weight on his injured leg and quickly pulled his hoof up because the second he put weight on his leg he felt a sharp, agonizing flash of pain. Cal and Mont looked at Ellsben with concern, and Ellsben indicated that he was all right.

More sweat beaded on Cal's forehead, and he wiped it away. When he reached up, he smelled the sour odor of the sweat from his armpit. He wished he was back at the pond he and Mont had discovered because nothing would feel better right now than to have cool pond water all around his body. He imagined himself diving down and touching the muddy bottom of the pond with his hand. Just thinking about the pond made him feel better.

From behind a group of nearby tents a deep voice suddenly said, "Yes, sir." Then there came the sounds of feet shuffling. The soldier who had stayed to watch Cal, Mont, and Ellsben started to move his head. He wanted to look back at the tents, but he stopped himself, keeping his gaze on the three of them.

A man wearing a general's jacket—dark blue with gold buttons—came from the nearby group of tents and walked toward Cal, Mont, and Ellsben. The man had two heavily armed soldiers, one to his right and one to his left, walking beside him. This was General Grintar. Cal recognized him from the drawings he'd seen of the general. Grintar had a round head, bright eyes, and a neatly trimmed reddish-brown beard. He had broad shoulders and was barrel-chested, but Cal was surprised to see that Grintar wasn't as tall as he'd imagined. Even with the thick-heeled boots Grintar was wearing, he was still slightly shorter than Cal.

Grintar crossed his arms and stared at Cal, studying his face. After a minute, Grintar loudly cleared his throat, and then he said, "They tell me you claim to be the prince."

"I am the prince," Cal said. "I'm Calton Lanshire."

Grintar's expression didn't change, and he didn't verbally respond to this. Cal had no idea what Grintar was thinking, but since he hadn't reacted, Cal had to assume that Grintar didn't believe him. Cal bent down and unlaced his right shoe. He took the shoe off and cradled it against his chest, reaching in and pulling back the bottom layer of the shoe. There was the heraldic crest, snug in the space Zinn had carved in the heel of the shoe. Cal reached in, and with the tips of his fingers, he pulled the crest out of the hole that it was resting in. He handed the crest to Grintar, and Grintar looked at it as if it meant nothing to him. He curled his fingers around the crest, enclosing it in his fist.

A panicky, sinking sensation attacked Cal's gut, making him feel as if he was falling from a huge height. If the crest was meaningless to Grintar, he had no idea what he could do now to convince Grintar that he truly was the prince. What if Grintar forced them to leave? No, Cal couldn't allow that to happen. Now that they had finally reached Grintar and his men, it would be insane to go back off on their own again and risk being captured or killed by Congressers or bounty hunters. If Grintar tried to send them away, Cal decided he would rush into the camp so that, hopefully, Grintar would arrest him. If he stayed Grintar's prisoner, and went with

Grintar and his men to Enara, Zinn would be able to prove Cal was the prince.

"You look like your father." It took Cal several seconds before he understood what Grintar had said to him because Grintar spoke in the Old Language. Cal had studied the Old Language ever since he'd started school, but he didn't have the natural ability to learn foreign tongues that some people had, and the Old Language was especially difficult to learn. The Old Language was the language that the people of the Ardonian Empire had used, and it had spread as the empire conquered new lands, and then it evolved into other languages during the centuries when the Ardonian Empire fell apart. However, the Old Language remained the language used for legal documents, and it was used as a second language of the upper class. To be fluent in the Old Language was a sign of social status. "You have your father's eyes," Grintar said in the Old Language.

"Other people have told me that too," Cal replied in the Old Language.

"I'm glad you made it here safely, Your Highness." Grintar bowed.

Cal felt weird because this was the first time anyone had greeted him with a bow, but he did his best to act natural. He knew this was something he was going to have to get used to. "General," Cal said, no longer speaking in the Old Language. "I want to introduce you to my friends." Cal introduced Mont and Ellsben to Grintar.

"You know," Cal said to Grintar, "I was afraid I wouldn't be able to convince you that I'm the prince."

"You're not the prince," Grintar said.

Cal looked at Grintar. He couldn't understand why Grintar would say that he wasn't the prince.

Grintar stared at Cal with a serious expression for a moment, and then he smiled. "You're not the prince," Grintar said. "Not anymore. Yesterday was your birthday. You're thirteen now. You're legally the king."

"Was it yesterday?" With all the traveling and excitement, Cal had completely forgotten about his birthday.

"May the kingdom prosper under your rule," Grintar said.

"Thank you," Cal said.

"Now," Grintar said. "I'm sure you'd all like to get cleaned up and have something to eat."

"We would," Cal said. "But first Ellsben needs to have his leg taken care of by a doctor. He was hit by a bolt from a crossbow."

Grintar tilted his head so that he could see Ellsben's injured leg. Then Grintar turned toward the guard who was standing to his right and ordered him to bring Ellsben to the medical tent. The guard saluted Grintar, and then he motioned for Ellsben to follow him.

"There's a man on the other side of the hills," Cal told Grintar. "He was killed defending me. We covered him with a blanket, but he deserves a proper burial."

Grintar nodded. "He will be given an honorable burial." Grintar ordered the guard who was standing to his left to get some men to retrieve the body, and to have the body buried in a proper spot with full honors. The guard saluted and quickly went back to the camp. Grintar turned his attention to the soldier who had stayed to watch Cal, Mont, and Ellsben while his partner had gone back to the camp to find Grintar. He told the soldier to have a tent prepared for Cal and Mont, and to have warm water for bathing made ready, and also to have clothes brought. The soldier saluted and immediately went to the camp to fulfill his orders.

"Would you like to have something to eat now?" Grintar asked Cal.

"I'm not hungry at the moment," Cal said. He looked at Mont, and Mont said that he wasn't hungry either. "I'd like to take a nap," Cal said. "I feel worn out."

"Rest is a good idea," Grintar said. He nodded. "We've got a lot of traveling ahead of us, and after today there'll be little time for rest. We have to reach Enara as quickly as possible. If you don't claim the throne within two weeks of your thirteenth birthday, that is considered a form of abdication, and you will no longer have a legal right to the throne. I figure we can make it to Enara in about a week, but it could take longer if we have to do battle with Congressers, or if Macton's men put up a heavy fight when we get near the capital. So we can't waste any time. We're going to have to cover as much territory as possible every day, and that means we've got some long, tiring days ahead of us."

Grintar brought Cal and Mont to the tent that had been prepared for them. He told them that the water for bathing and a fresh set of clothes would be brought to them shortly. Then he told them that he would have them woken up when it was time for dinner. He gave a quick, courteous bow to Cal, and then he disappeared.

The tent was big enough to accommodate half a dozen men, but it only had two cots in it. There was a small writing table in a corner of the tent and two small stools. On the table there was a lantern. Cal sat down on the edge of one of the cots and yawned. Mont's eyes were half closed. "It'll feel great not having to sleep on the ground," Mont said. Cal nodded.

"Hello," a voice called out from in front of the tent.

"Come in," Cal answered.

The front flap of the tent was pushed back, and a small, dark-haired centaur entered. The centaur looked around nervously. He was holding a bucket with one hand, and he had some clothes and towels clutched to his chest with his other hand. "I brought you wash-up water and some fresh clothes for you gentlemen." The centaur's deep Southern accent was so heavy, Cal could barely understand what the centaur had said.

"Thank you," Cal said. He introduced himself and Mont.

The centaur put the bucket and clothes down, and he shook hands with them quickly, nervously, as if he was afraid he was doing something wrong. He mumbled his name, "Kenton," and then he left the tent quickly, without giving Cal or Mont a chance to make small talk with him.

Mont went to the bucket and touched the side of it. "The water's warm. It's going to feel good."

"I almost can't remember the last time I had warm water to wash with," Cal said.

After they washed, Cal and Mont put on the fresh clothes. The clothes were the type of clothes farmers would wear; Cal had half expected that they'd be given military uniforms. Cal's pants were the proper length, but the waist was too large. He had to tighten his belt as far as it would go to keep the pants from slipping down. The sleeves on his shirt were a bit too long, and he remedied this by rolling them up. Mont's clothes fit almost perfectly.

"It feels strange being clean and wearing clean clothes," Mont said.

Cal agreed, and then he yawned. "I'm ready for a nap. I'm so tired right now, I could fall asleep standing up." Cal lay down on the cot, and a couple of seconds after his head sank into the pillow he was sound asleep.

Ellsben woke them up just before sunset. Cal sat up and stretched and yawned. He felt a lot better now that he had rested. Mont was sitting on the edge of his cot with his eyes barely open. The hair on the left side of his head was sticking out like a small wing. Mont yawned and rubbed his face. The tent wasn't tall enough for Ellsben to be able to stand up straight; he had to lean forward, and he looked uncomfortable.

"Look at my leg," Ellsben said. He turned so that Cal could see the fresh white bandage that was wrapped around his wounded leg. "The doctor found a piece of metal from the bolt in my leg. He had to give me a couple of stitches, and it hurt like crazy when he put the stitches in. I had to use all my willpower to keep myself from kicking."

"How does your leg feel now?" Cal asked.

"It's throbbing, but it feels better than before." Ellsben said he'd made friends with a couple of centaurs who worked for the doctor. These centaurs were outside the tent, and they were eager to meet Cal.

When Cal went out to meet the centaurs, they both immediately bowed and simultaneously said, "It's an honor to meet you, Your Highness." Cal smiled and reached out to shake hands with them. At first they were hesitant to shake his hand. They looked at each other as if they weren't sure it would be proper for them to shake hands with him.

Ellsben nodded his head, indicating to them that it was all right to shake Cal's hand. After they shook his hand, they nervously shuffled their hooves, and then they bowed and repeated that it was an honor to meet him. One of them said that they still had work to do, and they quickly departed.

Ellsben told Cal and Mont that dinner was almost ready. "I'll take you to Grintar's dining tent."

"I'm ready to eat," Mont said, patting his stomach.

"I'm starving," Cal said. "How about you, Ellsben?"

"I've already had dinner," Ellsben said.

"You must have really been starving," Mont said.

Ellsben shook his head. "I actually wasn't very hungry, but I had to eat when dinner was served."

"Dinner was already served?" Cal didn't understand. "I thought you said dinner was almost ready."

"*Your* dinner is almost ready," Ellsben said. "*My* dinner was served an hour ago."

"Why were you served dinner first?" Cal asked. "Why aren't you eating with us?"

"I can't eat with you."

"Why not?"

"Centaurs have to eat separately. Most of the men don't mind mixing with the centaurs, but some do, and so to prevent trouble, General Grintar has ordered that men and centaurs cannot dine together." Ellsben looked at Cal and raised his eyebrows. "It could cause a riot if the men saw me having dinner with the general and the king."

"That's not right," Cal said. "I can order—"

"No," Ellsben said, cutting Cal off. "Don't try to change this. You can't afford to have trouble right now. You need to keep the troops unified."

"I don't like it," Cal said.

"I know," Ellsben said. "But the best thing you can do right now is ignore it. Don't even mention it."

Cal nodded, agreeing to do as Ellsben had said, but he wasn't happy about it.

"There are about one thousand centaurs here," Ellsben said. "Most of them arrived after Grintar and his men had set up camp here. Word that Grintar was in the area spread quickly among the groups of centaurs who lived in the nearby provinces. Most of the centaurs are runaways who had been living in small scattered groups. They see Grintar as a liberator, and they treat him almost like a god. When they heard he was here, they came to volunteer their services. The centaurs have their own section of the camp, and that's where I'll be staying tonight."

Ellsben led them to the general's dining tent. Grintar was standing outside the tent with his arms crossed, smoking a cigar. When he saw Cal, he put out the cigar and held the front flap of the tent open.

"Goodnight," Ellsben said to Cal and Mont. "I'll see you in the morning."

There was already food on the table. A platter with sliced beef was in the middle of the table, and beside the platter there was a large bowl filled with salad, and next to the bowl there was a pitcher of water. The table was set for three, although it was large enough to accommodate a dozen people. "Please, sit down," Grintar said.

The food tasted excellent. As soon as they were finished eating, Grintar pushed back his chair and said, "We must get up just before the sun rises tomorrow. Everyone is going to be very busy. It's going to take a lot of work to disassemble all the tents and to get everything packed up properly."

"How long do you think it will take to get everything ready to leave?" Mont asked.

"One hour," Grintar said. "Maybe less if all goes well."

"That's fast," Cal said. "This camp is huge. I would have guessed that it would take all morning to get everything packed up and ready to go."

"This is the military," Grintar said. "We have to be able to move fast. When we're fighting the enemy, we have to be able to move our supplies rapidly forward, or, when necessary, backward. Speed is the key to winning battles."

"I'd like to see a battle," Mont said.

Grintar shook his head. "No, you wouldn't. Battles are horrible things. The blood and moans and screams of the dying will haunt my dreams for the rest of my life. The dead stay with me. When I close my eyes, I can see the shadows of ghosts on every battlefield."

Grintar hung his head for a moment as if saying a silent prayer. Then he abruptly pushed his chair back from the table and stood up. He told Cal that he needed to speak with him in private.

"I'll meet you back at the tent where we're staying," Mont said to Cal. "I'm still tired, so I might be asleep when you get back."

"Don't wait up for me," Cal said. "You should get as much sleep as you can."

Mont thanked Grintar for the dinner, and then he left.

"What did you want to talk to me about?" Cal asked.

"Let's go to my quarters," Grintar said. "I have something there for you to do."

General Grintar's tent wasn't far. Cal was surprised to see that the tent wasn't any larger than the tents the regular soldiers stayed in. In fact, there was nothing about his tent that distinguished it from any of the other tents in the camp. Inside, there was a cot, a writing table, a chair, and two trunks. "Please sit down," Grintar said, offering Cal the chair.

Cal sat down. Grintar took out a cigar and stuffed it in the corner of his mouth, but he didn't light it. He put his hands behind his back and paced for a moment, and then he pulled the cigar out of his mouth and said, "I've been told papers proving that Macton is a traitor have been intercepted. The papers are letters to Dengon from Macton, promising that once he becomes the king he will allow the Congressional provinces to secede from the kingdom. As the speaker of Parliament, Macton knows the law clearly states that it's treason for any member of the government, besides the king, to negotiate with enemies of the kingdom. He may think he's going to become the king, but he's not the king now, so his contact with the Congressers is capital treason."

"Did Macton sign these letters?" Cal asked.

"I've been told that he did," Grintar said. "Macton's obviously convinced that you won't be showing up to claim the throne."

"How much of a fight do you think the Congressers can put up?" Cal asked.

"Very little," Grintar said. He stuck his cigar in the corner of his mouth and lightly sucked on it for a moment, and then he pulled it out and dropped it in his pocket. "The Congressers have very few men left to fight. They're defeated. If your father hadn't been assassinated, Dengon would have surrendered. Defeating what's left of the Congresser military won't be difficult. Bringing the kingdom back together again, politically and emotionally, that's going to be your most difficult task."

Grintar began pacing. After a minute, he stopped pacing and faced Cal and said, "If you're going to bring the kingdom back together, you'd better choose your advisers wisely. The men you surround yourself with can help make your rule successful, or they can drag you down into the muck of failure."

Cal nodded.

"Your father was a great man. He ruled with strength and fairness. It was a great honor to serve him." Grintar bowed his head. "My father died when I was a young man," Grintar said softly. He looked up at Cal. "When I heard that the king had been assassinated, I felt the same anguish that I'd felt when I heard that my father had died."

Cal didn't say anything. He hadn't allowed himself to think about his father. He'd pushed what had happened to his father out of his mind because he'd needed to focus on finding Grintar and surviving. Now the painful feelings of loss came rushing back, and Cal felt a tightness in his throat and tears beginning to form. No. He wasn't going to let himself cry in front of General Grintar. He forced his mind to go blank.

Grintar went over to one of his trunks and opened it. He reached into the trunk and removed a wooden box that had beautiful, intricate carvings of vines all over it. Grintar opened the box and held it out so that Cal could see what was in it. Cal leaned forward and saw that the box housed the royal crown. Gently, Grintar set the box on his writing table, and then he reached into his pocket and removed the heraldic crest and handed it to Cal. "Put the crest back where it belongs," Grintar said. He carefully took the crown out of the box. Cal looked at the crown and found the spot where the heraldic crest belonged. When he pushed the crest back in place, it made a loud clicking sound. Cal felt the crest to make sure that it was firmly in place, and he found that it was. Grintar smiled and said, "Now the crown is ready for your coronation."

"It's still hard for me to believe that I'm going to be the king," Cal said.

"Soon you will be," Grintar said. He put the crown back in its box, and then he returned the box to the trunk. "Well, I think it's time to get some shut-eye. We've got to get up early tomorrow."

Grintar had a soldier escort Cal back to his tent.

Mont was already asleep. He had his blanket pulled up to his chin, and he was snoring softly. The lantern on the table was lit, and its light cast long shadows, and these shadows made Cal think of dark ghosts. He went to the lantern and put it out. Walking slowly, because he was almost blind in the darkness, Cal went to his cot. He got undressed and lay down on the cot and closed his eyes. He listened to the sounds of Mont's soft snoring, and then he heard men talking and laughing somewhere nearby.

Cal thought about his father. He wished his father was here now. It was almost impossible for him to imagine that he'd never see his father again. His father was gone, murdered. His father was never going to show up. The tears that Cal had held back earlier now gushed out.

"I'll bring the kingdom back together," Cal whispered. "I'll make you proud, Father. I promise."

EIGHTEEN

A HUGE TASK

C al stared at the castle. It was miles away, and yet it towered over the treetops like a lone mountain. The kingdom's red and blue striped flag was flying over the castle's north tower and over the castle's south tower. It had been four years since Cal had seen the castle, and it felt both like yesterday and a million years ago. Although the castle looked the same, he knew very little else would be the way he remembered it. A tremendous amount had changed during the four years he'd been away.

"We'll camp here for the night," Grintar said. "I don't want to march into the capital until I find out what's happened during the past couple of days. My spies will report to me this evening."

"Do you think Macton will attack us?" Cal asked.

Grintar shook his head. "It's unlikely he'd attack us militarily. Remember, he was a general. Macton knows he doesn't have enough men to be able to push back my troops.

He will put up a fight, but his fighting will be political, not military."

Cal dismounted the tall roan mare that he'd been riding. His thighs and lower back were stiff from five long days of riding. They'd covered a huge amount of territory. Cal was amazed at how quickly they'd reached Enara.

"Hey, Cal," Mont said. He ran up to Cal and grabbed his arm and smiled. Mont hadn't seen Cal since early this morning when they'd woken up and prepared to leave the area where they'd camped for the night because Mont had spent the day traveling at the back of the group with Ellsben and the other centaurs. During the time they had traveled to Enara, Mont had alternated days traveling in front with Cal, and traveling in the back with Ellsben.

"How are you?" Cal asked Mont.

"I'm a lot better today than I was yesterday," Mont said. "All those mosquitoes yesterday just about sucked every drop of blood out of my body. I was so happy there weren't many mosquitoes today."

"Me too." Cal nodded.

Cal and Mont helped put up their tent. While Cal was bent over pounding in one of the tent stakes, he heard hooves walking behind him, and he sensed someone staring at him. He quickly finished pounding in the stake and then stood up and turned around. He couldn't believe it. Zinn was on a horse, sitting in a saddle that had a special stirrup that was supporting his broken leg. Zinn put a hand over his heart and smiled, and then he saluted Cal.

"Zinn!" Cal called out.

A soldier who was accompanying Zinn helped him dismount. The soldier gave Zinn a pair of crutches. Cal ran to

Zinn and hugged him, and Zinn stroked the back of Cal's head. "I'm so happy you made it," Zinn said. "I'm so happy you're safe."

"How's your leg?" Cal asked.

"The doctor tells me there are several breaks just above the ankle. It will heal, but I'll probably always limp." The muscles around Zinn's mouth suddenly tightened, and his eyes appeared sad. He glanced down and then took in a deep breath and said, "I can't describe to you how angry I've been at myself."

"Why?"

"I'm angry at myself for letting this happen," Zinn said, indicating his broken leg. "I shouldn't have let this happen. I was supposed to lead you to General Grintar. I was supposed to be with you, I was supposed to protect you. And I failed."

"Your leg was broken while you were protecting me," Cal said.

An unhappy smile flickered across Zinn's face.

"You didn't fail," Cal said. "You allowed Ellsben to be my new guide, and he was the perfect choice. He kept me safe."

"I'm glad," Zinn said. "I didn't think that he was competent, but at the time there wasn't any other choice."

Grintar came over and saluted Zinn, and said, "It's an honor to see you again, sir."

"It's an honor to see you again, General." Zinn saluted back. "I have news." Zinn patted the breast pocket of his jacket.

"My quarters have just been made ready," Grintar said. "Let's go there. We can sit down and talk."

Cal and Zinn accompanied Grintar to his tent. Grintar had one of his subordinates bring in a small table, three chairs, and a footstool for Zinn to rest his broken leg on. After they sat down, tea was brought to them, and then Grintar ordered the men who were guarding his tent to make sure no one disturbed them unless it was an emergency.

Zinn took a thick envelope out of his jacket's breast pocket and put it on the table. Next, he put on a pair of reading glasses and opened the envelope. "These are several letters that Macton sent to Dengon," Zinn said. "This past week Macton grew overconfident. He was certain he was going to become the king, and because of this he was careless. He should never have signed these letters. They are tantamount to confessing to treason. He should have had one of the diplomats who work under him sign these letters—that way he could've denied any knowledge of them."

"Are these the papers you told me about?" Cal asked Grintar.

Grintar nodded. "Yes. These are the papers my spies informed me of. This is the first time I've seen them."

"How did you find out about the letters?" Cal asked Zinn.

"There are several aides to Macton who have remained loyal to the kingdom," Zinn said. "They told us about the letters and when they were going to be sent. Our men intercepted them after Macton's dispatcher got several miles outside of Enara."

Zinn took the letters out of the envelope and read them. Cal was surprised at how arrogant Macton sounded, how sure he was that he would be the new king. Macton referred to Cal's father as the "royal fool," and he claimed that even if he were constantly drunk he could do a better job running the kingdom than the royal fool had. He promised Dengon that the Congressional provinces could be an independent nation, with the condition that they agreed to have open, free trade with the kingdom.

Grintar pushed his chair back from the table and stood up. He grabbed a cigar from his pocket, put it in his mouth, and lit it. He paced and angrily puffed on the cigar. Then he abruptly stabbed the cigar out on the table and crossed his arms. "Macton's scum," Grintar said.

Zinn carefully folded the letters and put them back in the envelope. "With these letters we can have Macton arrested and removed from power. He will easily be convicted of treason."

"Without Macton as the speaker of Parliament, you will have a much easier time getting the Parliament to follow you," Grintar said.

"I will not make any deals with the Congressers," Cal said. "My father wanted them to surrender unconditionally, and that's what I want too."

"Yes." Zinn nodded. "They must surrender unconditionally. But once they surrender, don't attempt to punish them. They have to be treated fairly. Your father firmly believed this. If you oppress the Southern provinces, they will resist you, and the kingdom will never be able to heal." Zinn put a hand on Cal's shoulder. "Also, you're going to have to be careful with the centaur situation. Eventually, they'll have to be granted the rights of citizens of the kingdom, but you're going to have to be very careful how you do this and when you do it. If you grant them the rights of citizenship too soon, you'll be thought of as a naggie lover, and you'll have riots and rebellions throughout the South but also in parts of the North. However, if you wait too long to grant them citizenship, you'll almost certainly have a centaur uprising to deal with."

Cal nodded.

"You have a huge task before you," Zinn said.

"I know," Cal said. "It's going to be difficult, but I'm not going to fail. I'm going to bring the kingdom together the way my father wanted."

NINETEEN

THE NEW KING

The Parliament was being guarded by at least one hundred troops who were loyal to Macton. These troops were wearing clean, well-kept uniforms and were well armed. Grintar rode close to Macton's troops, stopped, stared at them for a minute, and then he ordered them to disperse. The troops ignored Grintar.

Cal was being guarded by a dozen of Grintar's best troops. These guards were surrounding Cal, and they had large shields that were being held up to protect Cal from arrows or crossbow bolts. Cal was on horseback, and Zinn, also on horseback, was beside him.

A tall officer approached Grintar. The officer had long, thick sideburns and a mustache. His mouth was drawn down into a deep frown, and his eyes were narrowed. The officer did not salute Grintar, and Grintar did not salute the officer. They stared at each other. After a moment, Grintar dismounted and walked up to the officer so that their faces were only several inches apart.

"Who is that?" Cal asked Zinn.

"That's General Dakton," Zinn said. "He served under Macton, and then he served under Grintar after Macton was relieved from his command. Grintar and Dakton were able to work together, but they never liked each other."

Cal remembered reading about Dakton in the newspapers that Mr. Alden used to buy. General Dakton was known for being a fierce fighter—he rarely lost a battle. However, he was also known for cruelty. It was rumored that he frequently tortured his prisoners of war, and it was well known that when he conquered a town he treated its citizens horribly. On several occasions he had burned entire towns to the ground because he suspected the citizens of the town were hiding Congresser soldiers who should have surrendered to him. General Dakton was so hated in the Southern provinces, several wealthy Southerners had made it known that they'd pay a large reward to anyone who killed General Dakton.

"Tell your men to put down their weapons," Grintar said to Dakton. "I have the rightful heir to the throne with me."

"You and your men are traitors," Dakton said. "You abandoned the kingdom in a time of crisis, after the king was murdered. Macton is the provisional head of the kingdom, and you refused to recognize his authority over you."

"Macton is a traitor."

Dakton put a hand on the handle of his sword, and lifted his other hand up and pointed it at Grintar and shouted, "*You're* the traitor!"

"That can be determined by the new king," Grintar said. "Now tell your men to put their weapons down. Let the rightful heir to the throne make his way into the Parliament."

Dakton spit, and his spit almost landed on Grintar's boots. He shook his head, and his expression was the expression of a man who had been deeply offended and was barely holding back his anger. "My men will never lay down their weapons for you," Dakton said. He turned and walked away from Grintar.

Grintar put his hands on his hips and stared at Dakton for a moment, and then, with his lips pushed down into a disgusted frown, he mounted his horse and withdrew his sword from its scabbard. He held the blade of his sword across his chest and shouted to Dakton's men, "I have the rightful heir to the throne. Put down your weapons so that the heir to the throne can safely make his way into the Parliament."

There was a mumbling of confusion among Dakton's men, and Dakton responded to this by angrily shouting orders to his men to prepare for battle. Immediately, Dakton's men readied their weapons and positioned themselves for battle; all signs of confusion completely dissipated.

Suddenly, Grintar shouted something, but Cal couldn't understand the words. Grintar's men spread out, and there was a tension that Cal could sense, like the way it felt seconds before a bolt of lightning was about to strike nearby. Grintar raised his sword over his head, held it there for several seconds, and then he swooped it down, slashing it through the air, and shouted, "Advance!"

Chaos exploded. Crossbow bolts and arrows whistled through the air, and men on both sides charged forward, yelling battle cries, and the ringing sounds of metal striking metal pierced the air as the opposing troops crashed into each other. Soon the agonized screams of the wounded and dying joined the other sounds.

The men who were guarding Cal moved him back, and they tightened their circle around him so that their shields were almost touching; Cal strained to see out through the thin slits in between the shields. All he saw was an occasional flash from the sun reflecting off metal, and at one point he saw a streak of red, which he was certain was blood pouring out of a wounded man.

It was difficult to estimate how long the battle lasted. The agonized screams and the ringing of metal striking metal seemed interminable, and it took all of Cal's willpower not to clasp his hands over his ears, but the battle stopped so abruptly Cal had a sense that it hadn't lasted more than three or four minutes.

There came a brief span of absolute silence which, after the battle's cacophony, seemed eerie, as if the dead had suddenly demanded the payment of silent respect. The air felt cold, causing Cal to shiver. Then there came the sound of a man moaning in pain, and then another painful moan, and another, and another. Grintar's voice could be heard calling out orders, and there were the sounds of his men responding.

Cal tried to block out the sounds; he tried not to listen to the moans and sobbing of the wounded. He stared down at his horse's thick black mane. After a span of time that felt like an hour but was probably only several minutes, Cal's guards abruptly lowered their shields, and the two guards directly in front of him moved away. Cal saw General Grintar walking toward him, and Cal could see maybe half a dozen twisted bodies on the ground behind Grintar. Cal focused his eyes on Grintar.

"We can enter the Parliament now," Grintar said. His hand went into his jacket pocket, probably searching for a cigar, but he quickly withdrew his hand from his pocket. His fingers twitched. The excitement of the battle must have made Grintar desperately want to smoke a cigar to calm his nerves, but right now he couldn't smoke because they were about to go into the Parliament.

Cal dismounted his horse. Several guards came over and helped Zinn get down from his horse, and as soon as Zinn was on the ground he was given a tall cane. Grintar put his hands on his hips and looked at the Parliament, and then he looked back at Cal and said, "Follow me."

They went slowly because Zinn was having a difficult time walking; he shuffled forward, leaning heavily on the cane for support. Four guards walked with Cal, one beside him on the left, one beside him on the right, and two behind him. To get to the main entrance of the Parliament, they had to walk through the area where Grintar's troops had fought Dakton's men. The dead and wounded were scattered everywhere, and this meant they couldn't walk directly to the entrance; they had to zigzag around the corpses and the severely wounded. Cal didn't want to see the corpses or the wounded, but he couldn't pass by without looking at them. A man made eye contact with Cal. The skin on the left half of the man's face was gone, and what remained looked like uncooked ground meat. The man silently opened and closed his mouth, and he lifted up his hands over his chest and twisted them as if he were trying to communicate some important thought with his hands. Cal looked away; he wished he could reach down and touch the man's face and heal it.

Up ahead, to Cal's left, Dakton's men, the ones with no serious injuries, were sitting in a long, single-file row with their hands on top of their heads. Many of Grintar's troops stood behind Dakton's men, watching them, making sure none of them would have the opportunity to run away or to make trouble.

Grintar suddenly stopped walking. "Wait here," he said. Grintar walked over to a corpse and stared down at him. At first Cal didn't understand what had attracted Grintar to this particular corpse, and then he saw the long, thick side-burns and realized that the corpse Grintar was staring at was Dakton. An arrow was sticking out of Dakton's gut, and a long gash from a sword stretched from under Dakton's chin to the middle of his chest. The sword had sliced through Dakton's shirt, undershirt, flesh, and muscles, leaving a wide gash that revealed part of three bloody ribs. Grintar nudged Dakton's shoulder with the tip of his boot, testing to see if Dakton would moan or twitch; it was as if Grintar didn't believe that Dakton could actually be dead. He nudged Dakton again, harder this time, and when there was still no response, Grintar gave Dakton a small salute, and then turned and walked back to where Cal and Zinn were standing.

The two doctors who had been traveling with Grintar were brought in to care for the wounded, and Cal watched as the doctors shouted orders to their medical assistants. It quickly became obvious to Cal that the doctors were assessing the wounded, and those who were considered to have terminal injuries were ignored because the doctors didn't want to waste their time on those who were soon going to die. The musky scent of sweat and the coppery odor of blood that filled the air seemed to become stronger, and this caused a wave of nausea to rush through Cal. He swallowed and told himself he was not going to throw up. He had to keep his composure.

As they walked up the stone stairs that led to the entrance of the Parliament, Cal noticed his boots were making an odd sound each time he took a step. The sound was like a piece of cloth being softly torn. Cal looked down and saw that his boots were leaving bloody prints. He'd inadvertently stepped in a puddle of partially coagulated blood, and the soft tearing sound he heard was the sound of the blood from the bottom of his boots sticking to the stone stairs.

There were two large wooden doors at the main entrance to the Parliament. Grintar tried to open the doors and found that they were both locked. He grunted, frustrated, and then he reached up and pounded on one of the doors with his fist and shouted, "Open these doors!"

A high-pitched voice answered, "I'm under orders to keep these doors locked."

"I'm General Grintar, and I have the rightful heir to the throne with me. I'm ordering you to open these doors."

Silence.

Grintar pounded on one of the doors again. "If you don't unlock these doors immediately, I'll have them smashed open, and if these doors have to be smashed open, you'll be arrested and put on trial for treason."

Immediately there came the sounds of bolts being slid open. One of the doors creaked open about a foot, and the head of a scared young soldier popped out. Grintar's eyes narrowed, and he stared at the soldier. The soldier's face went white, and he opened the door all the way and stood at attention. Grintar saluted, and the solider saluted back.

The hall that led to the Parliament's main chamber was long and wide and had a high ceiling. Both the floor and the walls were a beautiful gray marble. As they walked down the hallway their footsteps echoed, and the echoing footsteps were the only sounds Cal heard until they were near the Parliament's main chamber. The chamber's doors were closed, but the voices of the men debating inside could still, although only faintly, be heard in the hallway.

Grintar walked up to one of the chamber's doors, and Cal followed him. When Cal was next to the door, he could hear several voices debating what would be the best way to deal with General Grintar; the members of Parliament were obviously unaware that Grintar had entered the Parliament and was just outside the main chamber's door. One of the voices said that Grintar needed to be killed because once he was gone his followers would be left without a strong leader and wouldn't be able to stay together. Grintar quickly grabbed the door handle and started to push the door open, but Cal stopped him by firmly gripping his shoulder. "Wait," Cal said. "Let me enter the chamber first. I'm the king. I need to be the first to enter."

For a moment Cal didn't think Grintar was going to obey him. Grintar kept his hand on the door handle, as if he wasn't sure what he was going to do, and then he let his hand slip from the handle, and he took several steps back. "Yes," Grintar said. "Of course you should enter first."

Cal stepped forward. He gripped the door handle, and before any doubts could enter his mind, he twisted the handle and pushed the door open. He marched into the chamber, Grintar followed close behind him, and Zinn shuffled in after them.

The main chamber immediately fell silent. The seventy members of Parliament, sitting in their chairs, all turned their heads at the same time as if they were being operated by some mechanical device. They stared, confused, at Cal. There were thirty empty chairs interspersed among the occupied ones. Normally, the Parliament had one hundred members, plus the speaker, but when the Southern provinces seceded, the thirty members of Parliament from the Southern provinces resigned. Cal's father had ordered that the thirty empty chairs remain in place. He considered the empty chairs a symbol of the kingdom's incompleteness, and the empty chairs were left there to remind everyone that the kingdom would be brought back together and the chairs would be filled again.

Macton was standing at the speaker's podium, which was at least five feet above the floor of the chamber. When Macton saw Cal, his eyes flashed in fear, but he was able to quickly hide it. An angry, arrogant expression took over Macton's face.

Cal turned toward the members of Parliament and said, "I'm Calton Lanshire, son of Akron Lanshire. I'm your new king."

One of the members of Parliament stood up and faced Cal and started to bow, but before he could complete this motion, Macton shouted, ordering the member of Parliament to sit down. The member of Parliament froze and looked up at Macton, and Macton again shouted for the member of Parliament to sit down. Slowly, reluctantly, the member of Parliament returned to his chair.

Macton pointed at Cal. "How do we know this is in fact Calton Lanshire and not some imposter put up by our enemies to gain power? No one has seen Calton in years. He was moved to a secret place for his safety during the war. Why didn't Calton come to us immediately after our king, his father, was taken from us? Why is this supposed Calton only now appearing to claim the throne? I have strong suspicions that the real Calton was killed by enemies of the kingdom, and this imposter was found and trained by them to present himself as Calton so that our enemies could steal the throne."

The members of Parliament began speaking to each other, and their many voices filled the chamber with a sound that was like the deep growling of some gigantic animal. Cal tried to hear what individual voices were saying, but he could only hear pieces of conversations because the voices kept blending together. From what he could hear, he realized that the Parliament was confused. Some members believed what Macton had just told them, some members believed that Cal was in fact Calton Lanshire, and others were unsure what to believe. Sporadically, the members of Parliament who believed Macton would shoot a hostile look at Cal.

"Silence!" Zinn shouted. The members of Parliament quickly stopped their conversations and turned their heads toward Zinn. "General Grintar and I both are willing to swear under oath that this is Calton Lanshire, our new king," Zinn said. "There should be no doubt."

"But there is doubt," Macton responded. "General Grintar's word, even under oath, cannot be taken seriously. General Grintar should be tried as a traitor. He should have been under my command from the moment our king departed us. Instead of following the law, he abandoned this government and took as many members of the military as he could convince to follow him into the Western territories. General Grintar is a deserter and a traitor, and he should be—"

"You're the traitor," Zinn shouted.

"How dare you make such an accusation in this chamber." Macton's eyes narrowed, and he leaned forward. "I am going to have you and that deserter, Grintar, arrested."

"You don't have the power to have us arrested," Zinn calmly said.

"I am the speaker of Parliament and the provisional head of this government," Macton said. "And soon I will be the new king. Your lack of respect does not make me inclined to show leniency toward you."

"Your titles are about to be removed," Zinn said. "And you are about to be arrested for treason." Zinn reached into the inner pocket of his jacket and removed a thick envelope. He opened the envelope and removed the papers it contained. Zinn held the papers up, over his head, and told the Parliament, "These are letters from Speaker Macton to our government's enemy, the president of the so-called Congressional provinces, Dengon." Zinn lowered the letters and, squinting, he began to read them aloud.

Before Zinn could read more than three sentences, Macton shouted, "Forgery!" Zinn tried to keep reading, but Macton continued to shout over him, "Forgery! Forgery! Forgery!" Macton's eyes were wide, and his gaze darted around the chamber. He needed to see how the members of Parliament were responding to what Zinn had read.

The members of Parliament universally appeared stunned. They hadn't decided which side to believe yet. "Forgery!" Macton shouted again. He looked like an animal that knew it was about to be slaughtered.

Zinn tapped the letters with his index finger and said, "These letters are real. They have both Macton's signature and the official seal of the speaker of Parliament stamped on them." Zinn looked up at Macton and said, "Your arrogance made you careless."

"They're forgeries," Macton said, only now there was no conviction in his voice.

"You are a traitor," Cal called out. He walked toward the speaker's podium. "You betrayed the kingdom."

"I would never betray the kingdom." Macton tried to sound offended, but his shaky voice gave away the fact that he was sacred, not offended.

When Cal was several feet from Macton, he stopped walking and stared Macton in the eyes. Macton tried to keep his gaze on Cal, but he couldn't. It was as if Macton was afraid his thoughts could be read if he allowed Cal to look into his eyes.

"Guards!" Cal called out without taking his gaze from Macton. "Guards!"

SHADOWS OF GHOSTS

From two discreet, almost invisible alcoves at the back of the chamber two guards appeared. By tradition, the main chamber of the Parliament only had two guards, and their role was mostly just for removing any members of Parliament who got out of line while legislation was being debated or voted on. There had never been any need for strong security inside the chamber. Security was always strongest outside the Parliament building and, to a lesser extent, in the hallways that led to the main chamber and to the offices of the members of Parliament.

The guards quickly made their way up to where Cal was standing. They looked at each other, and then their gazes bounced from Cal to Macton. The guards were uncertain what they should do; they didn't know who they owed their loyalty to.

"Arrest the speaker," Cal ordered.

Nothing happened. The guards looked at each other and then at Cal, but otherwise they didn't move.

"Arrest the speaker." When Cal repeated these words, his voice was stronger and had an uncanny resemblance to his father's voice.

This time the guards obeyed immediately. They rushed up to the podium; one guard went to the left side of the podium, and the other guard went to the right side.

"Get back," Macton ordered, but the guards didn't obey. They grabbed his arms and dragged him toward one of the exits. "I'm innocent," Macton called out. "I'm innocent." None of the members of Parliament came to Macton's defense; they all sat silently in their seats and watched as the

305

guards removed him from the chamber. He was being taken to one of the holding cells that were located in the cellar of the Parliament.

As Macton was pushed through one of the exits, he glanced back at Cal with a hateful expression. Cal didn't react to this. Macton was pushed out of the chamber, and he disappeared from sight.

Behind and above the speaker's podium was the king's podium. The king's podium was where the king gave his annual State of the Kingdom address to Parliament, and where he spoke to Parliament when there was a major crisis. Cal ascended to the king's podium. He looked down at the members of Parliament, and they silently gazed up at him.

"My name is Calton Lanshire," Cal said to the members of Parliament. "I am the son of Akron Lanshire, and I'm your new king."

For a moment the chamber was possessed by a deep silence, and then, like a rapidly moving wave, the members of Parliament flowed up from their chairs, clapping their hands wildly and filling the chamber with a roar of enthusiastic applause.

TWENTY

NEW ADVENTURES

Cal's coronation was a simple affair. He cancelled all the celebrations and parades that traditionally took place after a coronation because he didn't feel it would be appropriate to have celebrations while the kingdom was still officially at war. Cal's coronation was before Parliament, and after he was presented with the crown, he asked that all the members of Parliament stand in silence for a minute in honor of his father.

The chief justice of the High Court read the king's oath, and Cal, with his right hand raised, repeated the oath; he swore he would carry out all the duties that were required of the king, and he swore to uphold all the laws of the kingdom. After Cal took the oath, the chief justice signed and embossed his seal on the necessary papers to legally certify Cal's coronation.

Mr. Alden resumed his role as Cal's tutor, and he also became, along with Zinn, one of Cal's most trusted advisers.

Two weeks and a day after Cal's coronation, President Dengon agreed to surrender unconditionally. Cal sent General Grintar to meet with President Dengon. When Grintar returned with the singed surrender agreement, he reported that President Dengon looked like a dying man. Before the war Dengon had been, for many years, the speaker of Parliament. He was known for his charm and his handsome features. He'd been a barrel-chested bull of a man. Now, Grintar reported, Dengon's charm was gone, and he behaved like a shy child who had been caught in the act of some wrongdoing. Dengon's face was no longer handsome, his eyes appeared sunken and had dark half-moons under them, and his once powerful frame had become shrunken and weak. His now thin shoulders perpetually drooped forward.

A week after the Congressional provinces surrendered, Macton was put on trial. His trial lasted almost two weeks, and it was full of emotion. Macton steadfastly maintained his innocence. Although most of his supporters abandoned him, there were a handful of men who came to the trial every day to show their support and loyalty.

Macton was convicted of treason, and when his conviction was read his supporters rushed toward the front of the courtroom, attempting to attack the prosecuting attorneys and judge, but they were immediately knocked down and arrested.

Macton was sentenced to execution, and he was to be hanged; however, Cal commuted his sentence to exile. Macton was sent across the Lanka Ocean to the kingdom of Sunan where his ancestors, three generations back, had immigrated from. The royal family of Sunan agreed to give him asylum. Macton's exile was permanent. If he ever traveled over the Lanka Ocean and landed on the kingdom's territory, he would be arrested, and his sentence of death would be reinstated.

Cal pardoned all of the leaders of the former Congressional provinces. The pardons only had one condition, and that condition was that none of the leaders of the former Congressional provinces could ever hold a government office. They could never become members of Parliament or even mayors or members of their local town councils. Even though these pardons were opposed by many senior members of his government, Cal decided these pardons had to be granted because he believed they would help the kingdom heal. If all the leaders of the former Congressional provinces were arrested and put on trial, each of the many trials would keep the divisive issues that had caused the war fresh in the minds of everyone, and the still raw emotional wounds that had developed during the war would deepen.

One of Cal's biggest challenges now was to integrate all of the freed centaurs into society. He planned to pass laws requiring equal rights for the centaurs, but laws couldn't change people's hearts. It would take a generation, probably several generations, before the centaurs would be accepted as equal members of society.

On a crisp, sunny morning, the day after Cal had commuted Macton's death sentence, Ellsben began his journey to find his family. He prayed that his wife and son had been able to stay together, but he privately told Cal that he had a painful suspicion his wife and son had been separated. "If they were separated," Cal told Ellsben, "they won't be much longer. Very soon you'll be together again."

"I hope it's soon," Ellsben said. "But I have a feeling that finding both of them is not going to be easy. I have a feeling that I have many difficult days of searching ahead."

Cal offered Ellsben a home on the royal grounds, and Ellsben enthusiastically accepted. "This would be a wonderful place to live," Ellsben said. "It would be a perfect place for my boy to finish growing up."

Two soldiers were sent to travel with Ellsben to protect him. The Southern provinces were still a dangerous place for centaurs, and Cal didn't want Ellsben traveling there without protection.

Mont decided, at the last moment, that he would also travel with Ellsben. "I need to find out what happened to Pap. I need to find out if he's still alive," Mont said. "I don't want to see him again, I don't want anything to do with him, but I need to know if he's still alive. I need to know if he survived the war. I don't want to put him out of my mind, assuming he's dead, and then have him suddenly show up. I need to know if he's alive or dead." Mont said that while he traveled through the Southern provinces with Ellsben, he would talk to people, and with luck, he would meet someone who knew, or had known, his pap.

Cal told Mont that he and his aunt could move to the royal grounds if they wanted to. Mont grinned, and then his expression turned serious. "I'd like that," Mont said. "But I don't think my aunt would want to move here. She's spent her entire life in Shua. She's only left the town three times in her entire life, to visit relatives, and each time she told me she wasn't gone a day before she wished she was back home. I doubt she'd be eager to move."

"You're both welcome to move here if you want," Cal said. "You'll certainly be treated a lot better here than you're treated in Shua."

Mont smiled and shook his head. "I bet I'll be treated much differently back home now that everyone knows that I'm best friends with the king."

When Cal said good-bye to Ellsben and Mont, he unexpectedly felt both jealous and lonely. He was going to miss his friends. He wanted to be with them, to be there if they needed help, and he wanted to share the adventures that they were going to have. But he forced himself to push these emotions and thoughts aside. He needed to concentrate on the kingdom's work.

Cal walked along the outskirts of the royal grounds. He stopped and looked back at the castle. The kingdom had many problems right now, and he had plenty of work ahead of him, but he felt confident.

READING GROUP GUIDE FOR SHADOWS OF GHOSTS

1. Who is your favorite character? Would you like to be this character? Why or why not?

2. Cal and Mont come from very different backgrounds. Their personalities are very different. Why do you think they become such close friends?

3. When the war starts, Cal is sent by his father to live in a remote village. Though this is for Cal's safety, he resents being sent away. He is angry at his father for sending him away. After his father is assassinated, Cal feels guilty for having been angry with his father. Explain how Cal overcomes the guilt he feels.

4. Ellsben loses his family when he is sold. Mont's mother abandons him when he is a young child, and his father

leaves him to fight in the war. Cal's mother dies when he is an infant, and his father is assassinated. Loss and abandonment are central themes in the novel. Compare and contrast how Ellsben, Mont, and Cal deal with the loss they suffer. What other characters in the novel suffer a loss or are abandoned by someone close to them?

5. Stro, the farmer who gives Cal, Mont, and Ellsben food and shelter, is a kind, generous man. However, he has fought for and supports the Congressers. This, from Cal's standpoint, means Stro is an enemy. Yet Stro is kind and generous. How does Cal's interaction with Stro change his view of the war? Is one side of a conflict always wrong? Can people on both sides of a conflict be good and decent?

6. What is your favorite scene or part of the story? Why?

7. Kozal betrays Cal. Later Kozal is killed while protecting Cal. Does this last act redeem Kozal? Do you think Kozal is a villain? Why or why not?

8. Cal hesitates when it's his turn to cross the bridge that goes over the snake-infested river. He has a bad feeling about the bridge. Ellsben and Mont have already crossed, and this makes Cal think he can't refuse to use the bridge. As Cal crosses the bridge it collapses, sending him down into the snake-infested water. How do you think Ellsben and Mont would have reacted if Cal had listened to the bad feeling he had and refused to use the bridge? If he didn't use the bridge, what other way could Cal have found to cross the river?

9. When Cal is bitten by the poisons river snake, he ends up unconscious and almost dies. After he recovers, he shows a newfound confidence. He makes wiser decisions and demonstrates the ability to be a strong leader. Why do you think coming so close to death gives him confidence?

10. There are many events and situations in *Shadows of Ghosts* that parallel events and situations from the US Civil War. How many parallel events and situations did you notice?

ABOUT THE AUTHOR

Stefan Haucke, driven by the desire to learn about other cultures and the need for adventure, has traveled to over twenty nations. He rode a camel near the pyramids in Egypt, swam with sea lions in the waters of the Galapagos Islands, climbed the Great Wall of China, hiked near the Acropolis in Athens, went dog sledding in northern Michigan, and photographed polar bears in Canada.

Along his many travels, Stefan has successfully worked as a deckhand, a shepherd, a dispatcher for an emergency services unit, an electric meter reader, and an office manager. He has also found the time to study the literature and history of ancient Greece, Russia, and the United States, and loves reading folktales, fairytales, and urban legends. He also enjoys astronomy, and on clear nights can be found gazing at the stars and planets with his telescope.